"LEMMY'S E... AND IT'S A...

D0752702

"Your friends the Ns are too much. What was it that Norbert guy said? His uncle had a bad ticker? Buddy Needleson didn't have a bad ticker, or if he did, he didn't die from it. The cops think Lemmy had something to do with it."

"Because of the car?" I asked. I looked down at my feet and studied my shoe, afraid to look Johnny in the eyes. He was right. It was all my fault.

"Yeah. Someone must have seen us dump the body and reported Lemmy's license plate number to the cops. They picked Lemmy up a few hours ago, surmising that anyone who would dump a body must have had something to do with its being dead. Lemmy told them someone had stolen his car, but the cops didn't go for that."

"So we've got to find out who murdered Buddy. If we get the murderer, maybe the cops won't care who dumped the body."

"Right, Brenda. Except for the 'we' part. Remember, I'll be filming day and night."

What a mess. It looked like I was going to be up all night for the second night in a row. I'd never get my spring line done.

THE BOOKWORM
Chester Pike, Norwood, PA
Between Winona and Amosland
Best Trades in Town

Other Brenda Midnight Mysteries by
Barbara Jaye Wilson
from Avon Books

DEATH BRIMS OVER

Avon Books are available at special quantity discounts for bulk purchases for sales promotions, premiums, fund raising or educational use. Special books, or book excerpts, can also be created to fit specific needs.

For details write or telephone the office of the Director of Special Markets, Avon Books, Dept. FP, 1350 Avenue of the Americas, New York, New York 10019, 1-800-238-0658.

Accessory to Murder

A BRENDA MIDNIGHT MYSTERY

BARBARA JAYE WILSON

This is a work of fiction. Names, characters, places, and incidents either are the product of the author's imagination or are used fictitiously. Any resemblance to actual events, locales, organizations, or persons, living or dead, is entirely coincidental and beyond the intent of either the author or the publisher.

AVON BOOKS
A division of
The Hearst Corporation
1350 Avenue of the Americas
New York, New York 10019

Copyright © 1998 by Barbara Jaye Wilson
Published by arrangement with the author
Visit our website at **http://www.AvonBooks.com**
Library of Congress Catalog Card Number: 97-93792
ISBN: 0-380-78821-7

All rights reserved, which includes the right to reproduce this book or portions thereof in any form whatsoever except as provided by the U.S. Copyright Law. For information address Curtis Brown, Ltd., Ten Astor Place, New York, New York 10003.

First Avon Books Printing: January 1998

AVON TRADEMARK REG. U.S. PAT. OFF. AND IN OTHER COUNTRIES, MARCA REGISTRADA, HECHO EN U.S.A.

Printed in the U.S.A.

WCD 10 9 8 7 6 5 4 3 2 1

If you purchased this book without a cover, you should be aware that this book is stolen property. It was reported as "unsold and destroyed" to the publisher, and neither the author nor the publisher has received any payment for this "stripped book."

Dedicated to my father,
Jay B. Wilson Jr.

ACKNOWLEDGMENTS

For enthusiasm, encouragement, hat facts, and more—thanks to Mimi Signor, Carol Lea Benjamin, Mary Lee Lewis, Jay B. Wilson Jr., Nora Novarro, Casey Bush, Ann Albrizio, Lyssa Keusch, Laura Peterson, Bob Zimmerman, Steven Martin Cohen, Peter Stathatos, Gene Daly, and X-Dot Potato.

1

The black car rumbled up First Avenue in the dead of night. I was in the backseat, sandwiched in between Norbert and Naomi.

"I'm freezing my ass off," said Naomi. She gave me a dirty look like it was all my fault. "How come it's colder inside this rattletrap than outside?"

Her brother Norbert leaned over me to explain. "That, my dear baby sister, is due to the wind rushing in through the hole in the floor."

I kept my mouth shut so no one could hear my teeth chatter and cursed myself for getting involved.

Up front, my ex-boyfriend, Johnny Verlane, was at the wheel. The car belonged to his agent, Lemmy—Lemon B. Crenshaw. Depending on your point of view, it was either a valuable antique or a bulky hunk of junk.

Dweena, riding shotgun, groped at the knobs on the cold metal dashboard. Her long platinum blond wig glowed in the dim light. Pulling one of the knobs, she turned and asked, "You people feel anything yet?"

Norbert pulled off a thick suede glove and felt around the floor of the car. "No good," he said. "Still ice-cold."

Johnny shook his head and said, "Lemmy warned me the heating system might be on the fritz."

"On the fritz," said Naomi. "That's the understatement of the century." She pulled the hood of her fake leopardskin parka tightly around her face until the only thing sticking out was the tip of her red nose and a couple of blond corkscrew curls. "This street gives me the creeps. I mean it's like Desolation Avenue or something. No stores, no restaurants, no people, no nothing but dark looming hospital buildings." She scraped a peephole through the frost on the window and looked out. "Yuck, Bellevue. Talk about depressing."

Dweena spoke up from the front seat. "This neighborhood's the pits, all right, but this being New York, and me being Dweena, I know hundreds of places open this late. Maybe when we get done with whatever—"

Naomi cut her off. "Thanks but no thanks."

I wished Naomi wouldn't act so snotty, especially considering how Dweena was doing the Ns—their last name being Needleson, that's what I call Naomi and Norbert—a huge favor by riding along.

Of the five of us, Dweena was the only one who had a valid New York State driver's license. With Dweena beside him, it was legal for Johnny to drive with his learner's permit. Dweena's license had been issued a few years back, when Dweena was still Edward, a successful stockbroker with a dashing but eccentric handlebar mustache. The picture on the license didn't do the new Dweena, the post-insider-trading-scandal Dweena, justice. But in a pinch, and we were most certainly in a pinch, it was the best we could do. The Ns were born and bred Manhattanites; they knew how to hail cabs, not parallel park. I'd let my license expire after moving to New York. The way I looked at it, one of the greatest benefits of living here was never having to drive. The only reason Johnny had the learner's permit was because he starred in the *Tod Trueman, Urban Detective* TV series and the producers, facing a tight budget, insisted he do his own driving except in the truly dangerous chase scenes.

Dweena, a soul far more sensitive than her demeanor would indicate, picked right up on the edge in Naomi's voice. She whirled her head around and glared at Naomi.

Naomi, who usually had trouble shutting up, retreated

even farther into her fake leopardskin hood. ''Dweena, Queen of the Night Scene,'' she muttered under her breath.

''Shhh,'' I said. Later, I'd have to talk to Naomi about her rotten attitude. After all, Dweena had taken off early from her job as a bouncer just to help us out. She worked at a trendy club in the meatpacking district on the fringes of the West Village. She was still dressed in work clothes—five-inch-high-platform shoes and a skin-tight red sequined dress that barely covered her butt. Talk about cold, Dweena was probably colder than any of us.

Dweena must have been thinking the same thing because she turned to Johnny and said, ''I could have got us a luxury car with leather interior, complete stereo system, *and* a functional heater.''

''Thanks for the offer, Dweena,'' said Johnny, ''but like I told you, we've got to be squeaky-clean legal. If, god forbid, we get pulled over with—''

''Shut up,'' said Norbert. He gripped the back of the seat and leaned forward so his mouth was right up against Johnny's ear. ''Don't tell her anything.''

''I heard that,'' said Dweena. ''I think it's about time somebody opened up and told me what the hell this is all about.''

Johnny, considerably more diplomatic than Norbert, patted Dweena on her large hand. ''I think it would be better if you didn't know.''

''It better not have anything to do with drugs,'' said Dweena. ''Dweena stays far away from nasty drugs.''

''Don't worry,'' said Johnny. ''This isn't about drugs.''

Before Dweena had a chance to ask what it was about, we were at Thirtieth Street. ''Here,'' I said. ''Make a right. The loading dock's around the corner.''

''Brenda, are you sure this is the right place?'' asked Norbert.

''I wouldn't have suggested it if I didn't know where to go.''

Johnny pulled up, killed the engine, and shut off the

headlights. Around us, New York was about as silent as it ever gets. We sat there for a while, breathing, fogging the air, shivering, no one saying anything, no one making the first move. Finally Norbert spoke. ''As long as we've come this far, kiddies, we might as well get it over with. Come on, everybody out. Except Dweena.''

''I just know it's drugs,'' said Dweena.

''It's not drugs,'' I said.

Norbert glared at me. ''Make sure she stays put.''

''You don't have to worry about that,'' said Dweena. ''It's not like I don't have plenty to do.'' She pulled a nail file out of her beaded evening bag and went to work on her inch-long dark red fingernails.

The rest of us got out and gathered around the back of the car. Johnny popped the trunk and slowly eased the lid open. I looked deep into the yawning cavity. Even though it was too dark to see much, I drew back instinctively.

Norbert took command, organized and directed our effort. ''On the count of three . . .''

We rolled the bundle out of the trunk, dragged it along the side of the building, then, with a heave-ho, flung it up on the loading dock. It landed with a thud.

We ran back to the car. I'm sure I wasn't alone in breathing a sigh of relief when Johnny got the old heap started on the first try. As we pulled away, Johnny turned on the headlights, illuminating the loading dock and our bundle.

''Oh god,'' he said, pointing. ''The blanket. It's unwrapped.''

Naomi turned her head away.

''Get the hell out of here,'' said Norbert.

''Damn right,'' said Johnny. He gunned the engine.

Dweena glanced up from her nails. In an instant she realized where we were and what we'd done. ''Jeezus H. Flipping Christ,'' she shrieked. ''A body. You fruitcakes dumped a body at the morgue.''

''Not just any body,'' said Naomi. ''It's our Uncle Buddy.''

''He had a bad ticker,'' said Norbert.

2

It's hardly my style to go around dumping bodies at the morgue in the middle of the night. I'm a milliner. I have a little hat shop on West Fourth Street in Greenwich Village. That's where I'd been that afternoon when Naomi called and begged me to help her out of a jam.

I'd have done the sensible thing and said no, but I owed the Ns a lot. It had been their parents, Howard and Zorema Needleson, who got me started making hats. If it weren't for them I'd still be working as an office temp. That's how I originally met them, a one-day assignment at Needleson Brothers, a feather importer, to help with inventory. They sure needed help. Howard's method of figuring out which feathers were in which boxes was to whack each box with a baseball bat until a feather flew out. I typed up whatever he yelled out. Zorema told me the prices. The work was okay except the place reeked of mothballs. When I complained about the smell, they sent me out to a millinery supply shop on West Thirty-eighth Street to make a delivery. The place was fascinating. I cruised up and down the aisles and checked out the merchandise. On the spot I decided to make hats. The timing was right. I'd just about given up making it as an artist. To make a long story short, I bought twenty dollars worth of hatmaking supplies, Howard and Zorema introduced me around to the trade, and I became a milliner.

So I owed Howard and Zorema. Of course, I also had Howard and Zorema to thank for introducing me to Norbert and Naomi, a friendship I was rapidly reevaluating.

Over the years Needleson Brothers bought out a bankrupt ribbon dealer, then a rhinestone guy, and gradually expanded from feathers-only to trimmings of all sorts. Howard said diversification was the way of the future. Then, a few months ago, Howard and Zorema, claiming they'd "had it up to here" with New York and the business, abandoned ship and retired to Florida, leaving their partner, Howard's brother Buddy, in charge of Needleson Brothers. Buddy Needleson, in his day an extraordinary salesman, knew nothing about the day-to-day running of the business. Norbert and Naomi got stuck with that job—the last thing in the world either of them was cut out to do.

Their hearts just weren't in the business. Naomi, cute in a pudgy, blond, bubbly kind of way, yearned to be a sultry lounge singer. Until the business got dumped in her lap she'd spent her days singing along, reasonably on-key, to Peggy Lee records and sewing frilly polka-dot dresses with huge circle skirts and matching accessories that she thought would look good when she finally got a gig. Norbert considered himself a scholar, and as such quite above working for a living. Each semester he combed the NYU catalogue and registered for the cheapest continuing education class. He didn't care what it was, as long as it got him the ID card that gave him access to the library, discounts on movies, and an excuse to ogle college girls half his age. His last class, a one-night seminar which he hadn't even bothered to attend, had been about how to find a job in a rapidly changing marketplace.

Despite the Ns' lack of business savvy, the recent craze for feathers had increased sales. Business was so good that Norbert and Naomi had dragged themselves into the showroom early this morning to catch up on back orders. That's when they found their Uncle Buddy, flat on his back on the floor beside Naomi's desk, dead as a doornail. Like Norbert said, he had a bad ticker. Naomi said the sudden surge in feather sales had simply been too much for him.

Why the Ns called me instead of the cops or 911 or the hospital or Buddy's wife Babette—I didn't have that part of the story quite straight. It had something to do with their uncle's hobby. Babette wasn't supposed to know about it and if she found out he was at the showroom after hours it'd make trouble for Howard and Zorema, who had allowed whatever it was Buddy was doing to go on behind Babette's back. Naomi said everything would be okay if they could just get the body out of the showroom. For that, they needed help.

At first I said no, but Naomi kept at me until I broke down and agreed to help. What harm could it do? It wasn't like a crime had been committed or anything.

It was impossible to explain all this to a really spooked Dweena. She'd been screaming hysterically, shaking her hands over her head, ever since we pulled away from the loading dock at the morgue. The Ns, not exactly happy themselves, jumped out of the car in front of their Fourteenth Street apartment building and hightailed it inside without so much as a thank-you to any of us. I noted their rudeness but didn't comment.

Johnny suggested I treat Dweena to breakfast at the Two-Four, an all-night diner close to Sheridan Square. "It's the least you can do," he said.

I agreed. Besides, I was a little spooked myself and wasn't yet ready to go home alone.

The Two-Four was famous for enormous crunchy waffles, high-caffeine coffee, and whacked-out West Village clientele. At five o'clock in the morning—transition time—the diner was filled with burned-out dressed-up half-asleep all-nighters on their way home after god knows what and burned-out sweatsuit-clad insomniac half-asleep early risers. Under the fluorescent lights everyone looked equally ghastly.

A table full of club-hoppers waved at Dweena, but she was too distraught to notice. A few people recognized Johnny, though they pretended not to notice. Johnny pretended not to notice them pretending not to notice. None of them fooled me for a second. Johnny's *Tod Trueman, Urban Detective* series was finally doing well in the ratings and ultra-cool Johnny with his high cheekbones, smoky gray eyes, and thick black hair was impossible to miss. I was glad when he found a booth way in the back of the diner where we'd be less noticeable.

A bubble-gum-popping waitress sauntered up to our table. "Whatchas havin'?" she asked out of the side of her mouth. She slapped large laminated menus on the table. Her nylon dress was pink and clingy, her eight-inch-high blue-black beehive hairdo sprayed hard as metal. She looked like she was auditioning for a waitress job in an uptown theme restaurant.

We ordered a round of famous Two-Four waffles and coffee. When the waitress left, I tried explaining things to Dweena. "It was the best thing the Ns—Norbert and Naomi—could have done for their poor dead Uncle Buddy."

"Dropping his body off at the morgue like thieves in the night is the best thing?" Dweena's voice cracked and changed pitch.

"It had something to do with keeping peace in the Needleson family," I said.

That struck a chord with Dweena. "Well," she said, pausing and shaking her wig dramatically, "I can *certainly* relate to that."

The waitress brought our waffles. I slathered mine with butter and drowned them in sticky imitation maple syrup. Something about the wee hours brought out my worst eating habits.

Halfway through her waffles, Dweena set down her fork and said, "There's one thing I still don't get. Why the morgue?"

Johnny spoke. "The morgue was Brenda's brilliant idea.

Norbert and Naomi wanted to dump their Uncle Buddy in the alley behind the showroom.''

''That's exactly what I would have done,'' said Dweena.

''It would have been easier,'' I admitted, ''but it would have been terribly disrespectful. I figured leaving him at the morgue would be like leaving a baby in a basket in front of a church. He'd be well taken care of.''

''Not many babies get left in front of churches anymore,'' said an oddly wistful Dweena. ''Just the other day I read about this three-hour-old baby boy. Somebody threw this tiny little guy down a compactor chute. If the building super hadn't been alert, the poor thing would have been squished. I tell you, sometimes Dweena doesn't know what this world is coming to.''

We pondered that thought, chewing our sodden waffles in silence. By the time we'd finished eating, Dweena was almost back to normal. ''Feathers are quite the rage,'' she said. ''Do you think your friends would comp me a feather boa for helping out tonight?''

''Oh sure,'' I said. Not nearly sure as I sounded.

We drove up Tenth Avenue to the Upper West Side to return Lemmy's car. The sun was up, the city alive, streets already clogged with the morning rush. Dead tired, I leaned my head against the window and dozed off in the backseat, half hearing Dweena's chatter about what color feather boa she wanted. I remember Johnny telling her turquoise was nice. She pooh-poohed turquoise as too midwestern.

The next thing I felt was the forward and backward jerking motion of Johnny attempting to parallel park in front of Lemmy's building, a feat his driving lessons obviously hadn't yet covered. By the time I was fully awake, he'd somehow wedged the car in between a NYNEX truck and a Dumpster full of cracked sinks and plaster chunks. We left Lemmy's keys with his doorman and hailed the first cab we saw headed downtown.

The driver, a guy with a scraggly ponytail and a nervous tic, kept eyeing Dweena in his rearview mirror. Finally he turned around. "Man, I've just gotta say something. You look awfully familiar. Didn't you used to work down on Wall Street? You know, before that insider trading thing?"

"Do I look like a stockbroker to you?" asked Dweena.

"Nah," said the driver. "I guess it must have been someone else. I'm sure I've seen you somewhere, maybe—"

"I get around," said Dweena, firmly ending the conversation.

The cab dropped Dweena off on Gansevoort Street and then wound its way through the Village, stopping on West Fourth Street in front of Midnight Millinery. I invited Johnny in to see what I'd been working on for spring.

Most people assumed that I named Midnight Millinery after myself. Actually, I named the shop first and then named myself after the shop. When the previous tenant, a deli, got closed down by the authorities for running a numbers game from behind the candy counter, the landlord wanted to gut the place and open up a Laundromat. I talked him into renting the storefront to me instead, promising I'd be no trouble and that I'd handle all the renovations myself.

The previous proprietor must have had a friend in the sign-painting business because, even though the place was just a dinky numbers-running side street deli, it had an elaborate hand-painted gold leaf sign on the window, OPEN 'TIL MIDNIGHT. It was so beautiful, especially in the sunlight, that I couldn't bring myself to scrape it off. That's how I came up with the name Midnight Millinery for the shop. I was going through a divorce at the time. I didn't want to keep my ex's name because he was a jerk. I wasn't all that happy about taking back my own rather forgettable surname, so I became Brenda Midnight. My lawyer, who was already getting a bundle for the divorce and the corporation papers, threw in the name change for free. Up until the time I inherited my best friend's nearby apartment, I'd lived in the shop and slept beneath my hat-blocking table.

* * *

I showed Johnny a strip of antique straw braid I got at a bankruptcy auction. The naturally golden straw was perfectly preserved.

"Nice," said Johnny, tracing his forefinger over the pattern woven in the straw, "but what can you do with it? It's no more than half an inch wide."

"Check this out," I said. I opened up an extra-large-size Midnight Millinery hatbox. Johnny watched with rapt attention as I gently unwrapped the tissue from the giant straw hat I'd been working on for over a week. "I already sold one of these," I said.

Johnny kept his eyes on me as I lowered the hat on my head. "My god," he said, "that hat must be a yard across."

"Brimspan thirty-four point five." I said. "All from that skinny straw braid."

He came closer and looked at the brim. "I get it, you coil the straw around."

"Yeah," I said, "about a million times for one this big. It's like making a coil pot out of clay, except upside down and a hell of a lot slower. Then I handstitch the whole thing."

"Why not use a sewing machine?"

I shook my head. "It yanks the spirit right out of a hat."

Johnny sighed. "You and your artistic integrity, Brenda. You're never going to get rich."

When I got home my little dog Jackhammer greeted me by jumping three feet off the ground. Then he crash-landed and jumped up again.

I bent over and scratched his head. "Sorry about last night, little guy, but I had to dump a body at the morgue."

Talk of dead bodies didn't seem to bother that Yorkie. He licked my hand, then rolled over on his back and thrashed around on the floor—my signal to scratch his belly.

I took Jackhammer over to Midnight Millinery and spent the rest of the morning trying to figure out how to speed up production on the straw hat. When that failed, I tried to come up with another, speedier idea for spring. When that failed too, I went home and conked out on the couch. I slept through the afternoon and evening. I probably would have slept through the night if Johnny hadn't called around midnight.

"Lemmy's been arrested and it's all your fault."

3

Lemon B. Crenshaw had been Johnny's agent for as long as Johnny had been an actor, which was ever since I'd known him, and that was a long time. If Lemmy was in trouble, Johnny was in trouble.

"I'm coming over," said Johnny.

Johnny lived a couple of blocks away on Bleecker Street. So close, I'd barely finished making coffee when the doorman buzzed to say that Mr. Verlane was on his way up.

Jackhammer, thrilled to have a late-night visitor, zipped full steam into the foyer to greet Johnny, only to be disappointed. Johnny hadn't brought any of his usual doggie treats. In fact, he barely acknowledged Jackhammer. He headed straight for the kitchen and poured himself a cup of coffee. His hands shook and some of the coffee sloshed into the saucer. He somehow made it across the room and into his favorite chair, an office swivel from the forties, without spilling any more.

"Your friends the Ns are too much. What was it that Norbert guy said? His uncle had a bad ticker? Buddy Needleson didn't have a bad ticker, or if he did, he didn't die from it. He croaked because somebody bashed his head in. The cops think Lemmy had something to do with it."

"Because of the car?" I asked. I looked down at my feet and studied a scuff mark on my shoe, afraid to look Johnny in the eyes. He was right. It was all my fault.

"Yeah. Someone must have seen us dump the body and reported Lemmy's license plate number to the cops. They picked Lemmy up a few hours ago, surmising that anyone who would dump a body must have had something to do with it being dead. Lemmy told them someone had stolen his car, but the cops didn't go for that. The cops say that unless Lemmy comes up with a better story, they have to assume he's the culprit, or at the very least a conspirator to murder. Oh yeah, get this—the cops keep asking Lemmy who's the dead guy."

"They don't know it's Buddy Needleson?"

"Guess not. Unless they're trying to trip Lemmy up."

I'd assumed there'd been identification on the body, but I sure hadn't checked. In fact, I hadn't even looked at the body. The Ns had it all nicely rolled up in a blanket when I got to the showroom.

"That's the least of our worries," continued Johnny. "Sooner or later they'll ID the body."

"I suppose so. How's Lemmy taking it?"

"Lemmy's in shock. Later he'll be pissed. After that he'll be really pissed. Right now he's mostly concerned that he was arrested at an inopportune time. He had a hot date with a new discovery, a beautiful big-bazoomed aspiring actress/singer/dancer. According to Lemmy, she's going to be the next big thing. Claims he was about to 'get lucky'—romantic music, soft lights, the whole bit—when the cops charged in, read him his rights, and carted him off to jail."

That might turn out to be a good thing. The last time Lemmy got lucky was just one more blip in a long history of disasters. Lemon B. Crenshaw had rotten luck with the opposite sex. Two of his ex-wives had left him for other women. His last girlfriend turned out to be an honest-to-god cloak-and-dagger-type spy who goofed up and got Lemmy confused with a nefarious UN diplomat who lived on the same floor in his building. As soon as the spy discovered the truth about Lemmy—that he'd never masterminded a terrorist plot to overthrow anything and probably never would—she dropped him like a hot potato pancake. All this made Lemmy a bitter, raging man. Johnny said it gave him the edge that made him a great agent. I doubted getting stuck in jail would do much for his agenting abilities.

It was a lot for me to take in at once. My brain tried to sort it all out. "Why didn't Lemmy rat on us?"

"Like I said, he's still in shock. Even after that wears off, he'll probably keep his mouth shut."

"Why?" I asked. "Lemmy's a nice guy and all, but nobody's that nice. Is he nuts?"

"No, Lemmy's not nuts. Nor is he all that nice. It's business, pure and simple. He'll keep his mouth shut because if he tells the cops he loaned me the car, I'll get arrested. If I get arrested before the next round of *Tod Trueman* episodes are in the can, the series will get canceled, my career will be shot, and Lemmy will lose his percentage."

Something finally made sense. "Once you're done filming, once the producers have sunk all the money, will he tell?"

"Probably. At that point, once the money is spent, it's like any publicity is good publicity."

"How long before you're done filming?"

"I don't know. A couple of weeks, maybe. They're bringing in some hotshot director from the coast, Sal Stumpford."

"So we've got two weeks to find out who murdered Buddy Needleson. If we get the murderer, maybe the cops won't care so much who dumped the body."

"Right, Brenda. Except for the 'we' part. Remember, I'll be shooting."

What a mess. I'd never get my spring line done. The worst part was that the whole thing really was all my fault. Jackhammer jumped up in my lap and licked my cheek.

"It's not the end of the world," said Johnny. "I'll help as much as I can, but you know how the shooting goes. Day and night."

Yeah, day and night.

"If you want my opinion, you should start with your friends Norbert and Naomi," Johnny suggested.

"I'm not feeling exactly friendly toward them now."

"I don't blame you. They must have known," said Johnny. "Either that or they're incredibly stupid. How could they not notice that their uncle's head was bashed in? No way that looks like a 'bad ticker.' "

"I didn't notice his head," I said, immediately feeling foolish in my halfhearted attempt to defend the Ns.

"That's because he was wrapped up like a mummy. Even when the blanket unfurled at the morgue, only his legs stuck out."

"You don't think the Ns murdered their uncle, do you?" I asked.

Johnny shrugged.

I was tempted to pick up the phone and give the Ns a piece of my mind. But what if the Ns *had* killed their uncle? If they had and if they knew I knew, would they be forced to shut me up? Our friendship only went so far. If they knew Lemmy was arrested, they'd know that I knew. I didn't know what to do. This was worse than any nightmare.

"Johnny," I said, "what's the procedure? Would the Ns know that Lemmy's been arrested?"

"Probably not yet. Here's the way it would work in a *Tod Trueman* episode: Cops find body, inform next of kin. Buddy Needleson had a wife, right?"

"Yes. Babette. She's some kind of consultant, I think."

"She'd be the one informed. Not the Ns. Then the cops pick up the suspect, Lemmy. They might or might not tell the next of kin the suspect's name. The next of kin might or might not tell the rest of the family."

"What do you mean, 'might or might not'?"

"Depends on the plot."

"Great. How about real life?"

"What the hell do I know about real life?"

I didn't know a whole lot about real life either, but I did

know one thing, and that was that Lemmy needed a good lawyer. "Who's Lemmy got for a lawyer?"

"Lemmy doesn't believe in lawyers."

"He's gotta have a lawyer."

"You tell *him* that."

Johnny was filming the next day at the crack of dawn, so I sent him home to get his beauty sleep and promised to leave a message on his machine if anything developed. After he left I downed another cup of coffee and set about getting Lemmy a lawyer.

I didn't know any criminal lawyers, but a partner in a huge law firm owed me a big favor for saving his butt. The fact that he was incompetent and, even in his more lucid days, knew only corporate law did not deter me from calling him. Maybe he had friends.

He picked up on the second ring. "Duggins is my name, law's my game."

"Mr. Duggins," I said. "It's Brenda Midnight. I apologize for waking you."

"Brenda, so good to hear from you. Don't worry. I wasn't sleeping. I've got an important case on."

I heard the Perry Mason theme song in the background. Mr. Duggins had taped every show of the long-running television series. He watched it constantly.

I got right to the point. "I need a favor, Mr. Duggins."

"Anything you want. You know that."

"I need to find a criminal lawyer, the best—"

"Perry Mason."

Mr. Duggins walked a thin line. I needed a real lawyer, not a fictional character. I tried to be diplomatic. "I need one in the city, Mr. Duggins. Doesn't Mr. Mason practice in California?"

Mr. Duggins sighed. "Ah, yes. Too bad. Hmmm. Let me think a minute. In New York. Okay, you got a pencil? Write this down. Winfield, Brewster Winfield. He's a little weird, but good, damned good. I don't have his number at hand, but he'll be in the book."

I wondered what weird meant to Mr. Duggins. "Thank you, Mr. Duggins. You're a lifesaver."

"Anytime, Brenda. How's that urban detective boyfriend of yours, Tod whatever?"

"Tod Trueman."

"Right, Tod Trueman, a good man, Brenda. You could do a lot worse, you know."

"Yeah, I know," I said, hanging up. It wasn't worth telling Mr. Duggins that Tod Trueman wasn't real or that Johnny was my ex-boyfriend.

Keeping my fingers crossed that Brewster Winfield was a real live lawyer, I looked him up in the phone book. Bingo. Mr. Duggins had come through. Winfield was listed with a lower Broadway address.

"You've reached the law office of Brewster Winfield," said a recording. The voice was rich and mellifluous. "There's no one here right now, but if you care to leave a brief description of your offense, someone will get back to you during office hours. If you're already a client, please mention your case number so we may serve you more efficiently."

After the beep I said, "My name is Brenda Midnight. My friend Lemon B. Crenshaw was arrested for murder. He didn't—"

I heard a clanking noise and high-pitched feedback. Then a live voice deep as the sea and smooth as honey. "You mean Lemmy Crenshaw the famous agent?"

"That's right." It never ceased to amaze me how absolutely everybody had heard of Lemmy.

"Fabulous," said Brewster Winfield. "Myrtle and I do this act . . ."

It looked like I was going to be out all night for the second night in a row.

I once read an article that said when the World Trade Center was built, Manhattan wind patterns changed and Broadway became the windiest street in the city. My personal experience coincided with that. I wind-tested my hat designs on Broadway and Eighth Street. Brewster Winfield's corner, a couple of blocks below Canal Street, was even windier.

I stood in front of the locked six-story loft building, hanging on to my hat for dear life, barely able to breathe as the wind slammed into me, and wondering how long it would take to freeze to death. Before long I heard someone call my name. I looked up.

A black man leaned out of a top-story window. Medusa-like coils of hair whipped around his head. "Catch," he yelled, and dropped a pink and gray argyle sock. It landed on the sidewalk in front of me. I picked it up. Inside was a set of keys that got me in the front door of the building.

The grim lobby smelled of fuel oil and dust. A fluorescent light flickered and buzzed in the ceiling. My boots crunched over gravel-size crumbs of plaster that had cracked off the gray-green walls.

The elevator, tiny and creaky and painfully slow, had a warped floor that gave a little when I stood on it. I looked out a round window at the passing cement wall and worried there would be a blackout. Please, Con Ed, I thought, I promise to always pay my bill on time if you'll just keep the electricity running long enough for me to get out of this death trap. By the time the elevator jerked to a stop on the top floor, I'd vowed to pay Con Ed six months in advance. Finally, with a horrible grating sound, the door opened and I found myself in the middle of a totally renovated, sleek, shiny hundred-foot-long loft. The thick plank floor gleamed.

"Brenda Midnight, I presume."

Brewster Winfield, round wide face, open smile, tall and dignified even in a white terrycloth robe and fuzzy plaid slippers, offered his hand. Two seconds into our handshake I noticed a strange movement in the coils of his hair. I yanked my hand away and jumped back three feet. Out of my throat came a sound, halfway between an eek and an expletive.

''It's only Myrtle,'' he said, stroking the orange and black snake entwined in his hair. ''She's a sweetheart, wouldn't hurt a flea.''

''I'm not a flea,'' I said.

Winfield gripped the snake around its middle, eased it off his neck, and placed it in a glass terrarium filled with sand and twigs and snake toys. The terrarium sat on a large wooden platform that was on wheels. ''Time to go beddy-bye, Myrtle. Tell the nice lady night-night.'' Myrtle slithered around her home checking things out, then rested her head beside a rock. Once Myrtle had settled in, Winfield turned his attention back to me. ''It's a little late for Myrtle to be up anyway. She had a grueling audition today.''

''Audition?''

''She does tricks.''

What did I expect? I asked myself, considering who'd recommended Brewster Winfield.

Motioning for me to follow, he led me through the loft. If the ability to spend lots of money with style and taste was any indication of lawyerly competence, maybe Winfield was all right. His space was divided into areas loosely defined by elaborately carved columns spaced every twenty feet or so. A tastefully muted color scheme and simple furniture of natural woods positively oozed elegance and wealth. The office area was in the front part of the loft, with high arched windows overlooking Broadway. A thick slab of glass resting atop four stacks of antique leather-bound law books served as his desk. It was bare except for a fresh yellow legal pad and an antique silver fountain pen.

He sat down at the desk. I sat in a leather chair opposite.

''Naturally I've heard of Mr. Crenshaw,'' said the lawyer. He interlaced his fingers, sat back in his chair, and smiled, waiting for me to say something.

I didn't know how much to tell him. I sure didn't want him to know about my involvement, or Johnny's, but without all the facts, the story didn't make much sense. So in the end I had to blab everything I knew, down to the last detail.

The whole time I spoke, Winfield tapped his desk with the silver pen, occasionally stopping to write something on the pad. He didn't interrupt. When I finished he stopped tapping the pen and looked out the window for what seemed like a long time. Finally he turned to me and said, "Our Mr. Crenshaw is a known commodity, a star in his own right. That helps. I also like the morgue angle. It gives the case an appealing morbidity. With some changes—we'll have to sex it up a bit—I think it can fly. I'll take the case." He stood up to shake my hand.

"Thank you, Mr. Winfield."

"Call me Brew." He settled back down in his chair. "Now, about my fees."

4

I felt a whole lot better with a lawyer on the case, even a lawyer who babytalked to a snake. Winfield assured me he'd get Lemmy sprung by lunchtime. "No prob," he'd said. "The cops have zilch. Somebody stole Mr. Crenshaw's car, dumped a body, and returned the car. Big deal. This is New York, stuff like that happens all the time. Doesn't mean diddly shit."

I hoped he was right because half a day was about all I could afford. Brewster Winfield did not come cheap.

I got home around breakfast time. Jackhammer glared at me through half-open eyes, but didn't budge off his bed. His well-chewed quilt was twisted underneath him. I straightened it out and covered him. "What's this," I asked, "no greeting, no flinging yourself at me in ecstasy, no begging for green beans?"

He snorted and burrowed under the quilt, turning so that he faced the wall. He didn't approve of my being out all night.

I patted him on the head. "Go back to sleep," I said, "and don't worry. It's in the lawyer's hands now. Everything will be back to normal before you know it."

I looked forward to the day when all of us could sit over a glass of wine at Angie's bar—Johnny, Lemmy, and me—

and laugh about the time Lemmy spent the night in the lockup.

I opened up the couch into a bed, smoothed out the sheets, and lay down, hoping to get a couple of hours' sleep before getting back to work on my spring line. No sooner had I fluffed up my pillow than I heard a pounding on the door. Cursing, I dragged myself into the foyer.

Like all New York apartments, mine had a peephole in the door. It's wide-angle lens brought six feet of peripheral hallway into view. Elizabeth, my across-the-hall neighbor, waggled her forefinger at me in greeting. When I opened the door, she zipped by me in a blur of red and slammed into the closet door. She grabbed the brass doorknob to steady herself.

"How's the Rollerblading going?" I asked, careful to keep my smile to myself.

She wore a bright red stretch unitard with black diagonal insets on the legs, black kneepads, and a black helmet decorated with white skull designs. Interesting attire for a woman in her early seventies.

"Fantastic," she said. "I'm about ready to hit the streets."

That's what I was afraid of. "Maybe you should take some lessons," I suggested. "Sidewalks are hard."

"Phooey," she said. "I don't need some frustrated power-tripping choreographer of an aerobics instructor telling me how to skate." She thumped her helmet. "I've got this, I've got kneepads, I'll be fine and dandy."

Back in what is now known as The Sixties, Elizabeth Franklin Perry had been a well-known artist and media darling, someone I'd actually studied in an art history class. At the height of her popularity, she quit making art to protest the Vietnam War. She hints there were other reasons as well, but she won't elaborate. For a short time last year she and my friend Chuck ran a computer graphics business out of a corner of Midnight Millinery. Fortunately that was over and we could be friends again. Now Elizabeth skates, concocts batches of very strange cookies, and, blatantly ignoring the rules of the condo, boards dogs. Before Jackhammer moved into my life, Elizabeth had boarded him for a man who had to give him up when he married a woman who claimed to be allergic.

Jackhammer adored Elizabeth. When he heard her voice, he roused himself, tore into the foyer like a cannonball, and hurled himself against her kneepads—the greeting I would have gotten if he hadn't been all huffy at me.

"Take off your helmet and stay awhile," I said.

"Don't mind if I do." With Jackhammer racing along beside her, she skated over to the chair by the window and fell into it. She took off her helmet, releasing a yard or so of silver and black hair. She sometimes wore her hair in a fat single braid tied off with a tiny bow at the end, but today it was hanging wild, frizzy, and crinkled from years of braiding. She looked at me and frowned. "You look like hell, Brenda. When was the last time you slept?"

"I had to dump off a dead body at the morgue late the other night. Ever since—"

She rolled her eyes. "Yeah, right."

"No, really—"

She interrupted. "Got any luggage?"

It was probably better not to tell her anyway. "Luggage? No. Why? You going somewhere?"

I could never understand why anyone would want to travel away from New York, the most interesting city in the world. Only under extreme duress did I ever venture off the island of Manhattan. For that matter, except for an occasional mission to the garment district for supplies, I rarely traveled above Fourteenth Street.

"Dude Bob wants me to meet him in Chicago," said Elizabeth. "I told him I'd think about it, but you know how he is. He went ahead and sent me a ticket. My plane leaves tonight."

In a weird way, the Dude was Elizabeth's boyfriend. They had met online and conducted most of their relationship typing at each other, computer to computer, modem to modem, in what they called cyberspace. Dude Bob had a real name that I could never remember, but Elizabeth referred to him by his Internet address, part of which was Dude Bob 43. According to Elizabeth that meant he was the forty-third person who subscribed to the same Internet provider who wanted to call himself Dude Bob.

I'd met the Dude briefly when he came to New York for a face-to-face meeting with Elizabeth. Their romance almost ended when Elizabeth discovered he'd been a hawk during the Vietnam mess.

"Why Chicago?" I asked. "Isn't it cold and windy enough for you here?"

"Convention," she answered. "Vietnam collectibles."

"With your politics? You've got to be kidding."

"My warmongering Dude says that the convention is for everyone—even 'commie pinko peaceniks' like me. After all, memorabilia is memorabilia. Some of the stuff I have, peace buttons and bumper stickers, could be worth a pile of money."

"Amazing."

"I've just got to figure out a way to get the stuff there."

"Luggage I don't have, but I just had four gross of Midnight Millinery hatboxes delivered."

Elizabeth smiled. "That's a great idea. A hatbox will be perfect, ever so stylish."

While Elizabeth prattled on about meeting up with Dude Bob, I got out my stepladder, dragged a couple of hatboxes out of the top of the closet, and handed them down to Elizabeth. "If these aren't enough, I can get more from the shop."

"These will do just fine," said Elizabeth. She rolled toward the door. "I hate to rush off and all, but I've got a ton of stuff to do."

By the time Elizabeth left, I was wide awake. Sleep was out of the question, so I munched on a couple of graham crackers for sustenance, grabbed Jackhammer, and headed over to Midnight Millinery. On the way I picked up the newspapers. I turned through every page—even the sports sections—but couldn't find any mention of a body dumped at the morgue or Lemmy's arrest.

Trusting that Brewster Winfield was earning his fee, I turned my attention to my spring line. I sketched hat shapes—big-brimmed, little-brimmed, no-brimmed, adding a flower here, a bow there. I filled up page after page, but nothing leaped off the paper screaming, "Make me, I'm spring." Still, it was satisfying work and got dead bodies, Lemmy, and lawyers off my mind. I'd almost convinced myself that the entire morbid mess had been a nightmare, a sign of overwork, a figment of an overactive imagination, when Dweena intruded, smashing that fantasy for good.

She stormed into the shop, resplendent in thigh-high white patent-leather boots, a chartreuse mohair miniskirt, and black leather jacket. Her wig, a perfect match for the skirt, fell thick and straight almost to her waist. Synthetic was my guess, probably from Fourteenth Street.

"What the hell's wrong with your creepy friends?" She stomped her platform heel on the bare floor.

"Which creepy friends?"

"The Ns," she said, "or whatever it is you call them. Those ghouls with the body. I called them up, you know, just like you told me to, and asked about the feather boa you said they'd give me. That Naomi person refused. She whined about hard times and told me ten percent above wholesale was the absolute best she could do. Plus I've gotta have a resale number. Resale number? Get real. I told her she owed Dweena big for helping out the other night. Know what she did? The pudgy little strumpet hung up on me."

What was wrong with Naomi anyway? Hard times? The Ns had just been bragging how this was their best season ever. "Hang on there a minute, Dweena. I'll get this straightened out." I dragged the phone into the storage closet for privacy. I'd get Dweena a feather boa if I had to buy it myself.

"Tell Naomi I'm traumatized, so now I want two boas, red *and* black," she said.

I shut the closet door and yanked the cord on the overhead light. I was surrounded by Midnight Millinery hatboxes and rows of antique hat blocks I got at the flea market. I kept them around as much for their magic as history. Now, alone with them in the closet, it felt like each wooden block was staring at me. Uncomfortable, I turned off the light and dialed in the dark.

Naomi answered, in her bubbliest business voice. "Needleson Brothers."

I froze. I'd been carried away by the moment. My anger at Naomi made me forget that she was the last person I wanted to talk to. Ever. She and Norbert had lied to me, set me up. Though it was hard for me to imagine, there was the possibility that one or both of the Ns had killed their uncle.

"Hello," said Naomi. "Hello, hello. Goddammit, who's there?"

Still I said nothing. If the Ns hadn't done it, who had? Not Lemmy. I was all mixed up. The only thing I knew for sure was that I didn't want to talk to Naomi. Hang up, I told myself.

"Brenda, is this some kind of joke?" All the bubble was gone from Naomi's voice.

I remembered too late. Naomi had trouble with a heavy breather, so for her birthday Norbert installed a Caller ID box on her phone. My own phone number had shown up on her display, betraying me. Caught, I had no choice but to answer. "Hi, Naomi. Sorry, I was distracted there for a moment."

"I thought you were this creep I met the other night. I never should have given him my number."

I didn't want to get into the trials and tribulations of Naomi's hapless love life or her on-again, off-again relationship with her boyfriend Fred. I tried to shut her up. "The reason I called—"

"But you know me," interrupted Naomi, telling me what I didn't want to know. "Fred's been a real jerk lately, but it's not like I'm going to stay home crying in my pillow.

Not this gal. So the other day I'm on a crosstown bus and I meet this real cute guy who says he's a record producer and he wants to hear my act. He's talking demo tape, so of course I gave him my number. It's been two weeks already and he hasn't called. I'm thinking maybe he's not a record producer at all. I think he was just after my body. . . .''

I tuned out and tried to figure out how to approach the situation. Murder could sure screw up a friendship.

Naomi interrupted my thoughts. ''. . . So, Brenda, what was it you wanted?''

First things first, I thought. I could worry about the murder some other time. ''Uh, it's Dweena. You know, she really wants that feather boa. She went all out for you guys the other night. Left her job early and everything.''

''Some job,'' said Naomi. ''Anyway, I already took care of Dweena. Imagine her nerve—and believe me I use the term 'her' loosely—calling and asking for a free boa, like they grow on trees or something. I did the only sensible thing. I hung up on her. Do you know how much a good feather boa costs?''

I didn't, but was willing to bet the best boa in the world wouldn't cost as much as one hour of Brewster Winfield's time. ''Look, Naomi,'' I said, ''I didn't think it would be that big a deal, one little boa, actually two. Without Dweena's license—''

Naomi jumped down my throat. ''Excuse me, Brenda but the morgue, and therefore the car, and therefore the need for Dweena, was all your idea. If Dweena wants a boa, then I suggest *you* buy her one.''

It felt weird yelling into the phone, closed up in a dark closet, but I did it—extraordinary times called for extraordinary measures. In the end, I convinced Naomi to throw in one boa for free if I bought the other at full price. After a squabble as to what constituted the full price, wholesale or retail (I won; Naomi agreed to wholesale), I informed Naomi that Dweena would drop by soon to pick out her boas. Naomi insisted I come with Dweena. Much as I didn't want to, it seemed like a good idea. No telling how the Ns would treat her.

Dweena was thrilled to hear I'd worked out a deal for two boas. She grabbed one of my hatboxes, I grabbed Jackhammer, and we set out through the streets of the Village, over to Sixth Avenue to wait a very long time for a bus in the freezing cold. To the north, beyond the spire of the Empire State Building, a stack of dark gray clouds poised, threatening snow.

Everyone on the street noticed Dweena. She attracted flirtatious winks, horn honks, flat-out stares, and one invitation to dinner by what seemed like a very sincere guy. It was probably the chartreuse hair or the miniskirt. Standing in her shadow, ignored, I felt a little dowdy, even though I had on my best-selling winter hat that never failed to look less than smashing. I hated the feeling.

When the bus finally came Dweena marched up the steps. With a dramatic flounce of her wig she sailed right by the bus driver, paying nothing. When the driver tapped on the fare box, Dweena winked and said, "I'm on the guest list." Then, nodding toward me, "My friend too."

The driver didn't go for it. "Guest list," he said. "Now I've heard everything." Again he tapped the box, this time more insistently.

"Hmpf," said Dweena, plunking her token into the fare box.

I was mortified, afraid I'd get caught sneaking Jackhammer on the bus, but the bus driver was so amazed at Dweena's brazenness, he didn't notice the wiggly bulge under my coat.

Needleson Brothers was in a run-down eight-story building. The lobby, never grand or even nice, was downright depressing. A grimy glass-covered board in the lobby listed the businesses in the building. Like Needleson Brothers, most were in the trimming trade—rhinestones, ribbons, buttons, feathers, beads. At the bottom of the list in big plastic letters, the terse warning TO THE TRADE ONLY was posted.

"I've been here before," said Dweena.

"There's dozens of buildings like this around here," I said.

"I'm pretty sure it's this one," she said.

I punched the elevator button. The fact that it didn't light up didn't concern me; I couldn't remember that it ever had. The fact that I heard no whirring of gears or clanking in the elevator shaft sent us into the stairwell. The door slammed shut behind us with a loud clang.

Dweena shuddered. "It smells like pee in here," she said.

"That's why I'm carrying Jackhammer," I said.

"He'd let us know if there was somebody in here, wouldn't he?"

"Oh sure," I said. I didn't let on, but I was greatly relieved that we made it all the way up without running into anyone other than a spider stringing a web between a water pipe and the third-floor wall.

The Needlesons had toned down the mothball odor considerably. Still, when I opened the door to the Ns' floor, Jackhammer's nostrils quivered.

"I know that smell," said Dweena. "I'm positive I've been here before."

Naomi heard us in the hallway and opened the door before I had a chance to knock. I knew her teeth were clenched behind her forced smile. "Dweena, how nice to see you again," she said. She had on a turquoise and white polka-dot dress with lace trim around the neckline.

"Likewise," said Dweena, sashaying into the showroom.

I put Jackhammer down. He scrambled around sticking his nose into every corner.

"Oh look, Norbert," said Naomi, "Brenda brought Jackhammer with her. I just love that little dog."

Norbert sat at his desk trying not to stare at Dweena. "That's nice."

While Dweena flitted from one gaudy display to the next, I tried to make polite conversation with the Ns.

"I am really creeped out," said Naomi, motioning me back to Norbert's desk.

"What's wrong now?" I asked.

"Mommy and Daddy called right after you did, you know, to find out the particulars about Uncle Buddy's funeral. So Norbert called Aunt Babette to find out."

"I know this is a difficult time for all of you," I said, not knowing what else to say.

"You don't know the half of it," said Norbert. "Babette was completely in the dark. She didn't know Uncle Buddy was dead, and there I was inquiring about the funeral."

"She thought he was joking," said Naomi.

"Some joke," I said.

"Right," said Norbert. "Babette says Buddy's on a sales trip. She doesn't expect him back until tomorrow."

Which meant the morgue still hadn't identified the body. I guess the cops hadn't been trying to trip Lemmy up after all. They really didn't know the body was Buddy Needleson's. "Did your uncle have identification on him when he was here?" I asked.

"I didn't look, but he usually carried a wallet," said Norbert. "Some bum probably stole it while the body was on the loading dock."

It pained me to think Buddy Needleson's body had been pickpocketed while on the morgue's loading dock. My idea of taking him to the morgue was to make sure he was treated nicely.

"Could be the killer stole it," said Naomi. She slapped her hand over her mouth.

"Goddamn it, Naomi," said Norbert, "don't you ever know when to shut up?" He turned to me. "My nutty sister doesn't know what she's talking about."

I didn't fall for that. Naomi had let the cat out of the bag. I now knew that they knew that their uncle had been murdered, and they now knew that I knew.

A red-faced Naomi fessed up. "We think he was bashed with Daddy's baseball bat. You know, the one he used for inventory."

The inventory bat. That thought was especially disturbing. "I just wish you'd told me," I said. "Murder changes everything."

"You wouldn't have helped if you'd known," said Naomi.

She sure was right about that. The three of us went at it for a while, screaming accusations back and forth. If anything good came out of the fight it was that I was finally convinced that neither of the Ns had anything to do with murdering their uncle. They might be liars, creeps, and snobs, but they weren't killers.

The battle was so intense, we forgot all about Dweena. When it was over we saw her staring at the three of us. She clutched Jackhammer close to her chest. "Can we leave now?" she asked.

Dweena and I walked back to the Village. I needed to clear my head; Jackhammer needed exercise. Dweena was just happy to be the hell away from the Ns. All together she had three boas. The red one the Ns gave her, the black one I bought for her wholesale, and a chartreuse one she'd stuffed into the hatbox when she thought no one was looking.

5

It really bothered me that no one had yet identified Buddy Needleson's body. Depending on the circumstances under which his wallet was stolen—at Needleson Brothers by the killer or on the morgue's loading dock by a pickpocket—that might have been my fault too.

His poor wife. How was she going to feel when her husband didn't come back from his sales trip and she found out Norbert wasn't kidding? I felt obligated to straighten this out. The Ns didn't give a hoot. The way they looked at it, the longer identification was delayed, the longer the funeral would be delayed, and the longer their parents would stay in Florida and not see the mess they'd made of their apartment.

An anonymous tip to the medical examiner's office seemed the way to go. I didn't want to get burned by Caller ID again, so to assure the call was truly anonymous, I went down to the laundry room in the basement to use the payphone. It was early evening, a slow time for laundry. I had the place all to myself. After a couple of false starts to get up my nerve, I finally let the quarter drop and dialed. My call was picked up immediately and I found myself lost in voice mail. I didn't want to hear the morgue's hours of operation. I didn't want the death statistics option or a brief history of the medical examiner's office. What I wanted was to leave an anonymous tip. I slammed down the receiver. I hated voice mail.

To do right by Buddy Needleson, I'd have to go to the morgue and identify his body in person. Either that or skip the whole thing entirely, which is exactly what I decided to do. Screw it. I'd already done enough. John Doe? Buddy Needleson? What the hell difference did it make? Dead was dead. If his own niece and nephew didn't care, why should I?

It nagged at me, the thought of Buddy Needleson moldering in a steel drawer, nameless and alone, perhaps to be buried as a pauper. It nagged at me in the shower, it nagged at me while eating a stale bread and cheese sandwich for dinner, it nagged me through my first glass of red wine. By the second, I couldn't stand it. I'd go.

I called Johnny, hoping to talk him into coming along, but he didn't answer. His filming must have run late.

A year or so ago a mouse died behind the wall of Midnight Millinery. I washed and scrubbed and sprayed but the smell of death lingered for days in the shop, in my clothes, in my hair, in my consciousness. If a tiny mouse could smell that bad, what would a morgue full of humans smell like? With that in mind, I walked through my building, checking the compactor room on each floor for garbage. On the seventh floor I snagged a red University of Oklahoma sweatshirt hanging on the newspaper recycling bin, on eleven a pair of dark green paint-stained sweatpants, and on fourteen a scarf with bright yellow sunflowers over a sky-blue background.

I tried Johnny again. Still no answer. Resigned to go alone, I put on the scrounged sweats, tied the sunflower scarf over my hair, and took off without my coat, not wanting to risk stinking it up. It'd be warm enough in a cab. Luckily, someone was getting out of a cab directly in front of the building. I jumped in. "Morgue," I said to the driver.

"Nice outfit," he said.

* * *

First Avenue was as creepy and desolate at seven-thirty in the evening as it had been at four A.M. two nights before. The cold weather didn't help any; neither did the knowledge that I was bound for the morgue, this time inside where they stashed the dead.

The cab driver left me off in front of the morgue, then peeled out, leaving black tire marks behind.

As I suspected, the day staff had gone home. The place was locked up tight. I cupped my hands around my eyes and looked through the glass door for signs of life. The reception area was dark and empty. I knew there had to be staff somewhere to take care of all the people who died in questionable circumstances after normal business hours.

An icy wind blasted down the street, tearing through my sweatclothes, making me wish I'd planned this out a little better. When I was about to give up and go home, I saw the tiny red glow of a cigarette far down a dark corridor. I pounded on the door. The red glow came closer. I heard a metallic click and the door opened.

"Oh you, huh?" said a husky voice. By the light of the street lamp I could just make out that the speaker was a blond freckle-faced man in his early twenties, dressed in a light blue lab coat.

Oh you. What did he mean by that? Was he expecting someone? "Yes," I said, playing it by ear.

"What year?" he asked.

I had no idea how to respond to that. "Year?" I asked.

"Year, you know. When did you graduate?" He pointed at my sweatshirt. "My second cousin went to oh you. I'd say from looking at you, he was there before your time, but you probably heard of him, they called him Einstein on account of how he ran down the football field—you know, relatively fast. Man, I remember when oh you went all the way to the Orange Bowl."

Oh you. He must have meant Oklahoma University. "Einstein? Sure I've heard of Einstein. A legend on campus." I smiled.

"Come on in, then, before you catch your death," said the second cousin of the football star.

He offered me a seat in the dark reception room. I held my breath as long as possible, but finally sucked in the air and was relieved to find it smelled no worse than any other reception room in New York. It was a bit stale, with an odd overtone that was not death. I sniffed again. Marijuana. My friend was higher than a kite.

"Thanks for letting me in," I said.

"You're lucky I saw you," he said. "I just came up here to sneak a smoke. Wacky weed. Want a hit?"

"No thanks."

"Name's Horace," he said.

We shook hands. "Jane," I said.

That about did it for the small talk. I sat and watched him smoke. He smoked and watched me watch him. He smoked until there was nothing left to smoke. "I best be getting back," he said, "unless, that is, I can do something for you."

"There is something," I said. "I came to see if a friend of mine is here, John Doe."

"We get a lot of those."

"Will you show me? I'd like to see them."

"Not so fast," he said. "You can't just come in here and look at our John Does. You've gotta come with a cop, or have some kind of authorization. I mean, can you imagine, with all the weirdos in this city, what this place would turn into if we just let anybody in to look at our bodies? Anyway, I couldn't help you if I wanted to, that's not my job. I'm just a lowly lab assistant working my way through school. Shit, I'd be in big trouble if they even knew I let you in, but I felt sorry for you out there in the cold like that. Plus you knowing my cousin and all."

I had no logical argument for why he should risk his job to help me. The situation called for deceit, for drama. I had to hope he had a soft heart and appeal to it. "Oh please," I said, bursting into tears.

He ripped a handful of tissues from one of the many

boxes in the waiting room. ''Jeezus lady, don't cry. All I need is for someone to hear you. We'll both be in a heap of big trouble.''

''I can't go to the police. You see, Buddy's married, and, and, and . . .''

''Oh, I get it. You and this Buddy, um, this John Doe . . .'' He winked.

I dabbed at my eyes and nodded.

''What makes you think he's here?''

''Just a feeling,'' I said. ''Sometimes I get these feelings.'' I started sobbing again, louder this time.

''Jeezus, lady. This isn't normal procedure, you know, but I guess maybe I can help you out. After all, you're almost a friend of my cuz Einstein.''

I blew my nose hard, looked up, and said, ''A legend, that Einstein.''

''All right, then. You wait right here.''

''Here? Alone?'' I asked. Too late, Horace had disappeared.

So I sat, all alone, in the morgue, in the dark waiting room, and watched cars stream by on First Avenue, wishing I could be in any one of them, going anyplace else. Bad as the waiting room was, I realized it would get worse. I still had to go somewhere and look at all the dead John Does. Maybe I'd get lucky and they'd show me Buddy Needleson first. I'd only seen him a couple of times alive: once at a Christmas party, and once when he tried to talk me into buying two gross of hot pink hackle pads he'd ordered by mistake. I was sure I would recognize him even dead, with his full head of wavy white hair and bushy black eyebrows.

About ten minutes later Horace came back. He carried a manila file folder. ''Come with me,'' he said, opening a door off to the side of the waiting room.

I hoped I didn't retch from the smell. Or faint. Losing consciousness in this place would be the absolute worst. Taking a deep breath, I followed him into the small room.

He flicked on an overhead light. ''No windows,'' he said, gesturing toward the cream-colored walls. ''We can turn on the lights in here so you can look at the pictures."

"What pictures?"

"The Doe family."

I sighed loudly. I wasn't going to have to look at bodies after all. Visions of rotting toe-tagged corpses vanished from my head. Pictures I could handle.

He looked at the expression on my face and laughed. "You didn't . . . you didn't think. Oh my god." He laughed some more. "Good lord, we don't do *that* anymore, not unless absolutely necessary." He handed me a stack of photographs. "Here, look at these."

I looked at the pictures out of the corner of my eye, not wanting to see. I didn't want to violate the privacy of dead strangers. When I caught sight of bushy black eyebrows, I looked at that picture directly. It was Buddy Needleson all right, with his head bashed in. I remembered to turn on the tears. "That's him, that's my Buddy."

"No shit," said Horace. "I never would have pegged this guy as your type. There's some papers you'll have to fill out and I'll need your signature."

"No," I said. "I can't fill out any papers. His wife—"

"Oh right." He thought for a moment. "Okay, here's what I can do. Tell me how to spell your boyfriend's name. There's a payphone down the hall. I'll call it in anonymously."

"That works?"

"You'd be surprised how much information comes in that way. You just have to know how to get through the voice mail."

"Thank you, thank you so much," I said, between sobs.

"Sure. Anytime. I guess that's about it, then, unless you want to see the body. We have a viewing room, for family and the like. It's got a little window, you can open it and touch him if you like, kiss him good-bye. I'd advise it. Given your special relationship to the deceased, you might not get another chance. Be kinda clumsy at the funeral, assuming the missus shows up."

I shuddered. "Thanks, but I don't think so. I'd rather remember him alive."

"I can dig it." On the way to the door, he said, "So lady, since your old man is like croaked and all, maybe you want to get in touch with my cousin, seeing as how you two have the same alma mater. He's not married." He handed me a slip of paper. "Here's his number. Give him a call."

"Thank you, I may just do that." I smiled, figuring I should be gracious if I expected him to make that anonymous call.

As soon as I got home I jumped in the shower. Then I shoved the sweatclothes and hideous scarf down the compactor chute. I thanked the Oklahoma University sweatshirt as it disappeared into the void.

I was surprised to find no calls on the answering machine. I had expected at least a thank-you call from Lemmy for getting Winfield to get him out of jail.

I called Johnny to see if he'd heard from Lemmy, but he either wasn't home yet or wasn't answering. Sometimes in the middle of filming Johnny got real weird and wouldn't talk to anybody. He claimed it put him out of character.

Much as I didn't want to trip the billing switch, I called Brewster Winfield. Just like last night, he picked up when I was speaking into his answering machine.

"It didn't go quite as planned," he said.

"What do you mean? Where's Lemmy?"

"Still incarcerated. The bureaucracy can be a real bitch at times, but I've put things in motion. Don't you worry yourself. Mr. Crenshaw will be back on the street soon, tomorrow afternoon at the latest."

6

The phone woke me.

It was Johnny. "What's going on?" he asked. "Lemmy's not answering his phone."

"I called you last night to tell you," I said, "but you weren't home." I mashed the receiver between my right ear and the pillow. "Everything's going to be all right. I found a lawyer for Lemmy, Brewster Winfield. He promised Lemmy'd be out by this afternoon." I left out the part about the lawyer promising to spring Lemmy the day before.

"I thought you didn't know any criminal lawyers."

"Mr. Duggins recommended him," I said. Johnny didn't have much faith in Mr. Duggins. If I'd been more awake I'd have lied.

"Duggins! That flake! Dammit, Brenda, this is important. This is Lemmy we're talking about. Remember I told you about this West Coast director, Sal Stumpford? Already he's asking questions."

"What kinda questions?"

"You know, questions like, 'Where the hell's Lemmy Crenshaw?' That kind of question."

"What did you tell him?"

"I don't know. I made up some crap."

"Aside from that, how's the filming going?"

Johnny sighed. "The usual. Grueling long day, grueling

long dinner, grueling long interview with a magazine. It'd be a whole lot better if Lemmy were around to smooth over the edges.''

''He'll be out soon. I think this lawyer's okay. The situation's under control.''

''I hope so, Brenda. I really hope so.''

''I straightened out that other thing too, about the screw-up at the morgue. I made sure Buddy Needleson's body was properly identified.''

''How'd you do that?''

If I'd known how upset Johnny was going to get, I would have kept my mouth shut about my second trip to the morgue.

''Jesus Christ, Brenda. Don't you realize how dangerous that could have been? That dope-smoking lab assistant could have been some—''

''He was okay. It worked out fine.''

''Next time, Brenda, please call me before you run off and do something stupid. Some places, you shouldn't go alone.''

''I did call you, Johnny. You weren't home.''

''Oh. Then you should have waited until I was home.''

'' 'Bye, Johnny.'' I hung up before he had a chance to protest.

Confident that Brewster Winfield was out there racking up billable hours getting Lemmy out of the hoosegow, and that the authorities had correctly identified Buddy Needleson, I went over to Midnight Millinery and turned my thoughts and efforts back to my spring line. Or tried to. I made a gallant effort, but it was impossible to think spring while looking out the storefront window at the cold gray day. Worse, every ten minutes or so, the blues show I was listening to on the radio got interrupted with warnings of the huge, potentially crippling snowstorm making its way toward New York City.

I gave in to the weather hysteria. It was time to lay in some food supplies. Jackhammer and I went shopping along Bleecker Street and got enough pasta, cheese, and bread to last through any storm. On the way back we passed by Johnny's apartment building. I felt a pang of loneliness. He'd been a lot more fun before he became Tod Trueman, Urban Detective.

The phone was ringing when I walked in the door. I dropped the groceries and made a dive for the receiver. I figured it would be Brewster Winfield with good news.

It was Brewster Winfield, all right, but the news was bad.

"I'm on a payphone," he said. "Can you hear me okay?"

"Perfect," I said.

"We've got trouble, big trouble."

"I don't understand," I said. "You said by this afternoon—"

"Look, there's no time to explain. You've got to come up with a place to stash Mr. Crenshaw. Someplace where nobody would think to look for him."

"Why? Where is he now?"

"I'll explain later. Just do it. I'll call you every fifteen minutes until you find a place."

I may not have understood the particulars, but I picked up on the urgency in Winfield's voice. Positive I could talk my friend Chuck Riley into hiding Lemmy for a few days, I said, "I already know a place. Give me an hour to set it up."

"Not one second more. I've got to get Mr. Crenshaw off the street."

I gave him Chuck's address.

"That's a hellhole," said Winfield.

Unlike the West Village, where the streets were so twisted up that West Twelfth Street intersected West Fourth Street, and streets like Charles and Horatio were jammed in between numbered streets, throwing off the logical numerical progression, the East Village was laid out so that it pretty much conformed to Manhattan's grid. Leave it to Chuck, though, to find the strangest street over there, the strip of East Fifth that dead-ended at both the Avenue A end and the Avenue B end, an accident that made the street uncommonly quiet by East Village standards.

The cab turned off Avenue B onto East Fifth Street and almost slammed into a black-primered car carcass that sat smack in the middle of the street. Every possible sellable tidbit had been stripped. A short muscular guy waited while his short muscular pit bull lifted his leg in front of a squatter-occupied building. Periodically the city declared war and chased the squatters out, but they always returned. Chuck lived in a boarded-up storefront across the street from the squat. Except for lack of natural light, it was actually quite nice.

He greeted me with a big smile and a bear hug. He'd forced his fuzzball cloud of red hair into a four-inch-long ponytail. Otherwise he looked the same—tall, skinny, freckled, dorky, and wired. Chuck Riley was an electronics genius, always on the intellectual edge. He hung out in cyberspace, East Village rock and roll clubs, and phone freak conventions.

Every square inch of his apartment was crammed full of computers and wires and sound equipment and old telephones and electronic parts and oscilloscopes—some ancient, some state-of-the-art cutting edge. Some worked, some didn't. The stuff that did work, worked in ways never intended by the original manufacturer. A collection of electric guitars, among them a much-coveted early Les Paul, hung from the ceiling.

A six-foot-high wall of old computer magazines divided the space into two rooms. Only Chuck could tell which was the bedroom and which was the living room.

He cleared snippets of copper wire off a wooden bench and motioned for me to sit down. "Can I get you anything," he asked, "beer, barbecued potato chips?"

"No thanks." I got right to the point.

When I finished explaining what I wanted, he looked at me and said, "No way."

"You can't say 'no way.' " I was surprised. I figured Chuck would jump at the chance to harbor a fugitive.

"Sure I can. I just did. I don't even know this Lemon character. What kind of name is Lemon, anyway? You say he's an agent?"

"Not just any agent, he's Johnny's agent," I said, hoping that might sway him. Chuck liked Johnny and never missed a chance to tell me how stupid I was to break up with him. "Without Lemmy," I added, "there'd be no *Tod Trueman, Urban Detective.*"

Chuck shook his head. "I don't know, it's like, look at this place, there's no room."

"It'll only be for a few days," I said, "until the lawyer gets everything straightened out."

"I don't think so, Brenda."

I could tell he was weakening. "You've got a perfect setup here," I said. "Lemmy could run his business. All he needs is a fax and a modem. You can rig it up so no one will know where the calls are coming from, can't you?"

"Piece of cake," said Chuck. A lopsided mischievous grin crinkled his face. "The problem is space, and the fact that I doubt Lemmy and I have a whole heck of a lot in common."

"Lemmy's really a cool—"

I was drowned out by a loud gritty guitar chord. It shook the whole building.

"That's Urban Dog Talk," said Chuck, "setting up for afternoon practice. They recently took over the whole third floor."

I was a fan of the band. In fact, it had been at one of their gigs that I met Chuck. He was their sound man.

The drummer started, then the bass guitar kicked in, then powerful screeching feedback, then dead silence. Chuck's lights blinked once and went out. The only light in the storefront came from the slivers that leaked in through the boarded-up front window.

The first thing I saw, when my eyes adjusted to the darkness, was Renard, Urban Dog Talk's six-and-a-half-foot-tall guitar player. He looked even taller in person than on stage. He had a couple days' growth of beard, closely cropped jet-black hair, dark, dark eyes, and a face that looked like it had been chiseled out of marble. He was dressed in all black. I'd had a crush on him forever.

"The freaking circuit breaker tripped again," he said.

"Of course it did," said Chuck. "You ran the synthesizers on the same line as the guitars again, didn't you?"

Renard nodded. "I had to. The keyboard player feels isolated all the way at the other end of the room. When she feels isolated, she can't play for shit."

"What can I say?" said Chuck. He threw his hands up in mock defeat. "Either spring for a goddamned extension cord or have the joint rewired." He got a key out of a drawer and handed it to Renard. "Here's the key to the basement. Go flick the breaker switch. I'd do it, but as you can see, I've got a guest."

"I noticed," said Renard. "It's Brenda, isn't it?"

I couldn't believe he remembered my name. I said something inane. My knees got weak and rubbery.

"So Brenda, what are you doing hanging out with the likes of Chuck?" asked Renard.

Chuck answered for me. "She's trying to talk me into aiding and abetting a fugitive from justice," said Chuck.

"Cool," said Renard. "Anyone I know?"

I signaled to Chuck to keep his big mouth shut.

He turned to me. "It's okay," he said. "Renard can keep a secret." Then he said to Renard, "It's some agent friend of hers."

"No kidding," said Renard. His eyes flickered with interest. "You've got an agent?"

I was too angry at Chuck to speak. Again he answered for me. "No," he said, "Brenda doesn't have an agent. She makes hats. It's Johnny Verlane's agent, you know, the guy in *Tod Trueman, Urban Detective*."

I couldn't believe Chuck was such a blabbermouth. I hoped Renard really could keep a secret.

Renard thought for a moment. "You mean Lemmy Crenshaw?"

"You've heard of him?" asked Chuck.

"Of course," said Renard. "Everybody's heard of super agent Lemmy Crenshaw. A fugitive? What'd he do?"

I spoke up before Chuck had a chance. "Nothing," I said. "It's a long story."

Renard looked from me to Chuck. "Chuck, old pal, please let Lemon Crenshaw stay with you. He'll hear us practice. He'll become our agent. We'll get discovered. We'll get a record contract. We'll actually pay you. It's our chance to make it big. I gotta go tell the band."

"Not until you get our lights back on," said Chuck.

"In a flash," said Renard.

After Renard left, Chuck assured me that Renard was cool. "He won't blab. It'd blow his chance of getting discovered."

"Then you'll let Lemmy stay?"

"Who am I to stand in the way of Urban Dog Talk's success? Lemmy can stay, but only for a few days. You've got to promise me that."

I promised.

I'd just finished filling Chuck in on some of the particulars when Brewster Winfield deposited Lemmy at Chuck's door.

"Sorry I can't stay," said Winfield, "but my Beemer's double-parked outside."

"A BMW? You've got to be kidding," said Chuck. We both stepped into the hallway so we could see out the front door. Winfield ran back to his shiny undented car, jumped in, and peeled out, leaving East Fifth Street behind as fast as possible. "I can't believe it," said Chuck. "A BMW, a dreadlocked lawyer in a two-thousand-dollar cashmere coat and six-hundred-dollar wingtips. The neighbors are going to freak."

From inside the apartment, Lemmy shouted, "Where's the goddamned lights?"

As if on cue, the lights came on.

Lemmy looked pretty bad. His suit was rumpled, his bald spot bigger than I remembered. He did a full three-sixty turn, taking in his surroundings. "What's with the wires?" he asked. "It's like I'm inside a freakin' television set."

I made the introductions and stood back and watched as Chuck and Lemmy assessed each other. Neither seemed to like what he saw.

Lemmy took tiny steps through the place like he didn't quite trust the floor. "What *is* all this shit?" he asked.

"Chuck's into electronics," I explained.

Chuck didn't say anything, but I detected tension in the set of his jaw and the throbbing vein in his forehead.

"No shit," said Lemmy sarcastically, "like I couldn't figure that out for myself. You know, Brenda, I've been patient, but this is really starting to piss me off."

"Please," I said. "Calm down and tell me what happened. I'm trying to get everything back to normal for you. I hired Winfield. He assured me that he'd fix everything. Next thing I knew, he calls, desperate to find a hideout. What went wrong?"

"What went wrong," said Lemmy, pacing back and forth, "is that by the time Winfield—who doesn't know a *habeus* from a *corpus*, by the way—finally figured out what to do about the bum rap, the rap wasn't so bum anymore."

"What do you mean? The cops had no evidence, except the car. Surely Winfield explained that away."

"Yes," said Lemmy, bobbing his head up and down, "even Winfield could do that. He got me released, a day late, a day wiser, a day more pissed off—but released. So he drives me home. All the way uptown he's yakking about selling my story as a movie of the week—some lawyer you got me, Brenda. He's going on and on about how we have to find a romantic angle, a counterpoint to the morgue bit. I'm bored as a gourd and don't like this opportunist infringing on my territory. I mean, if anybody sells my story, it'll be me. Then he starts in about his snake, claims it does tricks. All I want to do is get home, but two blocks before we get there, 'call me Brew' gets a call on his cellular. It's his answering service telling him the cops are looking for me again. I scrunch down in the seat and we drive by my apartment. What do you know, there's an unmarked cop car outside waiting."

"I don't get it. Why? There's no evidence, no motive."

Lemmy sank into Chuck's red plastic beanbag chair. It sighed as it puffed up around his body. "There wasn't. Then all of a sudden there was. At least there was motive, 'cause some jerkhole came along and ID'd the body, the John Doe. You know what, Brenda, the dead guy whose body you dumped at the morgue using my car, turns out to be Buddy Needleson."

I was the jerkhole who got the body properly identified. My gulp was audible, but Lemmy was too wound up to hear. "I knew that," I said. "He's my friends' uncle."

"The cops didn't know it at first. That's why they let me go. I didn't know either until the cops found out, but by then it was too late because the cops had figured out the connection."

"There's a connection between you and Buddy Needleson?" I hoped I'd misunderstood.

"Buddy Needleson is the SOB who's suing me."

"What for?"

"It was nothing," explained Lemmy. "I popped the jerk in the nose, that's all. It must have been two, three years ago. He tried to beat me out of a parking space on West Seventeenth Street during a Barney's warehouse sale. His wife sees blood and gristle and gets all hysterical and calls the cops. It's all on record."

All the time Lemmy talked, Chuck sat at one of his computers and typed up a storm. When he overheard the part about a fight, his interest was piqued, and he joined in the conversation. "Which was he suing for—a bloody shirt or a busted nose?"

"Both," said Lemmy, "and the kitchen sink. Then there's the mental anguish from the pizzas I had delivered to his apartment once or twice—well, three times max."

So much for Lemmy's maturity. "You really had pizzas

delivered to Buddy Needleson's apartment?''

''Sure,'' said Lemmy. ''Why not? Chinese food too, twenty separate orders of cold sesame noodles, all from different places, all at once. I had to do something after Needleson called me a couple of times in the middle of the night and breathed into the phone.''

''He did that?''

''Well, at the time I thought so. I found out later it wasn't him at all, it was Susan. Remember Susan? Such a sweet little thing, but easily ticked off.''

''You know,'' said Chuck to Lemmy, ''I'm beginning to like you.''

7

When I left Chuck's, he and Lemmy were yukking it up like a couple of fourteen-year-olds, comparing notes on harassment by food delivery. I knew they'd grow on each other.

Gray clouds moved fast overhead. Ice crunched under my boots. Not a cab in sight. I walked up a block and took Sixth Street over to First Avenue, watched three off-duty cabs pass, and gave up the cab idea. A brisk crosstown walk would give me time to think.

I'd sure screwed things up. The more I did, the worse things got. Like it wasn't bad enough that I got Lemmy in trouble for dumping a body he didn't dump, I had go make sure he got accused of murder too. I was up to my many hatbrims in trouble. If only life were more like a *Tod Trueman* episode.

"Brenda, wait up."

I turned around and spotted Renard, half a block behind, looking very good in a black leather jacket. While I waited for him to catch up, I reminded myself that I'd sworn off all actors, artists, and guitar players.

"I recognized you from a block away," he said.

Was that a compliment? "Oh," I said.

"Where you headed?" he asked.

"Home."

"Where's that?"

"West Village."

"Great. I'm headed to the B train. Going to see a guy in Brooklyn about an old Marshall amp."

"Tubes?" I asked. The question had exactly the effect I knew it would.

Renard did a double take. "You know about tubes?"

I nodded. "Sure."

"Yeah, it's got tubes."

Amazing how little knowledge it took to impress guys. Over the years I'd managed to get a lot of mileage out of a couple of basic facts about cars and guitars. I knew that before the transistor changed life on the planet, guitar amplifiers had contained tubes which caused a desirable distortion that was unobtainable with newer amps. I also knew that the big greasy thing that made a car move along the road was the engine, not the motor, an important distinction. And I could identify the make and model of any pre-seventies American car and make a good give-or-take-a-year guess as to its vintage.

We walked along for a ways. I tried to figure out a way to work car engines into the conversation and to keep Lemmy out of it, but didn't come up with anything.

Finally Renard spoke. "Looks like snow."

"Sure does. Weatherman says it's gonna be a monster storm."

After that, I don't remember what we talked about. I was relieved that Renard didn't quiz me about Lemmy.

At Sixth Avenue Renard descended into the subway. "Okay if I call you sometime?" he asked.

"Sure," I said. My warning bell went off, but I ignored it. After all, almost everyone in New York was an actor, artist, or guitar player.

I took a quick detour through Balducci's and looked at the luscious displays of out-of-season fruits and vegetables. I sprung for a bunch of five-dollar-a-pound asparagus, rationalizing it would help inspire my faltering spring line. Maybe, just maybe, I'd get this murder thing wrapped up quickly and manage to design spring before summer was due.

The minute I got home I threw the asparagus in the steamer. Jackhammer went berserk. He liked green vegetables even more than meat or Chinese takeout. Green beans were his absolute favorite, but asparagus, broccoli, and brussels sprouts were tied for a close second. He banged on the kitchen door with his paw and whimpered, but I didn't give in. Then he pulled out his ace card. Jackhammer was a smart dog. He knew that when he tossed his head just right, his hair fell over his eyes and he looked just like Elvis—the young thin Elvis—and he knew that when he did that he could get anything he wanted. One heavy-lidded stare through that drooping forelock and he got his very own stalk of asparagus. Two chomps and it was gone.

I ate a few stalks with some sliced tomato and thin slices of purple onion. I waited for spring inspiration to hit, but dead Buddy Needleson kept pushing his way into my brain, crowding out the flowers and other spring thoughts. It was useless. I had to figure out who killed Buddy Needleson and get Lemmy off the hook before I could do anything else.

I needed to know who wanted Buddy Needleson dead, which meant I needed to know a lot more about him, which meant that, much as I hated to, I had to call the Ns and pump them for information.

Naomi answered. "Brenda, you must have ESP or something. Just this very second I was thinking how I was going to have to call you to make sure we get our story straight before Uncle Buddy's funeral."

"What funeral? I thought there wasn't going to be a funeral."

"Of course there's going to be a funeral. What do you think we are, heathens or something? We always knew that sooner or later someone at the morgue would figure out who Uncle Buddy was. Norbert and I just hoped it would be later, much later. I don't know how they figured it out.

Norbert says maybe Uncle Buddy's fingerprints were on file, but I don't think so."

Or an anonymous phone call, I thought.

"Doesn't matter," continued Naomi. "The damage is done. The authorities contacted Babette. She went to the morgue and made a positive ID. Naturally, she's freaking out. She really believed he was on a business trip. With feathers so hot, she says if he had any business sense and was where he was supposed to be, doing what he was supposed to be doing, he'd not only have a bunch of orders, he'd still be alive."

"She has a good point there," I said.

"Maybe," said Naomi. "Anyway, Norbert and I came up with this idea."

"No," I said. I didn't care what their idea was. "Absolutely not, no way, a thousand times no."

"Don't be like that, Brenda."

I agreed to go to Needleson Brothers to talk to them. It was what I wanted in the first place, but I had a feeling what the Ns wanted to talk about wasn't at all what I wanted to talk about.

I got to the showroom just as Norbert and Naomi were sitting down to a late lunch of cold greasy chicken and spongy white bread. Norbert wore a tweed jacket with suede patches on the elbow, probably thinking it made him look professorial. He was dead wrong. Naomi was decked out in another of her full-skirted polka-dot creations, this one a green and red wool challis. It looked itchy. Neither of the Ns seemed concerned about anything other than feeding their faces.

"Pull up a chair," said Norbert. "We'll eat. Then we can talk."

Dozens of open condiment jars cluttered the sagging card table. I recognized sweet pickles, sour pickles, sweet-sour pickles, two jars of diet mayo, smooth yellow mustard, seeded brown mustard, ketchup, tahini, olives, pimientos, and raisins. In addition, several odd-shaped jars contained mysterious foods I'd never heard of, seen, smelled, or tasted. Nor did I want to. The pungent aromas mingled with the vague odor of mothballs in the background, resulting in a truly nauseating stench.

"Help yourself," said Naomi, gesturing with a knife slathered with something beige and sticky. "Make a sandwich."

"None for me, thanks. I just ate."

"Bullshit," said Naomi. "Anybody as skinny as you never 'just ate.' Maybe you had a bite but you didn't eat."

"She probably doesn't eat chicken and is just being polite," said Norbert.

"Of course she eats chicken," said Naomi. "Right, Brenda? It's not like it's meat or anything." She ran her finger around the inside of a nearly empty jar of tahini, scraping it clean.

"Chicken's exactly like meat," I said. "Chicken is meat. It walks, it talks, and if you're nice to it, it comes when its called."

"It's fowl," said Naomi, "not quite meat."

"It's full of feathers," said Norbert.

I didn't want to get into a philosophical or zoological debate with the Ns. "Whatever it is, I'm not hungry, but thanks anyway."

"Have it your way," said Naomi.

The Ns wolfed down their food. Both of them chewed loudly. Naomi dug her long pink fingernails into the white bread, leaving vicious indentations. She washed her food down with huge gulps of heavily creamed and sugared instant coffee. Norbert picked through the chicken, looking for morsels of dark meat. He sucked a generic-brand grape soda through a straw. For dessert they had cellophane-wrapped snack cakes à la mode.

"Like I mentioned on the phone," said Naomi, wiping her mouth with a napkin, "we need to get our story straight before the funeral so that when you meet Babette—"

"Back up," I said. "I can't lie to a grieving widow."

"You've gotta," said Naomi. "We can't let Aunt Babette know we found Uncle Buddy here."

"Why not? I mean, the authorities, especially now that—" I stopped myself two words before spilling the beans about Lemmy. I didn't know if the Ns knew or not and they certainly didn't know that I knew anything about anything. I planned to keep it that way as long as possible.

"Authorities? We don't want the authorities coming around," said Norbert.

"You can say that again," said Naomi. "Don't even say that word in my presence. If they discover that we found Uncle Buddy here, they'll start poking around, then they'll find out about the strip club, and then—" Naomi's face turned bright red. She clapped her hand over her mouth. She looked at Norbert.

He banged his hand on the table, rattling the condiment jars. "Goddammit, Naomi."

"Strip club?" I asked, wondering if I'd heard right.

"We were going to have to tell her sometime anyway," said Naomi.

"Not necessarily," said Norbert.

Naomi chewed her bottom lip and twisted a paper napkin in her hands. Norbert rubbed his forehead with his left hand. With his right he banged the table, at first slowly and methodically, then picking up speed until it became a frenzied machine gun rat-a-tat.

"Strip club?" I asked again.

"We didn't know," said Naomi, choking back a sob.

"Didn't know what?"

Norbert stopped banging and answered. "We didn't know about the goddamned strip club. At least not at first."

"We didn't know until after Mommy and Daddy cleared out of town," said Naomi.

"Please, somebody," I said, "start from the beginning."

"I guess it doesn't matter anymore," said Norbert. "You may as well know the whole sorry tale." He paused long enough to take a deep raspy breath. "As you've probably guessed, business hasn't been great lately."

Naomi piped up. "Until this season."

Norbert looked grim. "At this point, twenty good seasons wouldn't get us out from under. It's not just us, it's not just trimming, or feathers, it's the whole goddamned rag trade. It's like a bomb went off or something, leveling the garment district. Surely, Brenda, you've noticed the decline of Thirty-eighth Street?"

I nodded. Not so many years ago one block of West Thirty-eighth had dozens of specialized millinery suppliers—three stores just for veiling, a custom blockmaker, a felt guy, two buckram guys, on and on. Now few were left and the street was filled with costume jewelry showrooms and wholesale/retail clothing shops that appealed to tourists who veered off Fifth Avenue. I had to get many crucial supplies by mail order.

Norbert continued. "It's especially tough with the feather part of the business. We've got those idiot animal rights fanatics to contend with." He gave me a dirty look, like I might be part of the problem.

"Yeah, you'd think feathers were fur or something," said Naomi.

Or birds were animals, I thought. I kept my opinion on the subject to myself, though it was obvious Norbert noticed I rarely used feathers. Of course, I wasn't into any kind of surface decoration.

"Mom, Dad, and Uncle Buddy, carrying diversification to the extreme, came up with the idea to turn the place into an after-hours strip club for amateurs," said Norbert.

"You can just imagine what that was," said Naomi.

"Not really," I said.

"It's where any broad over the age of twenty-one," said Norbert, "no matter how fat or homely or grotesque, can hop up on a stage and strip naked in front of a bunch of adoring perverts."

"They're not all perverts," said Naomi, "and most of the ladies were quite attractive. See, the women got in free. Men paid a pretty penny to get in. Everybody paid through the nose for booze."

I was stunned. "A strip club? Here?"

Naomi corrected me. "An *amateur* strip club," she said. "Why not? Nobody uses this building at night. Even if they did, who are they going to complain to? The landlord? Everybody owes back rent. They're not exactly in a position to gripe about unsavory activity in the building. The cops? Don't make me laugh. Nobody wants the cops in here."

I still couldn't believe it. "Where do the strippers come from?"

Naomi looked at me like she couldn't believe how stupid I was. "You'd be surprised, Brenda."

"Most of our strippers were bored housewives who come in from the burbs, out for a night of adventure," said Norbert. "Although we'd started to attract a lot of Manhattan professionals blowing off steam."

"Blowing off something, at any rate," said Naomi.

"Don't mind Naomi," said Norbert. "She cops an attitude, pretends to be holier than thou, but I caught her working on a pink and black polka-dot G-string with matching pasties. If someone hadn't killed Uncle Buddy and ended the Needlesons' foray as impresarios, my baby sister would have been on that stage herself bumping and grinding to one of her stupid torch songs."

"I don't know what to say about any of this," I said.

"You don't have to say anything," said Naomi.

"In fact," said Norbert, "please *don't* say anything about this to anybody. If Aunt Babette finds out that Uncle Buddy was running a strip club out of here and that Mom and Dad and Naomi and I all knew about it, she'll never forgive us."

"Don't go blabbing to the cops either," said Naomi. "The stupid club made gobs of money. All we need is to have the IRS poking into our affairs."

I was curious. "How much money is gobs of money?"

"The books are such a jumble, I'm not sure," said Norbert. "One thing I can say for sure is that the club made gobs and gobs of money. Then the mob stepped in and took their gob. If you asked me, they're the ones who iced Uncle Buddy. The mob probably wanted a gob and a half."

"I can hardly blame Mommy and Daddy for packing up and hightailing it to Florida," said Naomi. "Things were heating up."

"I can't believe Howard and Zorema would leave you guys in the lurch with mob types and god knows what else on the scene," I said.

"They thought we'd be safe as long as we didn't know what was going on," said Norbert. "Uncle Buddy promised Mom and Dad he'd keep us in the dark, which we were until we came back to work late one night to straighten out the inventory."

"We walked straight into strip city," said Naomi. "I mean, I could not believe what I was seeing."

"I guess your Uncle Buddy had some explaining to do," I said.

"Explain he did," said Norbert. "We never even told Mom and Dad we knew—that is, until we found Uncle Buddy's body."

"Yeah," said Naomi. "Mommy and Daddy told us to get his body off the premises and play dumb."

I kept quiet while this all soaked into my brain. Two things made their story seem legit. One, the Ns weren't creative enough to make up a story like that. Two, I remembered what Dweena had said about being at the Ns' place before. At the time I thought she was confused.

"So," said Naomi, "let's talk about the funeral."

Like it or not, I had to go to the funeral. What better place to learn about Buddy Needleson? All his friends would be there. I hoped a few of his enemies would show up as well.

"Goddammit," said Lemmy when I told him, "I want to go to that funeral. I want to tap-dance on that jerk's grave like there's no tomorrow."

For Buddy Needleson there wasn't any tomorrow.

8

"Lemmy's on the lam," I said. I'd hoped Johnny would be out filming and I could get away with merely leaving a message, but he was home and I had to give him the bad news personally.

He wasn't any too happy and told me so, stringing together a whole slew of well-chosen, to-the-point expletives, ending with, "It's all your fault, Brenda."

As if I didn't know. I calmed him down by telling him how I'd made progress in finding out who killed Buddy Needleson.

"What did you learn?" he asked.

"Meet me at Angie's," I said. "I talk better on a full stomach."

Before I left I called Dweena and left a message for her to call me.

Ever since Angie's was written up in *New York Magazine* as the perfect neighborhood bar, it had been hard to get in because all the people from god-knows-where who wanted to hang out in Greenwich Village's perfect neighborhood bar came in droves, leaving no room for neighborhood people. But that night, the winter storm warnings scared the tourists off. Angie's was crowded but not impossibly so. Johnny and I founds seats at the dark, cozy bar. Tommy the bartender promised there'd be only a short wait for a table in the back.

Tommy was the perfect bartender for the perfect neighborhood bar. Tall, with fuzzy sideburns that made him look like he came out of the Wild West, he had a way with people. Three rumors circulated about Tommy: One, he actually owned Angie's. Two, he'd won it from the original Angie, a person not even the old-timers could remember, in a high-stakes poker game in a secret back room which was later destroyed during a period of expansion in the eighties when some idiot MBA decided to squeeze in two more booths. The third rumor was that Tommy had rigged the jukebox so that it played Frank Sinatra's "New York, New York" every hour on the hour. Three Franks and I usually knew it was time to leave.

Johnny and I ordered our usual—a red wine for me, dark beer for him—and stared at the brand-new twenty-one-inch TV Tommy had bolted into the wall above the bar. It looked sleek and out of place amid the cobwebs and old light fixtures covered with decades of bar dust. On the too-vibrant screen, a reporter in a brilliant red coat with glowing orange skin and windblown neon-yellow hair talked into a microphone, presumably about the coming storm. Behind her rolled a block-long line of hulking garbage trucks that had been retrofitted with snowplows.

Tommy took bets on how many inches of snow would pile up on the patch of sidewalk right outside the door. I put a dollar on twelve. Johnny went for eighteen. Minutes after the first "New York, New York" played on the jukebox, Tommy signaled us that our table was open.

We grabbed our drinks and headed to the back room, where we got our favorite corner booth. When the light was just right and I held my head at a certain angle, I could still make out a heart carved into the table with our initials in it.

Raphael, the waiter, had been around as long as Tommy. Another rumor circulated that he, not Tommy, owned Angie's and that Angie had given it to him as hush money.

Many theories were offered as to what he had hushed up about. My personal favorite was that he'd witnessed the murder of a vegetable delivery man who'd brought in a crate of unripe tomatoes.

Raphael smiled and asked, "The regular?"

We nodded and a few minutes later he brought out a grilled cheese with onion and no pickles for me and a cheeseburger with bacon, extra onion and double pickles for Johnny. He put the order of fries in the middle of the table.

After Raphael had gone, Johnny looked around to see if anyone was within earshot. Apparently satisfied the couple holding hands in the next booth was too self-absorbed to eavesdrop, he said, "Okay, Brenda, out with it. What the hell is going on?"

"Lemmy is safe at Chuck's."

"Chuck's? Jeezus." Johnny glanced over at the hand holders. They still appeared enraptured, so he continued. "You told me the lawyer you dredged up said he'd have no trouble springing Lemmy."

"That was before the cops came up with a possible motive."

"Which was?"

"Buddy Needleson was suing Lemmy because Lemmy busted his nose two years ago in a duke-out over a parking space."

"That's absurd," said Johnny.

"It's the truth. Lemmy admits it."

Johnny waved his arms at Raphael and ordered two more dark beers for himself and another red wine for me. I started talking. By the time I'd finished filling him in on the details about the lawsuit and Buddy Needleson's amateur strip club, Sinatra's "New York, New York" had played twice more and it was time to go. Johnny paid for both of us, a gallant move, especially considering how mad he was at me.

* * *

I couldn't sleep. I worried about Lemmy at Chuck's. I worried about the cops finding out about Lemmy at Chuck's. I worried about the size of Brewster Winfield's bill. I worried about my spring line. I worried that Renard would call. I worried that Renard wouldn't call. I worried that Renard would call and I would say something stupid. More than anything I worried about what to wear to Buddy Needleson's funeral.

I didn't want to blow my big chance to gather information because of a fashion faux pas. As a designer I had the responsibility to know proper dress for all kinds of special occasions, but the only funeral I'd ever been to was my grandfather's, when I was a kid. That funeral got interrupted halfway through when a devastating tornado churned through the tiny rural town. While civil defense sirens wailed, the funeral director ushered all of us mourners down to the cellar. Moments later the wind ripped the little funeral home right off its foundation. We were stuck beneath the rubble for hours. I remembered the dark, the sickening smell of sweet deodorant, the odor of fresh-cut pine. I remembered the sound of my scaredy-cat cousin whimpering that she'd lost her baby doll. When the rescue teams finally dug us out, there was no trace of my grandfather or his casket. I remembered all that as if it were yesterday, but for the life of me, I couldn't remember what the grown-ups had worn.

When I'd mentioned it to Johnny at dinner, he was no help. "Brenda," he'd said, "you're a New Yorker now, you've got a closet full of black clothes. You'll find something."

He didn't understand. Black was too obvious. I wished Elizabeth were around. At her age she'd no doubt been to a lot of funerals.

I was still tossing and turning when Dweena returned my call.

"Alternate-side parking rules, suspended or not for tomorrow?" she asked.

"I don't know. What's the radio say?"

"All confused, depends which station. They were suspended, but now they're saying it might not snow, in which case maybe they won't be suspended. Don't even ask about emergency snow route regulations."

I got to the point of why I'd called her in the first place. "Remember when we went to get the feather boas from the Ns at their showroom, you said you had the feeling you'd been there before?"

"Yes," said Dweena.

"Does amateur strip club ring a bell?"

"That's it," she said. "I knew I'd been there before. Dweena never forgets a venue. I went there with a friend. Her shrink recommended she strip to get over her shyness."

"Do you remember the man who ran the club?"

"Sure. Dweena never forgets a club owner either. Nice guy, white hair, bushy eyebrows."

"Buddy Needleson," I said.

"The dead guy in the trunk?"

"I'm afraid so."

"Too bad," said Dweena. "He ran a swell club."

"Do you know of any more amateur strip clubs in town?"

"There's a few, but the latest trend, if you can believe it, is all-night bowling, back again and bigger than ever."

"Will you take me to an amateur strip club? I need to get an idea what goes on."

"Sure. How about tomorrow? I can get a friend to cover for me."

"Tomorrow's good."

"I'll pick you up at midnight."

"Thanks, Dweena."

I was just about to hang up when I remembered. "One more thing, Dweena. I'm having a tough time trying to figure out what to wear to the funeral tomorrow."

"It depends," she said, "on which borough and whether it's a morning, afternoon, or evening funeral."

"Early afternoon, nondenominational, Manhattan, though I suppose the burial will be someplace else."

"In that case anything goes, though personally I wouldn't be caught dead in plaid or paisley."

9

Jackhammer walked up and down on my back until I woke up. I lay there and listened for the surreal muffled quiet that would mean the blizzard had come, but the New York buzz was as edgy as ever. I got up and looked out the window. No snow, plenty of sun, and not a cloud in sight. I flipped on the radio and listened to a weather report. The storm system was stuck somewhere in Pennsylvania and would be a day late and more intense than earlier predictions.

I nibbled on leftover asparagus while searching my closet for appropriate funeral wear. I was about ready to give up and wear black when I spotted a dark gray silk dress jammed way in the back. All it needed was a quick steaming.

Johnny called while I was getting dressed. "Remember that big-deal director I told you about, Sal Stumpford? He's got a big-deal hundred and three temperature, so today's shoot is off."

"Great," I said. "You can escort me to Buddy Needleson's funeral."

"I don't know, Brenda. It's like, you know, I don't much like funerals."

"Nobody much likes funerals, Johnny. Think of it as a fact-finding mission. Tod Trueman would go. He'd want to see who showed up."

* * *

The funeral parlor was on a seedy Chelsea side street, stuck between a burrito joint and a gay porno store. Its cinder-block facade was painted to look like cool gray marble veined with black. Etched into the heavy glass double doors was an elaborate art nouveau design. I stood back to get a better look. There were two ways to look at it. Either it intentionally depicted a traditional devil figure, pitchfork in hand, dancing around a bonfire filled with tortured humanity, or my imagination was working overtime. "It can't be," I said.

"Looks like old Beelzebub to me," said Johnny. He held the door open for me.

"Weird," I said. "Remind me not to have a funeral."

The place smelled like rug shampoo. It was probably something else because the oatmeal-colored wall-to-wall carpeting didn't look particularly clean. Neither did the pale green walls. We signed the leatherette-bound guest book that sat on an assemble-it-yourself reproduction Louis the Someteenth table. Also on the table was a stack of business cards, a box of tissues, and a dish of peppermint-flavored hard candy.

A dark-suited, noodle-thin, horse-faced man holding a cigarette with an inch-long ash watched us sign in. When we finished, he pointed us toward Buddy Needleson's chamber, then disappeared behind a wall of dusty drapery.

The chamber—a room with no view and a body in a laminated maple casket—was where the action was. This was both the viewing and the funeral, a combo job. Johnny said it was an unusual arrangement. "Cut-rate, I guess."

Norbert stood inside the door, a one-man receiving line. He wore a dark pin-striped suit that was an inch too short in the arms. "I'm warning you," he said, hugging us both, "bad vibes."

"What's the problem?" I asked. "I mean, besides the fact that your uncle is dead."

"Problems," he said, emphasizing the *s*. "I don't know how, but Aunt Babette found out about the strip club and, believe me, she's on the warpath. Then, to make it worse, Mom and Dad stopped on the way to stuff their faces and got here late. Babette says the least they could do is show up on time, especially since it's their fault her husband is dead because they ran off to Florida and left him alone to deal with the club and the mob. Mom and Dad are pissed at Babette because she didn't save them a front-row seat. They're pissed at Naomi and me on account of the big projection TV we bought and the fact that the apartment's a mess. Naomi is pissed at her so-called boyfriend Fred because he copped out at the last minute.''

While I was still trying to get straight who was mad at whom and why, Zorema Needleson spotted Johnny and me. She nudged her husband in the ribs with her elbow. ''Howard,'' she shrieked, ''will you look at who's here?''

''Good,'' said Norbert, ''maybe you can take their minds off their slovenly spendthrift offspring.''

Howard and Zorema Needleson had been in Florida for only a few months. Already they looked too tan and too silly, as if their brains had been fried along with their skin. Zorema had dyed her steel-gray hair a brassy red-blond, sported sky-blue eyeliner and big clanky jewelry. Howard obviously hadn't consulted anyone as knowledgeable as Dweena about his funeral getup. He had on a yellow and brown polyester plaid suit and a paisley tie. He hugged me. I felt a bulge in his chest and wondered if it was some kind of pacemaker device. When he saw me looking, he opened his jacket, patted his pocket, and said, ''Left-over pastrami sandwich. Who can blame Zorema and me for stopping off at the Carnegie Deli on our way to the funeral? Nothing in Florida comes close. So what if we missed the private family preview?'' He jutted his chin and rolled his eyes toward a woman in the front row. Perched on top of her bleached blond hair was a pillbox hat with a chin-length black veil.

''Babette, I presume?''

''That's my sis-in-law,'' said Howard, ''the widow.''

Zorema hugged me. She smelled of rose oil and pastrami. ''Brenda, if you aren't a sight for sore eyes. And who is your very handsome escort?'' She winked. ''As if I didn't know.''

''Johnny Verlane,'' I said, ''meet Zorema and Howard Needleson.''

''Don't be coy, Brenda,'' said Howard. He slapped Johnny on the back. ''You can't fool an old couch potato like me. I know Detective Tod Trueman when I see him. Never miss a show, son, not that I have a big projection TV like my extravagant kids. We're honored to have you here. If my brother knew a famous TV star was here at his funeral, he'd have a regular shit fit.'' Howard's loud guffaw drew attention to us.

Johnny smiled and looked uncomfortable. We were saved when some old friends of Howard and Zorema barreled over and hugged them. Johnny and I slipped away before anyone noticed.

We found Naomi standing near the casket dabbing at her red-rimmed eyes with a lace hanky. ''I didn't know she cared so much about her uncle,'' Johnny whispered.

''She doesn't,'' I whispered back.

She was dressed demurely, but still in polka-dots, tiny white ones on a navy-blue background. She wore navy patent-leather pumps, a matching handbag, and white gloves.

''Brenda. Johnny,'' she said, grasping our hands. ''How nice of you both to come.'' She burst into tears.

I patted her on the back. ''Naomi.''

''Can you believe it?'' she said. ''Fred promised to come, said he was looking forward to seeing Mommy and Daddy again, then at the last minute he calls and says there's a problem with a client and he can't get away after all. I can't believe he did this to me.''

We consoled her and then joined the fifty or so mourners who milled around the chamber, murmuring words of solace. No one went anywhere near the guest of honor's open casket. Except that there was no cheap wine, it was like an art opening where no one looks at the art.

''See anyone who looks like a murderer?'' I asked.

Johnny surveyed the crowd. "Nah."

"Anyone who looks out of place?"

"They all look like they've known each other and Buddy Needleson for decades."

"They probably have," I said. "We should go pay our respects to the widow."

"What for?"

"Protocol," I said. "Besides, we may need her help if we're going to solve this thing. She's one person who would know if her husband had any enemies besides Lemmy." I grabbed Johnny's hand and pulled him toward Babette Needleson, but before we got there I saw two familiar faces and stopped dead in my tracks. "What the hell are Detectives Turner and McKinley doing here?"

"Don't know," said Johnny. "They're out of their precinct."

"Maybe they're friends of Buddy Needleson," I said unconvincingly.

"I doubt it," said Johnny.

"We're about to find out, because McKinley just saw us." I waved halfheartedly at the detectives.

Detective Turner and Detective McKinley stood out like sore thumbs. For one thing, in a room full of rotten posture and rumpled suits, they stood tall and proud in impeccable custom-made fine wool suits. Also McKinley was black, and from what I could see, Buddy Needleson didn't have any black friends.

Turner and McKinley were Johnny's friends. In exchange for various freebies, they gave him lessons in how to act like a cop. I didn't remember whether I was currently in their good graces or not. In the past, I'd done them some big favors; then again, I'd also been a pain in the ass. As they approached, I plastered a smile on my face and hoped for the best.

"I can't believe my jaded eyes," said Detective Turner. "The lovely Village milliner Brenda Midnight and her consort Johnny Verlane several blocks above Fourteenth Street.

Must be the end of civilization as we know it.'' He made a big show of kissing my hand.

''I'm a friend of the family,'' I said. ''What's your excuse?'' I hoped they'd take that the right way.

''Murder,'' said Detective McKinley. ''This one got dumped in our laps, don't ask me why.''

''Actually,'' said McKinley, looking askance at Turner, ''coming here was my partner's idea. He insisted we go by the book. If you ask me, we're wasting our time. We already know who did the deceased. You can bet he won't show up here.''

''Really,'' I said, ''you know who did it?''

''It's kind of embarrassing,'' said Turner. ''Not only do we know who he is, we had him in custody for questioning, but some fly-by-night shyster sprung him. Then, after the perp's already gone—because that's the way the bureaucracy works in this city, slow as molasses—we got the real dirt. Turns out the guy's a hothead, couple of years ago he got in a street altercation with the deceased. Don't worry, we'll find him again, but not here. That'd only work in a *Tod Trueman*, right, Johnny?''

''You've been watching the shows?'' asked Johnny.

''Sure,'' said McKinley. ''You've learned well, Johnny. I'm proud to have had something to do with teaching you how to walk like a cop, talk like a cop, drive like a—hey, that reminds me—did you ever get a real license yet, or do you still just have that learner's permit?''

Johnny gripped my hand. The last time Johnny had driven was the night we dumped Buddy Needleson's body at the morgue. Did McKinley know something? Maybe he was trying to trick us into confessing.

To my great relief, McKinley continued. '' 'Cause if you don't,'' he said, ''I've got a friend down at Motor Vehicles who's quite a *Tod Trueman* fan. She'd probably be willing to look the other way if you still haven't got that parallel parking stuff quite right yet, as long as you're willing to part with a couple of personally autographed eight-by-tens.''

Johnny's grip on me relaxed. He smiled and said, "I may take you up on that, Detective."

"One thing that bugs me about the show," said Turner, "is the way Tod always gets the gorgeous girl in the end, as the closing credits roll. Don't you think that's a bit of a stretch?"

"Don't knock it," said McKinley, "that credit roll grope is my favorite part."

Organ music blasted out of tinny speakers on either side of the casket, signaling that the visitation was over and the funeral services were about to begin. We found four seats together in a middle row, near the aisle. McKinley went in first, then Turner, then me, then Johnny. I settled in and was checking out the hats in the crowd when Turner said to me, "You know, Brenda, I was thinking of you just the other day. My sister's kid is getting married soon and she's gonna need a veil."

"I don't do weddings," I said.

"Ah, come on," he said. "Can't you make an exception?"

I would not waver on this issue. "No, no, a thousand times—"

Johnny kicked my leg. I turned around to give him a dirty look, but saw that his expression was dead serious. He rolled his eyes toward the aisle. I followed his line of sight and was stunned to see, swaggering up the aisle, Lemon B. Crenshaw, fugitive from the law, looking ridiculous with a brown 1970s rock-and-roll shag-cut wig plopped down on top of his bald spot.

Turner and McKinley might not be the best detectives in the world, but that wig wouldn't have fooled anyone. They wanted Lemmy. He was the perp who got away. I had to divert the detectives. My resources were limited, time was short, so I did the only thing I could. I dropped my purse and let them help me gather up all the junk that spilled out. By the time they'd rounded up the last lipstick tube, Lemmy had settled into a seat a few rows ahead of us.

Amazingly, he had the good sense not to turn around and wave to Johnny and me.

A few of Buddy Needleson's friends stood up at the pulpit and said what a great guy he'd been. I was too worried about the cops spotting Lemmy to pay much attention. I hoped for a miracle, maybe a tornado like at my grandfather's funeral. Foolish thought. Tornadoes didn't happen, not in the winter, not in Manhattan.

If Lemmy got caught this time, he'd rat on me for sure. Who would take care of Jackhammer while I was in prison? What would happen to Midnight Millinery? In the midst of my fretting I began to notice an odd odor. At first I didn't think much about it. Funeral homes were full of odd odors. Then the odor intensified. I noticed other people beginning to sniff the air and squirm in their seats. Finally, from the back of the room, someone shouted, "Fire!"

Things rapidly deteriorated into chaos. People pushed, chairs toppled. Public servants Turner and McKinley rose to the occasion and helped in the evacuation.

10

We jostled along in the middle of the panicked crowd. Johnny and I kept Lemmy between us, out of sight of Turner and McKinley.

Lemmy, apparently oblivious to the fact that he was in danger of getting caught, was concerned only that Johnny was there. "You're supposed to be shooting with Sal Stumpford," he said. "What the hell gives?"

"Stumpford's got the flu," said Johnny. "Now shut up, keep your head down, and walk."

We exited the funeral parlor just as the first fire truck rounded the corner. While the rest of the mourners stood around and watched the firemen unfurl their hose, Johnny and I pulled Lemmy to the end of the block and around the corner.

"Lemmy, you're an idiot," said Johnny.

"Whadya mean, Stumpford's sick?" said Lemmy. "What's with the shoot?"

The man had a one-track mind.

"Forget about Stumpford," said Johnny. "We've got to get you out of here."

"I wanna stay."

"No."

The only cab in sight was double-parked in front of a deli halfway down the block with its off-duty sign on.

When the driver came out of the deli I was waiting for him.

"We need to get to the East Village quick," I said.

"So, why you telling me? Can't you read?" He jerked his chin in the direction of the off-duty light.

"There's an extra ten in it for you," I said.

"Hop in," he said.

I motioned to Johnny. He dragged a very reluctant Lemmy over to the cab. All the time Lemmy kept looking over his shoulder. "I wanna go back and watch."

Johnny put his hand on top of Lemmy's head and pushed him down into the backseat of the cab. "In."

"Goddammit," said Lemmy. He tried to twist free, almost losing his wig in the process.

I told the cab driver where we were going. He made me pay him the extra ten up front, then took off down Seventh Avenue, dodging fire trucks that were still arriving at the scene.

Once we were safely on the way, Johnny tore into Lemmy. "Dumb move, Lemmy, showing up like that."

Johnny was not only Lemmy's best friend, he was his best client and therefore responsible for a whopping percentage of Lemmy's income. Johnny could get away with calling Lemmy dumb and worse. And he did. Lemmy slouched down in the seat and pouted.

"I don't see what the big deal is," said Lemmy. "So what if I wanted to go to the funeral of an acquaintance to pay my last respects?"

"The big deal," I said, with as much patience as I could muster, "is that of all possible dead acquaintances, you're accused of murdering this particular one. Why do you think Turner and McKinley were at the funeral? They sure as hell weren't paying their last respects. They were looking to solve the case. According to them, that pretty much equals finding you."

Johnny spoke up. "You're lucky that when you waltzed in with that ridiculous rug on top of your head, Brenda had the resourcefulness to drop her purse. Her quick thinking gave Turner and McKinley the opportunity to crawl around on the floor and look at her legs instead of looking at you. If they'd seen you, fire or no fire, you'd be in the backseat of a squad car right now. It's a damned good thing you're a damned good agent, 'cause you make a damned lousy fugitive."

"I'll take that as a compliment," said Lemmy. "Thank you, Brenda, for having nice legs and dropping your purse, thereby saving me."

Except for the cabby's frequent bursts of expletives and fist-shaking at the atrocious state of Manhattan street repair, the driving ability of other cab drivers, and a guy on a call-in radio program, nobody said much for the next few blocks. Lemmy fussed with the wig and tried to get it properly resituated, front to front, back to back. I kept looking out the back window to see if we had a tail. Just because Turner and McKinley had been all wrapped up in getting people safely out of the funeral home didn't mean they hadn't seen us spirit Lemmy away.

Finally Lemmy broke the silence. "The more I think about it, the more I think this is bullshit. Admit it. You guys overreacted. Those cops never would have fingered me." He patted the wig. "Hell, with this baby on, not even my own mother would recognize me. Right, Brenda?" His brown eyes peeked out from beneath ridiculous fringed bangs.

I hated being put on the spot, being the one to tell him that he looked like a jerk in the wig and stuck out like a sore thumb, so I sidestepped the issue. "Although Turner and McKinley may not seem it, they're pretty sharp. I'm not saying they would have identified you. I'm saying it was too great a risk to take."

"Right," said Johnny. He reached over and yanked the wig.

Lemmy slapped at Johnny's hand. "Hands off."

When the cab pulled up in front of Chuck's, we all saw the BMW parked across the street, clean and shiny and out of place.

"Craparama," said Lemmy. "I don't want to see that lawyer. The guy drives me nuts."

Johnny had to threaten to pull out of the *Tod Trueman* series to get Lemmy out of the cab.

We hurried into Chuck's. I went through the unnecessary motions of introducing Johnny and Brew Winfield, both of whom already knew exactly who the other was. They made the proper nods and grunts. Then we got down to business.

Chuck apologized. "Sorry, guys," he said, "I had to go upstairs for a minute to ask Renard something about tonight's gig. When I got back, no Lemmy. *Pfft.* Vanished."

"No need to apologize," said Johnny. "Lemmy's an adult. If he wants to get arrested, there's not a damn thing any of us can do about it. Right, Lemmy?"

Lemmy made a face.

"What's that thing on your head?" asked Winfield. Not that he, who let a snake roam through his hair, had any right to talk about weird headgear.

"What's it look like?" said Lemmy. He threw himself into Chuck's beanbag chair and folded his arms, challenging us to come up with an answer.

We gathered in a circle around him and studied the wig with mock seriousness. To our credit, not one of us laughed or made jokes about synthetic roadkill. Finally Chuck said, "It looks like something you bought from one of the bums who sell garbage from blankets spread out on Second Avenue. What did you pay, two bucks?"

A little of the petulance washed off Lemmy's face. He looked genuinely sad when he said, "Three." Then he pulled the wig off and threw it at Chuck's antique oscilloscope. The oscilloscope withstood the impact; the wig fell to the table below. Lemmy hung his head. "I just wanted to go to the funeral, that's all. I don't see why you've all got to make such a big deal of it."

"Trust me," said Winfield, "murder is a big deal. Did anybody see you?"

"Nah," said Lemmy, waving his hand in the air, dismissing the question.

I told Winfield that it wasn't exactly "nah" and filled him in on Turner and McKinley and the fire. By the time I finished the story he was holding his head in his hands, massaging his temples. He looked up and said, "What's done is done. Let's hope the detectives didn't notice you. It shouldn't be necessary, but I'm obligated to remind Mr. Crenshaw that *Agent Serving Time in the Pokey with Hardened Crazed Criminals for a Murder He Didn't Commit* sucks. It's been done a million times. On the other hand, the concept I had in mind, *Fugitive Agent,* has got a lot going for it. Picture this: Wrongly accused innocent agent combs the underbelly of New York searching for truth and justice, along the way—"

"Stuff it," said Lemmy. "It's *my* story."

Winfield, a master of sweet talk, eventually got Lemmy to consider the possibility of a joint effort—a collaboration of two great minds at the top of their fields, is how he put it. Then Chuck got into the act. By the time Johnny and I left, the three of them were hovering in front of the computer, discussing the possibility of a *Fugitive Agent* web page.

One thing I'll say for Lemmy: Not once did he remind me that his predicament was all my fault.

On the way out, Johnny and I ran into Renard.

"Brenda," he said.

Although Johnny didn't have the foggiest idea who Renard was, Renard immediately recognized Johnny. "Tod Trueman, right?" He offered his hand.

"Pleased to meet you," said Johnny.

Renard turned his attention back to me. "Remember the amp I told you about yesterday?"

I nodded.

"It's a beauty. Works perfectly. Want to see it sometime?"

"Sure," I said.

"Great. I'm sorry about yesterday, rushing off like that. I mean, we could have had coffee or something."

I liked the idea of coffee with Renard. "Some other time," I said.

We made some small talk about the approaching winter storm. Then Johnny and I left. As soon as we were out on the street Johnny asked, "Who was that geek?"

"Renard," I said.

"I know that," he said. "I mean, who *is* he?"

"Ever heard of Urban Dog Talk?" I asked.

Johnny shook his head.

"He's their guitar player."

"Doesn't look like he could play his way out of a paper bag."

It was bad enough when Johnny and I fought about interior decoration. I wasn't about to get into it with him over rock and roll, so I let it go and changed the subject. "Winfield's okay, don't you think?

"Oh yeah, he's a real Perry Mason, that one," said Johnny sarcastically.

"Don't be so cranky," I said. "Just because Mr. Duggins recommended him doesn't mean he's not good. He got Lemmy out of jail, didn't he?"

"That he did," said Johnny.

Before Johnny and I parted company—me taking a detour through Soho and he heading straight home—he informed me that he wasn't about to let me go to the strip club alone.

"I'm not going alone," I said. "I'll be with Dweena. She knows her way around."

"That's what I'm afraid of."

"Anyway," I said, "don't you have to get your beauty sleep?"

"Nah. I doubt we'll be shooting tomorrow. This flu is a killer. Sal Stumpford will be flat on his back for days."

"Come along if you want, then," I said. "It's a free country. Dweena's picking me up at midnight."

"I'll be at your place at eleven." He looked up at the cool gray sky. "Are you sure you want to go to Soho? The blizzard could start any minute. Those boots of yours aren't much protection.''

What was his problem anyway? I was firm. ''Yes, I want to go to Soho.''

Johnny's weather prediction was right. No sooner had I turned down Broadway than snow started to fall—not heavy, but enough to swirl around and gather in the sidewalk cracks. By the time I got to Soho, big puffy flakes were sticking to the side streets.

I needed to check out what the competition was doing. The shop windows were already filled with spring stuff. Being New York, specifically downtown New York, the clothes were all black—shiny black, matte black, textured black, black on black—with an occasional light or bright color thrown in as contrast to make the black stand out. The hats were only so-so, but I had to hand one thing to the competition. At least their spring hats were out. Mine existed mostly in my head.

I walked up West Broadway toward home. The snowflakes fell fast and furious and the wind picked up considerably. By Houston Street it was piling up everywhere. I speeded up as well, making a stop at the coffee store on Bleecker Street to pick up a pound of their house blend.

The guy who measured out my beans had on an Urban Dog Talk T-shirt and dozens of tiny hoop earrings in and around his face. ''Gonna be a real blizzard. They say it might break the record of '47.'' He tapped the dark beans from a big metal scoop into a grinder, set it for fine grind, and turned it on. ''Radio says up to three feet.''

''In the city?''

''Yep. Even worse in the boroughs. And Jersey. Fuhgeddaboutit.''

11

Johnny came over early. This time he had treats in his pocket for Jackhammer. The two of them played a rousing game of Fetch the Chewy Toy while I dug through my closet. I had no idea what to wear to a place where the emphasis was on what people weren't wearing. At eleven-thirty I got panicky. Dweena was picking us up in half an hour and I still had on a sweatshirt and jeans.

"How about that backless silver lamé dress with the big slit that you found at the flea market?" said Johnny. "It's just the ticket, though it might be hard to get out of."

Johnny had become such a good actor I couldn't tell if he was serious. "Do you think I'm going to strip?"

He went back to playing with Jackhammer, completely ignoring my question.

At quarter to midnight I pulled a black stretch knit dress over my head. How could I go wrong in black?

"Good choice," said Johnny. "Now, which hat are you going to wear?"

"No hat," I said. "I don't want to be recognized."

When Dweena's Wall Street career suddenly ended, she'd briefly toyed with the idea of a life of crime, even going so far as to apprentice herself to a master car thief. A shouting match with a cheating lowlife chop shop manager brought that career to a halt before it got off the ground, and she eventually settled into her bouncer gig, only occasionally procuring cars for sport or personal use.

She pulled up driving a bright red sports utility vehicle. I knew better than to ask where she got the car. Her platinum-wigged head bobbed up and down to techno music that blasted out of enormous speakers. ''This baby's got four-wheel drive. Good for the snow,'' she said.

I sat back and enjoyed the ride as much as possible. We skidded through the blizzard down to a side street in Tribeca so obscure, neither Johnny nor I had ever heard of it. All the legal parking spaces were taken, so Dweena parked in a tow-away zone in front of an active driveway. ''Nobody's gonna need to use this driveway in the middle of the night in the middle of a blizzard,'' she said.

Before we got out she rummaged through the tapes and CDs on the dashboard. She derided most of them with a snort, but threw a couple into her big red purse. Then she opened up the glove compartment and looked inside. ''You wouldn't believe what people leave in these things sometimes,'' she said.

I guess this wasn't one of those times because she slammed it shut.

Broken-down anonymous six-story buildings lined the bleak street. Our footsteps mashing through the foot-high drifts broke the eerie silence.

Gesturing for us to follow, Dweena led us to one of the drab buildings. Except for tracks in the snow leading to it, the building was indistinguishable from all the others. Dweena banged her fist on the unpainted metal door. It opened an inch. A bloodshot eye peeped through the crack. The eye checked us out. Then the door creaked open all the way. I followed Dweena inside.

We were greeted by the owner of the bloodshot eye, an unsavory-looking middle-aged man wrapped up in an oversized bulky tweed overcoat. He had a five-day growth of beard, knock-'em-dead whiskey breath, and rotting tobacco-stained teeth. He looked us over, then stuck out his hand and said, ''Twenty-five bucks for the guy.''

''Highway robbery,'' said Johnny.

''This ain't no highway,'' said the guy.

Johnny grumbled about sexism, but handed over three tens. The man wadded up the money and stuffed it into his coat pocket. ''No change,'' he said.

I gave Johnny a five so he could make exact change, but the man wouldn't give him his money back. ''No refunds, no change.'' He slammed a rubber stamp into an inkpad, planted it on the top of Johnny's hand, and rocked it back and forth until the entire squiggly design had transferred. Then, with a grunt, he pointed us up a long wooden staircase.

Dweena stomped up the steps. Her high-heeled cowboy boots raised dust that hadn't been raised in decades. ''Unprofessional,'' she muttered to herself. ''I don't know what the world is coming to. Fools think they can hire any old bum to work the door.''

The second floor was quiet—four unmarked metal doors, each heavily padlocked. Same thing on the third floor. On the fourth-floor landing a man sat on a high stool. Dark beady eyes, prominent front teeth, receding chin, and slicked-back hair made him look like a rat. His outfit was straight out of the seventies—green polyester leisure suit, wildly printed brown and red nylon shirt, white shoes, and a thick white belt. It could have been tongue-in-cheek retro, but my guess was that he always looked like that.

''Well, well, well,'' he said in a high-pitched voice, ''what do you suppose we have here? Two ladies and a gent, I see. Or do I?'' He gave Dweena a hard look, pausing extra long at her large hands. Then he mumbled about how they didn't pay him enough, shrugged, checked for the stamp on Johnny's hand, and gave Dweena and me tickets.

''Drink tickets?'' I asked.

He gave me a blank stare.

I was all set to tell him I didn't appreciate the rude treatment, but Dweena pushed me through the door into the dim, smoky room. It took my eyes a few seconds to adjust to the darkness. Aside from a few candles scattered around, the only source of light was the white spotlight directed at a makeshift wooden stage where a dark-haired woman slithered to a vaguely familiar syrupy pop tune. A couple dozen men hooted, whistled, and clapped.

The woman mouthed the words along with the song's irritating infectious chorus. In the process, she fell off the beat and ended up stripping to an inner drummer. When the song ended, she stopped dancing. The men stamped their feet and shouted for more. "Take it off, take it off," they chanted, even though she had nothing left to take off except a pair of metallic green high heels. She shook her head shyly, bent over and popped a cassette tape out of a boom box that was chained down to the stage, grabbed a pile of clothes, and ran off into a group of giggling women, probably friends who had dared her to go through with it.

Next up, a fat woman in a gauzy yellow and purple tie-dyed muumuu. She put a tape in the boom box, adjusted the sound, and in one swift, surprisingly agile motion lifted the muumuu over her head.

Transfixed, Johnny edged closer to the stage. I didn't give a hoot about the strip acts. I wanted to get a feel for the club and the people who ran it. I wanted to understand what made Buddy Needleson tick. I wanted to find a motive for murder. I left Johnny with Dweena and went off to explore.

I started in the ladies' room. There was nothing but a cluster of women competing for primping space in front of a full-length mirror. The joint was squeaky clean, hardly the decadent scene I expected.

One of the women smiled and nodded hello to me. She looked familiar, but I couldn't place her.

I left the ladies' room and went off in search of the bar. I circled the big room twice but couldn't find it. There had to be a bar. I'd seen lots of people walking around with plastic cups in their hands. Finally a guy who looked as if he'd found the bar a few too many times staggered by. "Where'd you get that drink?" I asked.

He caught his balance, looked me straight in the eye, and said, ''What goes up, must come down.''

Ask a simple question, get an abstract answer. But it turned out the drunk was right on target. A couple of minutes later loud bells attracted my attention to a freight elevator at the back of the room. The doors slid open. Inside the elevator two bartenders in white shirts and red bow ties stood before a well-stocked bar. ''Bar's here,'' one of them shouted.

I considered using my drink ticket for a glass of wine, but a long line formed before I could get over there. A few minutes later the elevator doors slammed shut and the illegal unlicensed liquor establishment was history.

I wandered around awhile, then joined Johnny and Dweena at a table off to the side of the stage. Dweena, looking as bored as I felt, blew smoke rings. I didn't know she smoked. Johnny was watching a pale naked woman sway to insipid new age music. The music drifted off to nothing and the woman left the stage. The next act had livelier music, but not lively enough to keep me awake. ''Want to get going?'' I asked.

''Just a few more,'' said Johnny.

My ex-boyfriend never ceased to amaze me. ''Okay,'' I said, ''catch you in a little while.''

I looked around some more. The most notable thing about this illegal after-hours amateur strip club was how remarkably unsleazy it was, almost chaste. The goon at the front door and the man in polyester in the hallway were the only trashy elements and they were so stereotypical they could have come from central casting.

All of a sudden a flash of golden brown caught my eye. I couldn't believe it. There up on the stage one of my giant-brimmed straw hats undulated to the music. It was on the head of the woman I'd seen in the ladies' room. No wonder she'd looked familiar. She was a Midnight Millinery customer. As I watched, she flung pieces of her costume into the audience. When very little remained, she doffed the hat and danced behind it.

"Hats off, hats off," shouted the men in the audience.

Now, I'm pretty broad-minded, but I've got to admit, this threw me for a loop. I'm deeply connected to each and every one of my hats. When I sent this one out into the world, lovingly wrapped in tissue and cradled in a Midnight Millinery hatbox, I never in a thousand years would have guessed it was destined to become part of a strip costume. I wasn't quite sure how I felt about that.

For the last few seconds of her act, the woman put the hat back on her head and floated off the stage, buck naked. She headed straight into the ladies' room. When she emerged a few minutes later, fully and rather conservatively dressed, I was waiting for her.

"Hi," I said.

"I thought I recognized you," she said. "You're the milliner, right?"

"Brenda Midnight. I made that hat."

"Brenda. Of course. I'm Irene Finneluk. I can't begin to tell you how great your hat has been for my act."

"This isn't your first time?"

"Good heavens, no. Couldn't you tell? My act is much more polished than most of what you see here."

I hadn't noticed. "Too caught up in seeing my hat on stage, I guess." This lady was weird. I could understand how someone might strip one time, on a dare. But more than once? I took a stab in the dark. "Ever strip at a club in a feather and trimming showroom?"

"You mean Buddy Needleson's. Sure. It's where I got my start. Sad news, his death."

Boy, did I want to talk to her. I was trying to figure out how to convince her she should talk to me when I noticed she wasn't paying a bit of attention to me. Her eyes focused far across the room. "My god," she said. "I can't believe it. Don't look now, but I think that's Tod Trueman over there. My heart's a-flutter."

I introduced Irene Finneluk to Johnny. He told her how much he'd enjoyed her act. She told him how much she enjoyed his show. When I asked, she was more than willing to meet with me to talk about Buddy Needleson's strip establishment. "Here," she said, handing me a business card, "meet me at work tomorrow. We'll do lunch."

Finally Johnny agreed to leave. On our way out, Mr. Polyester Leisure Suit said, "Whoa there, girls." He stood in front of the stairway. "Get back in there."

I'd had enough of his rudeness. Again, I started to say something. Again, Dweena took action before I could. She shoved the man aside, grabbed my arm, ran down the stairs, and yelled, "Block him, Johnny." Dweena and I ran right past the downstairs bouncer and out the door. Johnny followed a couple of seconds later.

The bouncer didn't come after us.

"What was that all about?" I asked.

"Remember how we got in free?" asked Dweena.

"Yeah."

"The rule is that ladies get in free, but they have to strip. It's pretty much do or die. Those tickets we got weren't drink tickets. The numbers on them show it was our turn up on the stage."

"I told you to wear your silver lamé dress," said Johnny.

"That's not one bit funny," I said.

"I think we better clear out of here," said Dweena.

Easier said than done. Because of our dramatic exit we hadn't noticed the tow truck at the end of the block or the man struggling to hitch our car up. As we approached, he lost traction and tumbled into a snowdrift. He shook a clenched fist at the car. "Goddamned son of a bitch."

"Don't worry," said Dweena, "leave it to me. I can handle this guy."

She threw open her coat, revealing her plunging neckline and super short skirt and strutted over to the man. "Officer," she said in a sweet low voice, "what seems to be the problem here?"

Dweena must have known that the man was a police department employee, not a real cop, but she didn't let on.

"I can't believe it," said the man. "In the blizzard of

the century, we get a complaint about a goddamned blocked driveway. Normally, in this kind of weather, we'd ignore the call, but when the dispatcher checked it out, he finds out the goddamned vehicle in question is not only illegally parked, the goddamned thing is stolen. Wouldn't you think on a goddamned night like this the goddamned car thieves would take a goddamned break?"

"I don't know what the world is coming to," said Dweena. She shook her head sympathetically.

The man raved on. "The vehicle in question belongs to some goddamned big-shot designer that lives in the middle of goddamned nowhere on Gansevoort Street and I've gotta drop the goddamned vehicle there because the goddamned designer knows somebody at goddamned headquarters. Whoever heard of goddamned Gansevoort Street? I don't know where the hell it is."

"Will wonders never cease?" said Dweena. "This must be fate."

"What do you mean 'fate'?"

"Well, here you are wondering where Gansevoort Street is, and here I am, a resident of that very street. My friends and I are in desperate need of a ride home. Perhaps we can work something out." She batted her inch-long false eyelashes.

"It's against regulations, but I can hardly let you ladies—and gent—wait for a cab in this weather at this hour of the night, now, can I?"

Johnny helped the man and they got the car hitched up in no time. The four of us piled into the cab of the tow truck and drove through the blizzard to Gansevoort Street.

Later, when we were alone, I asked Johnny what would have happened if Dweena had stripped. "What is she anyway? I mean, does she—"

"Hell, I don't know, Brenda. Dweena's just Dweena."

12

A call from Elizabeth woke me early.

"Oh my," she said, "were you asleep? For the life of me, I couldn't remember if New York was three or four hours later than Chicago."

Elizabeth had a warped view of geography. She must have thought Chicago was somewhere between San Francisco and Honolulu. "One-hour difference," I said. "It's six here."

"Sorry," she said. "You get any snow in New York?"

I dragged myself out of bed and pulled the phone over to the window. White, everywhere I looked. "Lots of it. Two, three feet and still coming down strong."

"It's been doing that for the last two days in Chicago," said Elizabeth. "O'Hare is shut down. The Dude and I are stuck here until meltdown. The convention's swell, so I don't mind staying for the whole thing. I've got a favor to ask, though. Would you mind checking on my cactus? He probably won't need water, but he likes attention. His name is Spike."

"Sure. I'll go tickle Spike's needles."

"Thanks, Brenda. You're a lifesaver. I called you last night as soon as we found out we were stranded, but you weren't home. I hope that means you had a hot date with Johnny."

"Not exactly," I said. "Johnny, Dweena, and I went to an illegal after-hours amateur strip club."

"In the blizzard?"

"Storms stop planes, close schools, and screw up the mail, but nothing stops New York nightlife."

"God, I miss New York," said Elizabeth. "Much as I like the convention and the Dude, I'm homesick as hell. Tell me all about the strip club."

"There's not much to tell."

"Why did you go?"

When I'd told Elizabeth about the morgue, she hadn't believed me. I never had gotten around to telling her about the murder charges against Lemmy. It was way too much to explain over the phone. "No reason, really," I said. "Dweena thought it would be a hoot."

"So, did you strip?"

"Of course not."

"Did Dweena?"

"Nope."

"Oh."

"And Elizabeth," I said, "the answer to the question you're too polite to ask—I don't know. Like Johnny said, 'Dweena's just Dweena.' "

My doorman Ralph, who lately seemed to be working all the shifts, took one look at Jackhammer and burst out laughing. "That's some snowsuit you've got there, little guy."

Jackhammer strutted through the lobby, showing off the fake leopardskin coat I'd made for him. Even I thought he looked a little silly.

The super had already shoveled a narrow path through the snow and scattered a chemical deicer on the sidewalk, turning the snow into bright blue slush. I didn't want Jackhammer to get the stuff on his feet, so I carried him over to a clean drift. The top two inches of his favorite fire hydrant poked through the snow. He had such a great time thrashing around, I hated to take him in, but I had business to get to. Once upstairs, I wrapped Jackhammer in a big towel and dried him off. Then I got down to work.

Irene Finneluk's business card said she was a real estate broker at a firm I'd never heard of in the West Seventies. I called to confirm our lunch appointment. She said if I could get uptown in the snow, she'd be glad to see me.

"No problem," I told her, thinking it wouldn't be, but of course it was. During the time I waited in the blinding snow for the number ten bus, three out-of-service buses roared past. After twenty minutes I gave up and hoofed it to the subway a few blocks away. The sidewalks weren't bad, but the intersections were hell. The snowplows had pushed snow out of the middle of the street, over to the curb. I guess they had to put it somewhere, but it meant I had two choices at the intersections: either climb over the six-foot snow mounds or walk around them in the middle of the slippery street, mixing it up with the skidding, out-of-control traffic. I opted to go over.

Once I got to the subway and down the treacherously slick steps, an express train screeched into the station and zipped me up to Seventy-second Street in minutes.

Irene Finneluk's real estate firm was located in a beautifully maintained brownstone. A receptionist with bruise-colored fingernails greeted me. She sat behind a slab of black marble cluttered only by a phone and a computer monitor. "Renting or looking to buy?" she asked.

"Neither," I said. "I'm Brenda Midnight. I have an appointment to see Irene Finneluk."

The receptionist called Irene and told her I was waiting. She pointed me toward an eclectic, well-coordinated grouping of chairs. "Make yourself at home," she said. "Ms. Finneluk will be with you momentarily."

I took my coat off, settled into a Barcelona-type chair, and looked through a huge three-ring binder. It had page after page of full-color eight-by-tens of luxury properties. Prices ranged from too expensive, to ridiculously expensive, to you've-gotta-be-kidding expensive.

I was thinking how real estate was a weird day job for

an amateur stripper when Irene Finneluk came out. I barely recognized her. The elegant woman striding toward me in a classic Chanel knockoff didn't look anything like the straw hat stripper. By day Irene Finneluk wore her hair slicked back and tied with a velvet bow, her makeup was subtle, the overall effect low-keyed.

She shook my hand, a hearty, sincere, trained professional shake. "Sorry you and Tod—"

I corrected her. "Johnny Verlane."

"Right. Johnny. I'm sorry you and Johnny had to leave so early last night. A couple of new dancers chickened out, so I took another turn."

"Our ride was leaving," I said.

"I still can't get over the fact that I actually met Johnny Verlane in the flesh. What a thrill. It must be fantastic to have him for a boyfriend."

"He's just a friend," I said.

She didn't even try to hide her smile. "In that case, you tell Johnny for me that I'd be delighted to put him on the guest list any old time. I perform two or three times a week."

"I'll mention it," I said.

"Thank you," she said. "I'll be forever grateful." She glanced at her watch. "Now, did you have anyplace special in mind for lunch?"

"I don't know the neighborhood," I said. "Maybe you should pick."

"If you don't mind, I'd like to get a pizza and run over to see an apartment. It's a brand-new listing, just came in this morning. I want to get a look at it before the competition, if you know what I mean. It's a fabulous three-bedroom co-op on Central Park West with a highly motivated seller. We can eat and talk at the apartment."

"Fine with me," I said, wondering what would highly motivate someone to sell such an apartment.

Irene was a trouper. She not only managed, in thigh-high snow, to hail the only cab within miles, but she convinced the driver to wait while she picked up the pizza. ''I'll just be a second,'' she said. She hopped out and ran into the pizza joint. A couple of minutes later she was back, pizza in hand. ''Want a slice?'' she asked the cabbie. ''Cheese and mushroom.''

''No thanks,'' he said, ''I'm off dairy.''

The cab turned south on Central Park West and pulled up in front of a massive dark stone building. The walls must have been two feet thick. While Irene flipped through a wad of high-denomination bills looking for change to pay, another cab pulled up in front of us. An impeccably dressed slender man with carefully styled blond hair got out first and helped a woman out of the cab. The woman was draped in a full-length red fox coat. Together they walked toward the building. Irene leaned forward in her seat to get a better look at them. ''I'll be goddamned,'' she said. She shoved a fifty in the driver's hand and tore out of the cab like it was on fire. ''Keep the change.''

With me following, she broke into a trot and got ahead of the man and the fox lady and stationed herself between them and the door.

''Look what the old tomcat dragged out of the alley,'' said the man with a smirk.

With a scathing edge to her voice, Irene said, ''What rock did you crawl out from under, Gerard?''

''Same rock as you, dear.''

Fire burned in Irene's eyes. ''I'm afraid you're wasting your time if you've come to see Seven East. My client''—she jutted her chin in my direction—''is ready to make an offer.''

I smiled tentatively, not sure what else to do. No one noticed.

''We'll see about that.'' Gerard reached in front of Irene and opened the door. ''See you in hell,'' he said.

I figured Gerard was the competition.

The immense lobby was presided over by a silver-haired doorman. Real brass buttons and red braid decorated his dark gray uniform. He directed us to an old-fashioned wood-paneled elevator manned by a white-gloved elevator operator. On the way up, no one said a word, though both Gerard and Irene breathed purposefully loud. At the seventh floor they bolted from the elevator.

With fox coat and me trailing behind, Irene and Gerard made a left turn off the elevator, another left where the hallway bent around into a little alcove, then stopped in front of a door. Fingers poised over the buzzer, they locked eyes. Gerard blinked first; Irene pushed the buzzer.

A woman wearing green silk lounging pajamas opened the door. Her face was puffy, her eyes red and full of tears. She blew her nose. ''Three to five years,'' she said between sobs. ''Can you believe it? I wanted to keep this place, rent it until I get out, but the goddamned lawyer demanded all the money now. I ought to sue the bastard.'' She stepped aside and we all filed into the apartment.

The lady in the fox coat let out with an ''Oh my god'' under her breath and, I have to admit, so did I. The enormous living room had fifteen-foot ceilings and fireplaces at both ends. High arched windows framed a breathtaking Christmas card view of Central Park in the snow. Except for a curvy brown velvet couch that the crying woman dramatically sank into, the place was empty.

The competition went north; Irene and I went south. Our footsteps echoed down a long hall. At the end was the master bedroom suite, with its own fireplace, solarium, and dressing room. Irene whispered in my ear, ''She was forced to sell off the furniture piece by piece as the trial progressed.''

I didn't keep up with the news on a regular basis, so I didn't know what she was talking about, but I nodded my head as if I did. ''A shame,'' I said.

''Thank god the murder didn't take place here,'' said Irene. ''There's no stigma attached to the property.'' She put the pizza box on a window seat. ''Grab a piece and come with me. We can talk while I do a quick walk-through. Feel free to ask me anything you want about the strip clubs.''

I followed Irene into a bathroom that was two times the size of my entire apartment. She turned the gold-toned faucets and watched water flow down the drain of the pink marble sink.

I didn't want to beat around the bush. "Why do you strip?" I asked.

"I have a great talent," she said. "If there were any money in stripping, I'd turn pro." She flushed the toilet with her foot and smiled at the rapid rate of water return. "Good water pressure for an old building."

"Are there many amateur clubs?"

"None of them lasts very long. That is, except for Buddy Needleson's. His club was an institution. The women loved the place, despite the mothball stench, because Buddy ran it on the up and up. He was a good man."

"Up and up? An illegal club."

"Well, about as up and up as an illegal club can get. I guess what I mean is he treated the strippers fair and square. He wanted a good venue, not merely to get rich."

"Do you think the club made money?"

"Oh sure. Lots of it. Even after paying off the cops, the mob, whoever gets paid off these days."

"So he definitely made payoffs?"

"I never actually saw anything like that, not with my own two eyes, but he must have been. I mean, no one ever closed the place down."

"Did he have any enemies that you know of?"

"I don't know. Maybe the competition."

Irene tested the tub and shower. "Not bad at all," she said. "Pipes can be a big problem in these prewars."

I had plenty of experience along those lines. Periodic floods, constant seepage, cracked and peeling plaster were common in my building, but I was surprised to hear that three-million-dollar apartments also sprung leaks. "What about blackmail?" I asked.

"Blackmail?"

"Sure, I mean, here you've got a bunch of women and maybe they don't want the whole world to find out what they did. Husbands, boyfriends, employers—''

Irene shook her head. ''Where have you been? Nobody bats an eye at a naked lady anymore. Prime-time TV has nudity. Personally, I can't wait until Tod Trueman broadcasts his cute little butt all over the land. Do you know if that's coming up this season?''

''Not that I've heard.''

''Damn.''

No matter what she said, I still thought blackmail was a good possibility. Maybe not all the strippers would be so nonchalant. ''Do you think any other strippers would be willing to talk to me?''

''I can give you names of some of the regulars and you can see for yourself.'' She wrote the names down on a napkin from the pizza place and handed it to me. ''Why do you care so much?''

''A couple of hard-headed cops think a friend of mine killed Buddy Needleson. I know he's innocent. To prove it, I've got to find the real murderer.''

13

"It's a cover-up," I said. "Irene Finneluk is hiding something."

"She sure wasn't last night," said Johnny.

I didn't laugh. "I can't believe you can joke about this. After all, Lemmy's your agent and best friend. I shouldn't have bothered to call you the instant I got home. I could be soaking in a hot bubble bath right now."

"Settle down, Brenda. You left yourself wide open with that cover-up statement. I couldn't resist."

"Johnny, you're no comedian."

"I may not be a comedian, but you, Brenda, you've got no sense of humor."

Before the conversation completely deteriorated into a battle of who did and did not have a sense of humor, I got back on subject. "Irene doesn't think Buddy Needleson was blackmailing anybody. She said stripping's not a big enough deal for blackmail."

"Makes sense to me," said Johnny. "Who cares who's naked anymore?"

"I'm not convinced," I said.

"Who does Irene think killed Buddy Needleson?"

"She doesn't know. She did say something kind of interesting, though. The club never got closed down, apparently rare in that kind of business. She figures Buddy

Needleson had to have been paying off the cops, the mob, somebody.''

''It wouldn't be the cops,'' said Johnny. ''The mob, maybe. I like that angle.''

''Why do you always defend the cops? Just because you play a detective on TV doesn't automatically make you part of the brotherhood of blue. I remember one *Tod Trueman* where a bad cop blew his brains out after you discovered he was taking payoffs from a drug-dealing pizza shop owner.''

''Episode Six,'' said Johnny. ''I know bad cops exist, but cops on the take don't bite the hand that feeds them, nor do they bash in its skull. My guess is it was the mob.''

''That's pretty much what Norbert said when I talked to him,'' I replied. ''But I disagree. The mob wouldn't use a baseball bat for a rubout. That's hardly their weapon of choice.''

''Mob's not what it used to be,'' said Johnny.

''It could have been a jealous competitor,'' I said. ''Buddy Needleson's club was very popular.''

''Nah,'' said Johnny.

We knocked around some more ideas, then Johnny excused himself to take a nap. ''Stumpford's temperature is down, he's out of bed. We'll probably be shooting again tomorrow. I've got to be in top form for the last scene. It's got a tight close-up as Tod deals with some pretty weighty emotional issues.''

''Oh yeah,'' I said. ''Weighty issues? Tod Trueman? Like what?''

''Like in the obligatory car chase, the drug kingpin bad guy loses control of a classic red 1956 'Vette and smashes it into an overpass. The vehicle explodes, the bad guy gets creamed, and Tod is silhouetted against the churning red and yellow flames. It's truly a poignant moment as Tod reflects on the forces of good and evil.''

''I'm moved,'' I said.

* * *

I finally took that bubble bath and got down to some heavy thinking. I didn't know how to proceed. Should I talk to the strippers Irene told me about? Go after the mob? Investigate the police? Scrape up dirt on the competition? Interrogate the Ns?

I needed to do something fast, before Lemmy did something stupid again, before Brewster Winfield's bills wiped me out, before Johnny's *Tod Trueman* episodes were in the can, before Lemmy ratted on Johnny and me and we landed in jail. Meanwhile, I needed to work on my spring line so I could keep Jackhammer in kibbles, a roof over my head, and Midnight Millinery's rent paid so I wouldn't end up out on the street, unable to find out who killed Buddy Needleson.

I added more bubbles, blasted them with hot water, relaxed, and thought hard. It boiled down to two problems: Lemmy and my spring line. I wasn't making much headway on either.

The phone rang. I vowed not to get out of the tub, not to pick up, no matter who it was or what they said, but when I heard the message, I broke my vow. Chuck was on the "so call me" part of his message when I grabbed the receiver with a dripping wet hand. "Lemmy what?" I said.

"Oh," said Chuck, "you're monitoring your calls."

"I was in the bath," I said. "What's this about Lemmy?"

"Lemmy shaved his head."

On a cosmic level the fact that Lemmy Crenshaw had shaved his head was insignificant. There was a tiny possibility that by shaving his head, Lemmy would attract a woman who would bear his child. That child would grow up to discover an almost extinct, very slimy pond animal, and that when the slimy pond animal's tummy was tickled, it would secrete a gooey substance that, depending on its processing, was a strong wood glue, a cancer cure, or a substance capable of blowing up the entire universe as we know it. Only a tiny possibility. On a less cosmic level—this I had to see for myself.

"I'm coming over," I said.

* * *

Chuck came to the door holding a bag of bright orange puffy cheese-flavored snacks. "Want one?"

"No way," I said. "I don't eat anything that glows in the dark. What I want to see is Lemmy's head."

"Lemmy's head, and the rest of Lemmy, is upstairs at an Urban Dog Talk rehearsal," said Chuck.

"Oh," I said.

"You can go up if you want. Renard won't mind. He's kind of sweet on you."

"I don't know."

Renard played a Flying Vee guitar. The thought of seeing him play it up close was too much. Once again, I had to remind myself I'd sworn off actors, artists, and musicians, especially guitar players, especially guitar players with Flying Vees who looked like Renard and played like—well, played like Renard, and that was very, very good.

"Go ahead," said Chuck. "When you get back, I'll show you Lemmy's web page."

I wavered. "I don't think so."

"You've got nothing to lose."

What did Chuck know about what I had to lose?

I walked up the narrow staircase very slowly, still not sure I wanted to go. That's not exactly right. I wanted to go. It's just that I thought I shouldn't go. With every step the music got louder, and by the time I got to the third floor, I couldn't turn back.

I knocked on the door. No one answered; no one inside could possibly have heard my knock. For that matter, no one inside could have heard a nuclear blast a block away. I opened the door a crack and a palpable concussion of sound, a blast of pure energy, whooshed out. I jumped inside and pulled the door shut behind me.

A tangle of thick cables covered the white-painted floor. The room was jammed with guitars and amplifiers and keyboards and mixing boards and computers. Tiny lights blinked, needles rose and fell with the level of sound. With Chuck on the first floor and Urban Dog Talk on the third, it was no wonder an occasional fuse got blown in this building.

Renard smiled at me and for a brief but thoroughly fantastic instant I let his smile wash over me with the music. Then the warning bells in my head went off. I should have stayed away.

To break the spell I turned my attention to the rest of the band. Except for a new bass player, a tall redheaded woman, they had the same lineup I'd seen before: a tiny woman with short-cropped black hair played various configurations of keyboards and synthesizers, a lanky guy played drums, and a short guy with a ponytail down to his waist played rhythm guitar. As far as I was concerned, they were all background to Renard.

Lemmy was sitting in a fat green chair bopping his bright shiny new head to the rhythm. I balanced on the arm of the chair. He said something. I couldn't hear, so I bent down and put my ear close to his mouth. He cupped his hands around his mouth and yelled, "Did you find the murderer?"

I cupped my hands and yelled back, "No."

"Shit."

For that, I read his lips.

"I'm getting close," I yelled.

"That's good, Brenda. Keep up the good work." He nodded his head toward the band. "Not bad."

I smiled and nodded. Maybe he really would become Urban Dog Talk's agent.

I'm not sure how long the rehearsal lasted or how many songs they played or if they played a lot of songs once or a few songs over and over. I remember that when they were finished Renard came over and asked how I liked it. I think I said something stupid like great or cool when I should have commented on the Marshall amp or his vintage Flying Vee. Actually what I should have said was good-bye. I had another chance when he mentioned he owed me a coffee, but instead of good-bye I said, "Anytime."

Then Lemmy and I left. He walked down the stairs in

front of me, which gave me an excellent view of his shaved head.

I thumped it with my forefinger. "How come you shaved your head?"

"Because I got sick of being another guy with a piddly-assed bald spot and a pathetic attempt at a comb-over. Now I say, if you don't got it, flaunt it."

"It looks good," I said, surprised that I meant it.

"Thanks, Brenda."

"The band's great, don't you think?" I asked.

Lemmy turned around so I could see his smirk. "I think the bass player is a stone fox, that's what I think."

Chuck must have heard us coming down the stairs. When we got to his place, he was standing in the doorway with a huge smile spread across his face. "Hot dog, I'm on a roll. The Fugitive Agent web page is up on the Net."

Lemmy touched the top of his head. "Did you delete my hair?"

"Yes, I deleted your hair, and the bags under your eyes too. I took your old picture into my handy dandy photo retouch program and used the airbrush tool to—"

"Please," said Lemmy, "spare me the gory details. Let me see the page."

"Whatever you say, Chrome Dome." Chuck sat down at his computer. "You guys better pull up a chair. We've got a lot to explore."

A few keystrokes and a lot of gurgling, farting, sputtering, and whistling sounds got us connected. Then Chuck clicked his mouse and his monitor filled with the words "Lemmy Crenshaw, Fugitive Agent" in big bold bright red type. Beneath the words was a small picture of Lemmy without hair. "Watch this," said Chuck. He clicked on a bright red button on Lemmy's chest and the picture moved. Lemmy waved to a cyberspace audience.

"That's me," said Lemmy. He clapped his hands like a gleeful three-year-old.

"Cool, huh?" said Chuck. Next he pointed to a column of blue buttons that ran down the right side of the screen.

"Click on these to see your clients in action." He pushed the mouse across the table to me. "Here, pick one."

Naturally I clicked Johnny's button. The picture on the screen showed his publicity shot. I clicked on another button and a little two-inch movie started. It showed Tod Trueman scaling up the side of the Empire State Building on a rope, including the melodramatic action music.

"That's nice," I said, "except it's not Johnny. That was a double."

"Yeah, well, Tod's fans don't know that," said Chuck. "Anyway, it's low-res."

It occurred to me that maybe this web page wasn't such a good idea. "Isn't this dangerous?" I asked. "Lemmy's supposed to be in hiding and here you've got his face all over the Internet."

"Don't sweat it," said Chuck. "Any contact will be through an anonymous electronic remailing service. No one can trace Lemmy, yet he can advertise to the entire world."

"Still seems risky to me," I said. "What's Brewster Winfield say?"

Chuck smiled. "Brew thinks it's the best thing since sliced bread, the transistor, and the answering machine, and he hasn't seen the animated version yet."

14

I got lucky. Just as I was leaving Chuck's, an empty cab cruised by. I grabbed it. Then I realized maybe I wasn't so lucky after all.

The driver, a dark-eyed, straggly-bearded madman, hunkered down over the steering wheel and plowed his dented yellow vehicle through foot-high slush, laughing all the way. He was like a thin, young, demonic, speed-addled Santa at his day job a few weeks after Christmas. He ho-ho-hoed and swerved merrily across Sixth Avenue four inches in front of a careening double-decker tour bus full of gaping out-of-towners.

I hung on for dear life. At Seventh Avenue the driver slammed on the brakes halfway through a red light, hit an icy patch and spun through the intersection. I took the opportunity to get out while the getting was good. "You know," I said, "it's such a nice day, I think I'll get out right here and walk the rest of the way." I kept my voice steady and calm so as not to excite the driver more than he already was. Given the gray bleakness I don't think he believed the nice day bit, or maybe he didn't understand it, but he took the wad of singles I thrust through the payhole and let me out.

I walked along Bleecker Street toward home. On the way I passed by Johnny's building. Brown paper covered the windows of the ground-floor storefront. Another business belly up, about the hundredth failure in that spot in the time I'd known Johnny.

When Johnny and I first met, the store was a coffee shop, a relic of Greenwich Village's beatnik days. The owner, an exuberant man named Luigi, served tiny cups of strong espresso and flaky custard-filled pastries to a black-sweatered, bongo-thumping clientele, most of whom had long straight hair and a tendency to scribble poetry on the napkins.

Johnny took me there on our first date. At the time I was working as an office temp and Johnny had just landed a role in a twenty-second aftershave spot. We sipped espresso and talked for hours. A year or so later, Luigi died in somewhat mysterious circumstances. Since then, every business that dared rent that space had failed within a few months of opening. There'd been a sandal shop, a used bookstore, a dirty bookstore, a dirty poster and T-shirt shop, an ice-cream store, a frozen yogurt store, a muffin shop, a copy shop, and one very popular restaurant that I'd never gone to because, for the entire six months of the restaurant's existence, Johnny and I weren't speaking to each other and I avoided that strip of Bleecker Street entirely. Neighborhood lore had it that Luigi's ghost put the whammy on each new business for reasons that were anyone's guess, but probably had something to do with those mysterious circumstances surrounding his death.

I was so caught up in reminiscing I misjudged a harmless-looking patch of ice. It turned out to be a thin veneer covering a deep puddle. I broke through and icy slush filled my boot, instantly numbing my toes. I'd had frostbite in the past and knew that my toes needed immediate care.

Normally I wouldn't have considered dropping in on Johnny unannounced, but this was an emergency. I walked back to his building. Then I paused, finger hovering over the button next to Johnny's name, and considered the magnitude of what I was about to do.

It's like this: Nobody but nobody drops by unannounced and uninvited in New York City. It's a no-no, a big fat faux pas, a breach of the social trust. Anyone fool enough to just drop by better be ready for anything. Anything like maybe the droppee will slam the door in the dropper's face. Or, maybe the droppee will turn down the sound on the TV, douse the lights, drop to his knees, and crawl around for the next half hour, carefully staying well below the windows, pretending to be out. Then there's the chance that maybe the dropper will discover something she'd rather not know about the droppee.

With all this in mind, I pushed Johnny's buzzer. He answered immediately. The signal-to-noise ratio of his intercom was heavily weighted in favor of noise. I couldn't decipher the sounds coming out of the intercom, but since they were accompanied by a buzz from the door signaling the lock's release, I assumed it was human speech inviting me up. So up I went.

Johnny's door opened a couple of inches. "Brenda?"

"Yeah, sorry to drop by without calling, but my toes . . ." I gave the door a little push but it didn't budge.

"Uh," said Johnny from behind the door, "it's like, uh . . . it's not a good time."

The reality of the situation hit me. I was mortified. I'd broken the rules, all right, and it looked as if I'd stumbled onto something I'd rather not have known. Johnny had somebody there—probably a guest starlet. I doubted they were going over their lines, at least not the ones in the *Tod Trueman* script.

There was no graceful way to proceed. I made a flash decision to get the hell out of there, maybe pretend the whole thing had never happened. I'd turned to go when Johnny's kitchen timer gonged loudly.

"Shit," said Johnny, "my soufflé." He ran off, leaving the door slightly ajar and me in the hallway.

Johnny's building was over a hundred years old. Over time it had settled, twisted, and sagged so that Johnny's door no longer hung evenly on its hinges. Left unlatched and unattended to deal with gravity all by itself, it swung open all the way, revealing a sweeping view of Johnny's apartment.

What I saw caused me to burst into laughter. Tears rolled down my cheeks. There stood Johnny in his kitchen tending his fallen soufflé. He was dressed head to toe in a fuzzy pink and white bunny rabbit suit, complete with big ears.

I stepped a few feet into the apartment. When I saw no evidence of any starlet, I went all the way into the kitchen. I couldn't talk. All I could do was point at Johnny and laugh.

"It's not funny," said Johnny. His ears flopped when he talked.

It was funny. Still laughing, I retreated to the living room, sat down on the couch, took off my boots, and rubbed life back into my toes. I'd just about settled down when Johnny gave up on his soufflé and sat next to me on the couch, squashing his fluffy white tail. I was about to make a carrot joke when he started talking.

"Zipper's stuck," he said. "I can't get the damned rabbit suit off."

"How long have you been a bunny?"

He glared at me. "Since this morning. It came in the mail, a gift from a fan. I put it on as a goof."

"Strange gift," I said. "What were you going to do if I hadn't happened by?"

"I didn't want you or anybody to happen by. I was gonna cut it off just as soon as my soufflé was done. Think you can you fix it?" He sat on the floor in front of me so I could get to the zipper.

While I fiddled with the zipper I asked Johnny about the storefront downstairs. "What's the deal?"

"I don't know," said Johnny. "Yesterday, a candle store. Today, gone. Poof. Vanished in the middle of the night."

"What do you think it'll be next, a Laundromat?"

"Actually, we've got a lottery going in the building. It's five bucks to join. So far we've got three votes for a Seattle-style coffee shop."

"That fad's over," I said.

"I agree," he said. "Then we've got two votes for another condom shop, but again I don't think so, not with one half a block away, and one vote apiece for video rental, sneakers, vintage clothing, burritos—"

"No," I said. "Poetry, live poetry."

"My money's on a skate shop."

"Put me down for poetry," I said.

"It's your money," said Johnny, "but don't say I didn't warn you."

I got the zipper back on track, promised Johnny I wouldn't breathe a word of this to anyone, and left.

I was badly shaken by the situation at Johnny's. Not by Johnny in the dopey bunny suit, but by what I'd thought was going on—Johnny with someone else. Not knowing what else to do, I ended up going to Midnight Millinery. I wasted an hour staring at my wooden design head block trying to come up with something new for spring, something that didn't take three days to make. The big straw braid hat might be okay for a store window, or a magazine layout, or a strip act, but the line needed guts, something real people would wear. Then again, the way the wind chugged up Fourth Street, slammed into the building, and rattled my big storefront window, I wasn't convinced there'd ever be a spring.

When I couldn't stand it anymore, I went home. A message from Naomi waited on my answering machine. "Call me," she said.

Against my better judgment, I did.

I hadn't talked to her since Johnny and I ran out of her uncle's funeral, a fact that did not make her happy. If she'd had any idea we'd absconded with Lemmy, the man wanted for her uncle's murder, she'd have been even less happy.

"You know, Brenda," she said, "it's not like the funeral was called off or anything. As soon as the firemen left, it started again."

"Really?" I said.

"Don't play the innocent, Brenda. You didn't see anyone else leave, did you? Face it, you guys were rude."

"I'm sorry."

"No you're not. I can tell. Anyway, by leaving early you not only missed a beautiful service, you missed some really cute firemen. What is it about firemen anyway? Why are they always so gorgeous?"

"I don't know, Naomi. It's an enduring New York mystery, like how come no one ever sees baby pigeons? Or where does the steam in the street come from?"

"All I can say is," said Naomi, "you should have been there. But the reason I called is to invite you to Uncle Buddy's burial."

"Wasn't he buried after the funeral?"

"That got all screwed up. Because the fire delayed everything, the funeral home refused to drive the hearse to Queens without going into double overtime since they'd hit rush hour on the way back. Naturally, Babette threw a fit. She threatened to sue since the fire was the funeral home's fault. That got the funeral director all huffy. He claimed the best he could do was to squeeze Uncle Buddy into tomorrow's schedule. Babette still may sue. Meanwhile, we've got to give him a proper burial. Babette's driving Mommy, Daddy, Norbert, and me. It's a big car. There's plenty room for you."

"To Queens?"

"Sure. Everybody gets buried in Queens."

I made a mental note to have my lawyer put a clause in my will specifying cremation. "Thanks for the invitation, but tomorrow is impossible. If only I'd known sooner, maybe I could have gone."

"Have it your way," said Naomi. "Mommy and Daddy will be disappointed they didn't get to see more of you. They're flying back to Florida right after the burial. I mean, you know, it's like we'll already be right by LaGuardia."

"Maybe next time," I said.

"Next time?" said Naomi. "Uncle Buddy's only going to be buried once."

"A figure of speech," I said.

Naomi snorted and hung up the phone.

I didn't care if she was mad at me. She couldn't possibly be more mad at me than I was at her. All I'd done was leave a funeral early. She'd dragged me into this whole mess. No way was I going to spend the day driving around Queens with the Ns, Howard, Zorema, and the grieving widow.

Besides, the fact that the entire Needleson family would be spending much of the day in Queens gave me an idea. Friends or not, I still didn't trust the Ns a hundred percent. Maybe I'd find out why if I took the opportunity to snoop around their showroom.

My stomach growled, but nothing in the kitchen looked good. Elizabeth was still in Chicago, I couldn't bring myself to call Johnny, and Renard hadn't called, so I took Jackhammer out and picked up some cold sesame noodles with an order of broccoli floating in garlicky grease from the local Chinese takeout. That's when I knew I was depressed because it's what I always eat when I'm feeling sorry for myself because I hate Chinese food. To really rub it in, they left out the fortune cookie.

Sometime in the middle of the night Jackhammer jumped out of bed and puked up his half of the cold sesame noodles. When I got up to get a glass of water, I stepped in it.

15

Jackhammer and I got outdoors early the next morning, before anybody had a chance to throw more deicer on the sidewalks. The weather prediction was for a continuing warming trend, but from the looks of the sky, I didn't believe it.

The garbage hadn't been picked up since the storm. Big black plastic bags of it were piled high at the curbs. According to a sanitation department spokesperson on the news, regular pickups would resume "as soon as possible." For now, though, Jackhammer was doubly thrilled. He had mounds of snow to play on and heaps of extra garbage to check out.

Apparently he'd learned the lesson of the cold sesame noodles the night before. He turned up his nose at garbage in front of the Chinese restaurant and trotted on down the street to the Italian restaurant. There he tried to get his teeth around a half loaf of garlic bread lying on the sidewalk. I tugged him away, but all the way down the block he twisted his head around and looked forlornly back at the bread until a brief, bloodless skirmish with a passing Chow got his attention off scavenging.

When we got back upstairs, I called Elizabeth in Chicago. Looking for sympathy, I told her I was confused about Johnny.

"Look, Brenda," she said, "if you don't snap him up,

believe me, somebody else will. Take a word of advice and cut this 'just friends' crap. Get with the program. Wake up and smell the coffee. The early bird gets the—''

''So,'' I interrupted, ''how *is* Chicago?''

''Cold and windy as hell. More snow.''

I'd expected as much. ''And Dude Bob 43?''

''Now, *that* is a story for another time. Suffice it to say we're not letting that old Vietnam War come between us. Not only that, I'm making out like a bandit. Get this, some collector offered me two hundred dollars for one of my peace buttons.''

''What is it, encrusted with diamonds?''

''It's rare. You had to be a member of this group to get this particular button.''

''Which group?''

''Some group that walked across the country, you know, to protest the war.''

''You were a member of that group?''

''I think so. It's hard to remember that far back.''

''That's nuts. You can't remember if you walked across the country? I'd sure remember something like that.''

''It's one of those things where I've told the story so many times, the story seems more real than the experience and I start to wonder if I made the whole thing up.''

''But you've got the button.''

''Yes, I do. So, maybe I did walk across the country.''

I called the Ns at home and the showroom. When there was no answer, I assumed they were safely on their way to Queens to bury their uncle. Much as I hated to, I had to take action. I'd never get another opportunity like this with both of them gone most of the day. Sure, I was uncomfortable with the idea of snooping around Needleson Brothers behind the Ns' backs. However, it was all their fault. They'd brought it on themselves when they dragged me into this mess.

I had a set of keys to the showroom from the time the entire Needleson family had taken a lavish European vacation disguised as a tax deductible buying trip. While they were supposedly buying ribbon and feathers on the Riviera, I stopped in every couple of days to pick up the mail and water the office sweet potato plant. They'd never asked for the keys back.

Since I had keys, I figured it wasn't really breaking and entering. At least there was no breaking involved. Still, I was very, very cautious. I cruised by the front of the building a couple of times to make sure no one saw me go in. Then I ducked into the lobby and studied the building directory as if I were looking for a suite number, just in case somewhere someone was watching. As a last dodge, I took the elevator to the floor above Needleson Brothers and walked down a flight. I hung out in the stairwell for a couple of minutes listening to be sure the coast was clear before tiptoeing out into the hallway. A hot sauce distributor rented the only other office on the floor. He was rarely there, but in case this was one of those rare times and he was peeping out his peephole, I ran through a little act. I rang the Ns' bell, paused, and then, as if someone had said something to me, talked back to the door. "Okay, Naomi," I said, "I'll let myself in."

Which is exactly what I proceeded to do. The top lock, a serious deadbolt assembly, opened smoothly. The bottom lock was a temperamental piece of junk. I jiggled the key, pulled it out, stuck it in again, jiggled again, finally got the door open, and officially trespassed. Quickly I pulled the door shut behind me.

The showroom was a mess, but no more than usual. I wandered into the back room. It seemed as good a place to start as any. Lopsided cartons of ribbon and rhinestones and feathers were scrunched together, stacked precariously high. I tried not to think about Howard Needleson's baseball bat inventory system, or that his missing bat had probably bashed in his brother's head.

In the middle of the room was the shipping and receiving department. It consisted of a rickety table, a postal scale, two rolls of strapping tape, a ball of twine, a felt marker, and a pad of gummed labels printed with the Needleson Brothers logo. A half-size refrigerator was plugged into an extension cord that hung down from a light fixture on the ceiling. Inside were leftovers sealed in plastic containers, jars of condiments, and a six-pack of generic-brand grape diet soda.

If I'd known what I was looking for I would have looked for it. I kicked a few of the cartons. Feathers flew out and drifted slowly to the floor. What else did I expect? Looking at the room as a whole, nothing seemed out of place.

I moved on into the front room, a combination reception area, showroom, office, and illegal after-hours amateur strip club. Two molded plastic chairs—one orange, one turquoise—and a stack of outdated trimming trade magazines defined the reception area. In the showroom proper feathers and ribbons of every color and variety imaginable were thumbtacked to the wall.

The Ns had brought their old TV to the office. It occurred to me that maybe that was what Howard and Zorema had been mad about at the funeral, not that the Ns had spent too much money on their new set, but that they were sitting around watching the tube when they were supposed to be working.

Their desks were regulation gray metal, the kind that sell for about a dollar seventy-five at the flea market. I went through Norbert's first. In his top drawer, under an unused ledger book, was an old issue of *Penthouse*. His side drawers contained the usual mess of paper clips, rubber bands, cheap ballpoints, plastic coffee stirrers, and packets of sugar. A big file drawer was full of videotapes. At least they weren't watching soap operas all day.

Needleson Brothers was not computerized. An old IBM Selectric sat in the center of Naomi's desk. Underneath it, I found eraser crumbs and blueberry muffin crumbs. She kept stationery, invoices, and, amazingly, a package of carbon paper in her top drawer. I didn't know they still sold the stuff. In her side drawer were several romance novels with broken spines and, way at the back of the drawer, a set of keys to the Ns' apartment.

I picked the keys up. Did I dare? No. I put them back and slammed the drawer shut. It was one thing to check out the scene of a crime to which I'd been given keys, but quite another to let myself into someone's personal home with keys I'd stolen. For thirty seconds I debated the moral implications. I couldn't possibly invade their privacy. Then again, the Ns had lied to me. I didn't owe them anything. I grabbed the keys out of the drawer, turned off the lights, and split.

I checked my watch. I'd been at Needleson Brothers for less than an hour. There was plenty of time to get in and out of the Ns' apartment before they got back from Queens.

The Ns lived in a gigantic building on Fourteenth Street. The lobby was a hotbed of activity. Delivery men, maintenance men, tenants, dogs, and visitors all streamed through at the same time. I sailed right by the harried doorman and onto the elevator.

Howard and Zorema had moved into the sixteenth-floor one-bedroom after Norbert and Naomi were already grown up and out on their own. Then, when Howard and Zorema moved to Florida, Norbert and Naomi moved into the dirt-cheap rent-stabilized apartment and claimed they had lived there with their parents since day one and had a right to assume the lease. The landlord wanted the Ns out so he could slap a fresh coat of paint on the walls and rent the apartment for its market value, which was triple what the Ns were paying. He had to prove the Ns had never lived in the apartment and therefore didn't have a right to the lease. The last I'd heard, the situation was at a standoff.

I listened at the door. Silence. I knocked. No answer. Briefly, I considered chickening out. Then I unlocked the door and went in.

The Ns must have been waiting until they got the lease problem settled before they spent a dime on the place. How else could they have moved in and not painted the dingy water-stained walls? Or ripped out the carpet? I couldn't tell if it was a greenish stained brown or a brownish stained green. On every possible surface, and there were a lot of them, sat dust-covered cutesy ceramic knickknacks. The furniture was covered with ill-fitting slipcovers made out of leftover dress fabric. In the center of the room, directly across from the couch, was their brand-new very expensive enormous projection television.

Most of the living room floor was taken up by an inflatable mattress and Howard and Zorema's suitcases. The suitcases were open, so I peeked in and discovered Zorema's brand of deodorant, that she'd put the cap back on crooked, and that Howard took blood pressure medication twice a day.

Naomi's bedroom, which used to be Howard and Zorema's, was a jumble of fabric, much of it pink. Her sewing machine was set up in the corner. Frilly polka-dot dresses and matching accessories hung from hooks and hangers, were draped over chairs, piled up on the floor, and exploded out of her closet. A gold-tone heart-shaped frame with a photograph of her boyfriend Fred sat on the dresser. In the picture Fred reclined on an artfully rumpled navy blue satin sheet. He wore red and white polka-dot boxer shorts, no doubt one of Naomi's creations. I learned more than I wanted to, none of it useful.

Norbert's bedroom used to be the dining room. He'd blocked it off from the living room by stringing up draperies from the ceiling. A small dresser contained three drawers of obsessively folded underwear. Norbert had piled his jeans and shirts on top of the dresser, probably because there was no closet in the dining room. A rickety bookshelf full of philosophy books leaned against the wall. The only other furniture was a mattress. I checked underneath. Nothing.

In the kitchen a herd of cockroaches roamed the countertop, feasting on toast crumbs and patches of sticky red jelly. More lurked in the cabinets behind dinner plates and cereal bowls and soup cans. I checked the freezer because in one of the early *Tod Truemans*, Johnny, acting on a hunch, found stolen diamonds in a package of frozen spinach. Norbert and Naomi had no frozen spinach, only frozen pancakes. Once again, life proved to be completely unlike a *Tod Trueman* episode.

There was a drawer for silverware, a drawer for dishtowels, and a junk drawer, where I found more keys. These were tagged with Buddy and Babette's name and a Battery Park City address.

This time I didn't ask myself if I dared. I didn't debate the moral implications. All I cared about was time.

16

I jumped into a cab in front of the Ns' building. ''Battery Park City,'' I told the driver.

Battery Park City, a relatively recent bulge on the Manhattan shoreline, owed its existence to the World Trade Center, which, until it got beat out by Chicago's Sears Tower, had been the tallest building in the world. To build the World Trade Center, a very deep hole was dug in lower Manhattan. All the dirt and garbage, dead bodies and busted radios from that hole got dumped in the water off the end of Manhattan, making ninety-two brand-new acres of incredibly valuable real estate. After years of bureaucratic battling, Battery Park City, a modern complex of mixed-usage buildings, rose atop that landfill.

I couldn't imagine why Buddy and Babette Needleson lived down there. Most of their neighbors were Wall Streeters who were decades younger than the Needlesons. Maybe it was good for Babette's consulting business. Or it could have been the low crime rate that attracted them. Maybe they just didn't like New York. The sanitized planned community of Battery Park City didn't have much in common with the rest of the city.

Buddy and Babette lived in one of the largest buildings in the complex. A hyper-alert doorman perched just inside the entrance gave me a thorough looking over. I didn't have on an eight-hundred-dollar, dress-for-success, man-styled suit with low pumps. I didn't carry a briefcase. I didn't look like a maid. In other words, I could be trouble.

He was polite but firm. No way was I going to slip by him. "Can I help you?"

"I sure do hope so," I said, sighing deeply. "It's about Babette Needleson."

The doorman shook his head and said, "Such a shame about the mister. A man like that, cut down in his prime."

Quite a bit after his prime, I thought. I sighed again and, borrowing a phrase from Dweena, said, "I don't know what this world is coming to."

"You can say that again."

I didn't. Instead I said, "I'm sure you already know that Mr. Needleson's burial was delayed due to that unfortunate situation at the funeral home. Now it looks like things are about to get all messed up again. You see, Babette—that is, Mrs. Needleson—called me from the grave site all the way out in Queens. Wouldn't you know the funeral home sent the wrong paperwork? Babette, who is understandably distraught, left her copy at home, never thinking she'd need it. She trusted everyone else to do their job right. If I could just get into her apartment and fax the proper paperwork, she could straighten out the problem and finally lay poor Mr. Needleson to rest."

The doorman furrowed his brow. "I'm not supposed to give out keys."

I clasped my hand to my chest and tried to look shocked. "I'd never ask you to do such a thing. I already have a set of keys from the time I did some work for Mrs. Needleson. That's why she called me." I got the keys out of my purse and dangled them in front of his face.

The doorman smiled. "In that case, go on up."

I started toward the elevators.

"Just one thing," he said.

What now? I turned around and was relieved to see a smile on his face. He rummaged behind his desk and came up with two small blue packages.

"As long as you're already going up," he said, "would you mind taking these with you? The mailman brought them after Mrs. Needleson left. I'd rather not bother her when she gets back, you know, at a time like this."

The elevator whooshed me and the blue packages up to the twenty-fifth floor, much higher, in my opinion, than anybody should ever live. I got in with no trouble, locked the door behind me, and checked my watch—almost twelve-thirty. The Needleson family would probably stop for lunch after planting their loved one, but I didn't want to push my luck. I gave myself a one o'clock deadline.

The packages posed a problem. I couldn't leave them in the apartment or Babette would know someone had been inside. I decided to leave them just outside the door, as if the doorman had given them to a neighbor to take up. In the meantime, I left them on a table in the foyer.

It took me a minute to adjust to the idea of being in the apartment of a total stranger. The Ns' place hadn't been so bad. I'd been there before. I knew the Ns well. Anyway, I figured, after all they'd done, they deserved it. Snooping around Buddy and Babette's was more difficult to rationalize.

I stepped through the foyer into the apartment. Nice place. Except that Buddy Needleson ended up with a bashed-in head and a burial in Queens, he and Babette had done all right for themselves. Whatever kind of consulting Babette did, she must have been very good at it, because even with amateur stripping, the trimming business wouldn't buy an apartment or furniture like this. The thirty-foot living room had a unobstructed floor-to-ceiling view of the water and the Statue of Liberty. Expensive streamlined furniture enhanced the view. Personally, I preferred not to be reminded that I lived on a tiny island surrounded by questionable waters, but I'm not like everybody else.

The sparkling clean kitchen was equipped with every known labor-saving device, though none appeared ever to have been used. There were no cockroaches hiding in Babette's orderly cabinets. No dirty dishes in the sink. No secrets in the silverware drawer. No diamonds in the freezer.

Babette used the smaller of two bedrooms for her office. The name of her company, according to some stationery, was Lucky Liberty Productions Limited. A computer and a laser printer sat on a large solid oak table. There were no files in the office. She probably kept her records on the computer, but I wasn't about to turn it on. Next to the computer was a stack of blue boxes like the ones the doorman had given me. That solved that problem. I got the two boxes from the foyer and added them to the stack. She'd think they'd always been there.

Next stop was the master bedroom. In there, the magnitude of what I was doing really got to me. I didn't want to know the intimate secrets of Buddy and Babette's marriage. I took fast peeks in the bureau drawers and closets, saw nothing out of the ordinary, glanced into the bathroom, and got out of there. Some sleuth I turned out to be. In the future, I promised myself, I'd stick to millinery.

The doorman saw me on my way out. He smiled and said, "You can use my fax if you want to."

That caught me off guard. "Huh?"

"You know, for the paperwork."

"Right, the paperwork." I'd forgotten my ruse to get past him. "Thanks," I said, "but Mrs. Needleson has a fax machine. I used hers."

A string of cabs waited to take laid off ex–Wall Streeters to job interviews and networking lunches. I'd planned to take the bus up to the Ns' apartment, but with the rotten weather getting rottener fast and no time to lose, I splurged for a cab. I picked the one with the sanest-looking driver. He turned out to be another honking, lane-switching maniac. Aided by a good tail wind, he got me back to Fourteenth Street and the Ns' apartment building faster than I would have dreamed possible.

For the second time that day, the Ns' doorman paid no

attention as I passed by. Once upstairs, I listened at the Ns' door, then, just to be sure, I knocked. No one answered, I let myself in, deposited Buddy and Babette Needleson's keys back in the kitchen drawer, and took off.

My next stop was the showroom. I let myself in again and put the Ns' apartment keys back in Naomi's desk. Then, confident I'd covered all my tracks and returned all keys to their proper places, I locked up and left. For the time being, my life of criminal trespass was over. I let out a big sigh of relief.

Only to take it back.

The hot sauce distributor across the hall—the one who was never there—was, in fact, there and coming out of his office. I froze. I heard him unfasten his chain lock. I saw the silhouette of his body moving behind the pebbled glass window in his door. I ducked into the men's john next to Needleson Brothers, a heartbeat before he opened the door and stepped out into the hallway.

Not the best choice, maybe, but given the circumstances pretty much my only choice. I hightailed it into the single stall, jumped up on the toilet, crouched down, and waited for the hot sauce guy to come in, rip open the stall door, and ask me what the hell I was doing there.

It didn't happen.

I heard the elevator arrive, its doors open and clang shut, then silence. I straightened up and stood there for a moment, listening. Then I climbed down from the toilet, opened the door a crack, and checked out the hallway. Empty.

I started to leave, but something I'd seen registered in my brain. It's nothing, I told myself, but the more I thought about it the more that nothing might just be something. I went into the men's room again and got back up on the toilet. From that vantage point, I was eye level to a vent. Like a million other bathroom vents in a million other old buildings, this vent was covered by a hexagon-patterned metal grate. Unlike all those other vents in all those other buildings, there was something behind this one.

I couldn't reach the grate from the toilet. A wobbly sink was closer. Hoping it would support my hundred pounds, I climbed up on the sink. Teetering on the edge, hanging on to an exposed pipe for balance, I flipped a metal latch on the grate and opened it. Behind the grate, bolted to the wall, was a video camera pointed straight into the Needleson Brothers showroom next door.

That camera changed everything. I'd been right. No matter what Irene Finneluk said, Buddy Needleson must have been blackmailing his strippers. Was there ever a more perfect motive for murder? To get the real lowdown I'd have to talk to the strippers Irene had told me about.

Of course those scheming, lying Ns had known about the camera all along. I let myself back into the showroom, gathered up the videos from Norbert's desk, and went home.

17

My TV reception is lousy. Three overlapping shadow signals compete for space on my nine-inch black and white screen. The sound doesn't work at all, but Chuck helped me rig it up by running a cable out of the earphone jack, sticking on an adaptor, and plugging it into the back of my stereo. I used to run it through a boyfriend's spare guitar amp, but when we broke up he took the amplifier back. Aside from Johnny's *Tod Trueman* show and occasional disaster coverage—earthquakes, terrorist bombings, hurricanes, and plane crashes—I don't bother with TV, and I don't have a VCR.

The point is, I needed someplace else to watch the videotapes I'd swiped from Norbert's drawer. Elizabeth didn't have a TV. Johnny didn't believe in VCRs. Chuck had every electronic gizmo known to mankind and could easily play the videotapes, but I wanted someplace closer. I called Dweena.

"What kind of videotapes?" she asked.

"I don't know. Aren't they all alike?"

"That depends," she explained, "but it probably doesn't matter. I've got a standard VCR, a standard adapter, and a brand-new video camera. Your tapes will fit in one or the other. Get here before I leave for work at midnight and I'll set you up."

With that taken care of, I pulled my boots off and prepared to relax. Jackhammer looked mournfully toward the door, then at me, then back at the door. I spread out newspapers and detailed the abominable weather conditions. Sometime during my exhaustive explanation of the windchill index, he stopped paying attention, walked over to the papers, gave me a dirty look, and lifted his leg.

After that I dozed off. I woke up to the sound of Naomi's voice coming out of my answering machine. She did not sound one bit happy.

"Goddamm it, Brenda, I know you're there. Pick up. It's an emergency. Where've you been all day?"

The first thing that went through my head was that I'd triggered an alarm somewhere and she was on to me. Or maybe the hot sauce guy had seen me. Much as I wanted to ignore the call, I had to answer to find out how much hot water I was in.

"Hi, Naomi. I got home just this second from shopping."

"Yeah, right," said Naomi, "on a crappy day like today, Brenda Midnight shops. You don't expect me to believe that, do you?"

"Well . . ."

"You're home now. I suppose that's all that matters."

I gathered up my courage and asked, "What's the problem?"

"You know my Fred, don't you?"

I felt like I knew him well because of the way Naomi was always going on about their volatile relationship, but other than that photo of him in polka-dot undies on Naomi's dresser, I'd never actually seen him. "Not really," I said.

"Oh. Well, I suppose that's no problem. See, I was supposed to meet him tonight at La Reverie."

"La Reverie? It must be a special occasion." La Reverie was one of the top romantic restaurants in town.

"Yeah, like really, La Reverie. Brenda, I'm positive Fred

was gonna pop the question tonight. I mean, it's about time. Why else go to La Reverie?"

"That doesn't sound like a problem, Naomi. Don't you want to marry Fred?"

"Of course I want to marry Fred. He's handsome, has a good job, and he adores me. The problem is that I'm stuck in Queens with my mean brother, asinine parents, and poor Aunt Babette, all in one roach-ridden motel room which only has two chairs. So guess who gets to sit on the vibrating bed with her parents? Norbert keeps reminding me how lucky we were to get a room, and how we did so only because he knew somebody who knew somebody else who owed another somebody a favor and somehow somebody knew the motel clerk."

"I don't understand," I said. "Why don't you come home?"

"You mean you don't know?"

"Don't know what?"

"Turn on your crummy little TV, Brenda. There's like two more feet of snow that plopped on Queens in two hours. Streets and highways are closed. Trains are shut down. Nobody but nobody is going anywhere anytime soon."

"It's not that bad here yet," I said. "How about your uncle? I mean, did he get buried?"

"Uncle Buddy is in the ground. It was a bitch, but the deed is done. However, I didn't call to talk about Uncle Buddy. I need to ask a favor."

"Whatever it is," I said, "the answer is no. No, no, a thousand times no. No, no, no, no, no." I had learned my lesson well.

"Come on, Brenda. You owe me."

I didn't owe Naomi a blasted thing. I should have hung up, claimed we got disconnected by the storm, but I figured she'd keep hounding me.

She sniffled and went on. "I've been calling Fred all afternoon, to break the date. First his secretary tells me he's in a meeting, then she says he's at lunch, then she says he went home early, so I tried him there. No answer."

"Where do you think he is?"

"I don't think anything, I know my Fred. He's out buying an engagement ring. It's just like him, to put it off 'til the last possible minute. So what you've gotta do, Brenda, because you owe me, is show up at La Reverie and explain to Fred why I can't be there."

I prided myself on my strength and independence. So it was hard for me to admit that deep down inside, like millions of other red-blooded New York females, I yearned to be wined, dined, and romanced at La Reverie. It was an institution, silly as a heart-shaped bathtub at a honeymoon resort, with okay food, mountains of fresh flowers, and candlelight. Going there alone to break someone else's date was not exactly the way I'd envisioned going.

Dressed to kill in a clingy black dress, red velvet cocktail hat, heavy wool coat, and insulated rubber boots, I plowed through deep snow and arrived ten minutes before Naomi was supposed to meet Fred. I checked my boots and coat and slipped on a pair of black satin pumps. The hostess told me to wait for Fred in the piano bar. I sat at the end of the bar, adjusted my hat in the mirror, and ordered an overpriced, mediocre red wine.

One after another, couples in fine clothes glided by me and descended a dramatic curved stairway to the peach-colored dining room below. No one came in threes, fours, or fives. Absolutely no one came to La Reverie alone. Except me.

Every fifteen minutes or so I checked with the hostess to be sure Fred hadn't slipped by and gone down to the dining room to wait for Naomi. Each time she told me he hadn't. Finally, exasperated, she said, "You know, we can't hold this reservation forever."

"Fifteen more minutes," I said, and returned to my bar stool. Face it, I thought, Fred wasn't coming. Even though I was just a stand-in, it was awful being stood-up at La Reverie. Smiling, self-confident women passed by with devastatingly handsome dates and looked at me with pity. If I thought being a stood-up stand-in was rotten, what happened next was a whole lot worse.

To avoid the stares of passing couples, I focused on a pile of lime wedges in a saucer behind the bar. In fact, I was focused so intently I probably wouldn't have seen them at all, except for the hush that fell over the room. But when the hush happened—the hush that could only mean someone prominent had come in—my head twisted toward the front door just like everyone else's.

I was pretty sure Johnny didn't see me, but I sure as hell saw him—smiling, dressed to the nines, arm-in-arm with a busty redheaded guest starlet. I recognized her as the damsel in distress from one of the *Tod Trueman* episodes. Tod had rescued her by diving off the Brooklyn Bridge onto a garbage barge where she was being held prisoner. In a flurry of dancelike self-defense movements, he single-handedly freed her from her sadistic captors.

It felt like someone had reached into my chest, ripped my heart out, and slammed it, broken and bloody, against the wall. I didn't stick around to wait for Fred.

In no shape to go anywhere or see anyone, I somehow forced myself to take the videotapes to Dweena's.

She took one look at me and asked, "What's the matter? Your baby blues are blood-red."

"It's nothing," I said. "A little cold. I fell into a puddle the other day."

She frowned. "I hope you're taking your vitamin C."

"Oh sure." I forced myself to smile. I knew she knew I was lying about the red eyes, but she was too much of a lady to make a big deal out of it.

Dweena's second-story apartment was right smack in the middle of the meatpacking district on Gansevoort Street. "When I can't sleep," she told me, "I lean out the window and count the sides of beef swinging from hooks circling on the rack below."

"Like counting sheep," I said.

"Yeah, but it's cows and they're dead and eviscerated. It helps me to get back to sleep, except in the heat of the summer when it's too smelly to open the window."

In any other city in the world this would have been considered way on the wrong side of the tracks. In New York, where the rules don't count, the meatpacking district was terribly trendy. Dweena rattled off the list of famous designers, writers, and artists who were her close neighbors ". . . and that's on Gansevoort Street alone," she said. "If you count Washington and Horatio . . ."

Dweena continued to drop names. I tuned out and looked around. Her apartment was large by New York standards and much more normal than I had expected. Except for the all-cement ceiling, walls, and floor, the fact that the ridged floor sloped to a drain by the dining room table, and that rails traversed the ceiling, I'd never have guessed that the former tenant had been a meatpacker.

I sat down on a red couch that probably doubled as her bed and eyed a stack of expensive foreign fashion magazines on a coffee table. On top of them, folded into quarters, was the *Wall Street Journal*. Dweena still kept up with the market. In fact, the only hint that Dweena was maybe just a tad unusual were three new feather boas draped over her bathroom door and dozens of brightly colored, elaborately styled wigs lined up on a shelf. It would have been an interesting challenge to design hats to sit atop those.

Dweena finished her rundown of neighborhood luminaries and said, "Give me those tapes and I'll get you started." She showed me how to fast forward, freeze frame, and change tapes. "Make yourself at home. I've got to get ready for work."

Hands on her hips, Dweena stood before her wigs for quite some time before choosing a short yellow pixie style. Then, with the wig in one hand and a hairbrush in the other, she danced around the room, brushing briskly and belting out words to a song I didn't know.

I started the first tape. My hunch was right. It showed a stripper. Because of the camera's fixed position, the stripper occasionally danced out of range and I'd see nothing but wall. Then, a few seconds later, she was back minus a piece of costume.

It didn't take long to get bored enough to remember how depressed I was. So, with one eye watching the videotapes, I flipped through a fashion magazine. Unfortunately, the magazine didn't take my mind off Johnny and the guest starlet. To my eye every male model had Johnny's features, his body, his presence. The fashions didn't make me feel any better either. Each page had at least one fabulous spring hat that was not mine. I was squinting at the tiny print credits on a two-page spread to see who had made a whimsical straw hat when Dweena danced by, suddenly stopped, and said, "What's that?"

"This hat?"

"No. That guy on the video."

She rewound the tape and played it back.

We watched a well-toned stripper in a silvery glitter costume begin her act. Before she had a chance to take anything off, a man in dark sunglasses and a snazzy fedora grabbed her, wrapped her in his overcoat, and dragged her offstage. The stripper kicked and screamed and flung her arms. She knocked the man's hat off his head, ripped his sunglasses off his face, and then, as a finale, pulled at his thick wavy grayed-at-the-temples black hair. It came off in her hands, revealing a hairline that started at about the center of his head. The stripper looked as surprised as the man did.

"Bad rug," I said. "Very uncool."

"Wrong," said Dweena. "That guy should be very cool by now. He's been dead for three years."

18

Dweena zeroed in on the few seconds of tape that showed the man without his wig. "That sneaky, slimy son of a bitch."

"What's wrong?" I asked.

"Where'd you get this?" she asked.

"Bottom drawer of Norbert Needleson's desk at the showroom. I found a video camera hidden in the men's bathroom. Guess it's obvious now that Buddy Needleson secretly taped the strippers, then blackmailed them. Since he ended up dead, I'd say he blackmailed one too many."

"No," said Dweena. "He wasn't blackmailing strippers. If anybody was getting blackmailed it was the man on that tape, Brink LeHalle."

"Brink la what?"

"Brink LeHalle. He's the bastard who scammed Wall Street. The man who, when he got caught, brought down one of the oldest, most prestigious investment houses of all time. I was his boss."

"Back when you were Edward?"

"Yes. I was Edward, the brilliant aggressive broker who, through no fault of my own, got promoted to management. I, as Edward, wasn't cut out for management. 'Stay on top of things,' they told me. How was I to know Brink LeHalle was a crook, a pathological liar? He seemed like an okay sort of a guy. Kept to himself. Generated piles of money.

My department's profits went through the roof. I was happy. The firm was happy. Nobody asked questions. It never occurred to me that the incredible profits were due to LeHalle's thumbing his nose at a couple of very serious securities laws. Very, very serious. We're not talking parking tickets here, you know?''

I nodded.

Dweena continued, ''The shit just had to hit the fan. When it did, when the Feds were closing in, LeHalle smashed his hundred-thousand-dollar pleasure boat into a bridge abutment, demolishing the boat and, it was thought, Brink LeHalle. Now I know why his body never turned up. He faked the whole thing. With Brink presumed dead, I—that is, Edward—got all the heat. I got booted out of the firm, no severance, no nothing.''

''But you didn't know anything.''

''No way to prove that. Besides, I *should* have known. It happened on my watch. The firm threatened to prosecute me if I didn't go quietly. So I left, laid low for a while and took stock of my life.''

''Rotten luck,'' I said.

Dweena shrugged. ''It wasn't such a bad thing, really. It was time for a career change.''

Some career change, I thought, from Edward the Wall Streeter in three-piece suits to Dweena the bouncer in three-foot-long wigs.

''Are you absolutely a hundred percent positive the guy on the tape is Brink LeHalle?'' I asked.

Dweena gestured at her shelf of wigs. ''Do I know disguise, or what?''

''Maybe the tape was made before LeHalle's boat hit the bridge,'' I suggested.

''No,'' said Dweena. ''He's aged and put on a little weight. That's a recent tape, all right. Brink LeHalle is alive and well. I'd bet my last wig on it.''

I called Chuck from Dweena's.

''You and Lemmy still awake?''

"Yep."

"Something's come up," I said. "I'm on my way over."

I played the video for Chuck and Lemmy.

"So," said Chuck, "what's the big deal?"

"Yeah," said Lemmy, "so what if some insecure loser with a two-thousand-dollar hairpiece yanked his babe off the stage?"

"Ever heard of Brink LeHalle?" I asked.

"Name sounds familiar," said Lemmy.

"Wasn't he one of those Wall Street guys who got busted a few years ago?" asked Chuck. "I think he croaked."

"He didn't quite croak," I said. "That's him on the video." I told Chuck and Lemmy what Dweena had told me. "She's positive it's LeHalle," I said, "and she's positive it's recent."

"What's that mean?" asked Lemmy.

"It means," I said, "that even if Buddy Needleson didn't blackmail the strippers, and I'm still not totally convinced of that, he might have been blackmailing Brink LeHalle."

"For what?" said Lemmy.

"For being alive when he was supposed to be dead."

"So you think Brink LeHalle offed Buddy Needleson," said Chuck.

"I'm saying there's a good chance he did. Either Buddy Needleson recognized LeHalle and tried to blackmail him or else LeHalle found out about the tape on his own. Maybe Buddy Needleson tried to blackmail LeHalle's girlfriend, she told LeHalle, and he realized how dangerous the videotape was. Whichever way it happened, LeHalle would go after the videotape."

"But if he went after the videotape, why didn't he get the videotape?" asked Chuck.

"Good question," said Lemmy.

"I already thought of that," I said. "LeHalle confronted Buddy Needleson. They argued. In a fit of anger LeHalle picked up the baseball bat Howard Needleson used for inventory and clobbered Buddy with it. LeHalle's a scammer, strictly white collar, not a killer. When he realizes what he's done, he panics. He knows he's got to get out of there fast.''

''Could be,'' said Chuck.

''Call my lawyer,'' said Lemmy.

Chuck had rigged up his computer so that when he placed the call to Brewster Winfield, anyone who might be tapping the line would think the call was coming from either Tokyo, Japan, or Trimble, Missouri, depending on the kind of equipment they were using. Even so, when Winfield answered, Chuck chose his words carefully. ''Get your ass over here,'' he said, and hung up.

Fifteen minutes later Winfield showed up carrying a leather satchel. ''Wait'll you get a load of Myrtle's new trick,'' he said. He started to unzip the satchel.

''I already told you,'' said Lemmy, ''I don't handle animal acts.''

''Her new trick is a humdinger.''

''Forget snake tricks and check this out,'' said Chuck. He started the videotape.

Winfield watched it to the end. ''So what? You can hardly blame the gentleman if he doesn't want his lady to get naked in front of a room full of degenerates.'' His hand moved toward the zipper his bag. ''Now, take Myrtle here—''

I cut him off. ''Except in this case, the gentleman who doesn't want his lady getting naked is Brink LeHalle.''

''Now, that's a familiar name. Do you mean Brink LeHalle, the Wall Street criminal?''

I nodded.

''A pity. That would have been some trial if he hadn't perished. A boating accident, if I remember correctly.''

''That's right,'' I said. ''Except he didn't perish.''

Winfield put Myrtle's satchel at his feet, sat back, and listened closely as I told Dweena's story. When I finished, he nodded solemnly. "You say this Dweena person is positive?"

"A hundred percent positive."

Winfield let out a long whistle. "Holy shit."

"Pretty heavy, huh?" said Lemmy.

"We'll get a movie out of this yet," said Winfield.

The easiest, quickest, and most direct thing to do would have been to take the video straight to Turner and McKinley and let them handle the situation. But if I did that, they'd wonder how I got the videotape. I figured it was only a matter of time before they made the connection between Lemon B. Crenshaw, the man they wanted for murder, and Johnny and me. I didn't want to push my luck.

The four of us sat down to discuss what to do. Winfield took Myrtle out of her satchel. She slithered up his body and draped herself around his neck. Lemmy edged his beanbag chair out of the snake's range. I picked a different seat altogether, as far away as possible, hoping I didn't insult anybody. Chuck brought out a value-size bag of barbecued potato chips and a jug of screwtop red wine. He didn't seem to mind Myrtle at all and offered her a chip. "She doesn't eat that crap," said Winfield.

We crunched chips, chugged wine, and knocked ideas around for an hour or so and came to the obvious conclusion: To get the heat off Lemmy we needed to prove that Brink LeHalle killed Buddy Needleson, which meant we had to find Brink LeHalle, which meant we had to talk to those other strippers Irene had told me about. "We" pretty much meant me. Lemmy couldn't do it, he was in hiding. Chuck couldn't do it, he had to make sure Lemmy stayed in hiding. Winfield could do it, but for a fee.

"I guess that leaves me, huh?" I said.

"Where's Johnny?" asked Chuck. "He could help you, that is if he's not off with some other woman."

"I don't know," I said.

"He's shooting episodes with Sal Stumpford," said Lemmy.

I wasn't so sure about that.

Winfield stood up and stretched. "I'm glad that's all straightened out. Brenda, you keep me informed of your progress." Using both hands, he disentwined Myrtle from his neck. "Now I think we all deserve some entertainment. Myrtle, let's show the nice people what a smart little lady you are. How much is two and two?"

Was I ever surprised when that silly snake lifted up her head and bobbed it four times. Then she turned her head from side to side as if she were basking in audience appreciation.

"I'll be goddamned," said Lemmy.

Winfield patted the slinky genius on her flat head. "Very good, Myrtle. Let's try another one, harder this time. What's two times two?"

Again Myrtle bobbed her head four times.

"Wait a minute," said Chuck. "I smell a rat. No matter what you say she's gonna bob her head four times. It's like, four bobs is what she does."

Myrtle hung her head. Then she slithered down Winfield's body, across the floor, and into her satchel.

"Now look what you've gone and done," said Winfield. "You hurt Myrtle's feelings."

Chuck bent down and talked into the satchel. "I'm sorry. I didn't mean to hurt your feelings."

Myrtle poked her head up out of the bag, bobbed four times, and retreated.

"She doesn't hold a grudge," said Winfield, zipping the bag.

"Not bad," said Lemmy, rubbing his chin, "not bad at all."

After Winfield and Myrtle left, Lemmy raved on and on about Myrtle. "Maybe an animal act wouldn't be such a bad idea," he said. Then he passed out.

With him out of the way, Chuck and I got down to the details of the plan.

"I need some kind of a ruse," I said, "something to get the strippers to talk to me."

"Got anything in mind?" asked Chuck.

"It would have to be something not too official sounding, not like the government or anything. How about if I say I'm doing research for the sociology department of some college. Can you whip me up some credentials?"

Chuck flashed me a huge smile. "Does a bear shit in the woods?"

We invented Brenda Miller, Research Assistant from the Department of Sociology, Tochin College, Tochin, Iowa. Chuck sat down at the computer. I looked over his shoulder as he designed a Brenda Miller business card and letter of introduction from the dean of Tochin's sociology department. He then created an official-looking seal for the fake college. An oval of leaves intertwined around the silhouette of a man who looked exactly like Chuck with deflated hair and a pointy beard. Chuck arranged the words TOCHIN COLLEGE around the oval and added a banner with the words ESTABLISHED 1876.

"Good," I said. "I like an institution with a long history of academic excellence."

Chuck beamed, obviously proud of his handiwork.

Lemmy woke up. He stumbled by on his way to the bathroom and stopped to look at the design. "Way cool," he said.

Both Chuck and I gave him a weird look.

"I never heard Lemmy talk like that before," I said. "Where'd he pick that up?"

Chuck shrugged his shoulders.

While I thumbed through a computer magazine, Chuck printed out a dozen business cards on a single sheet of heavy card stock, then cut them down to size with a razor blade. When Lemmy finally emerged from the bathroom, he had a square of toilet paper stuck to the top of his freshly shaved head.

"Cut yourself shaving?" asked Chuck.

"Yeah," said Lemmy. "I hate this part. However, the

results are worth it.'' He walked over to me and bent his head down. ''Feel it. Go ahead, feel it.''

I touched his head.

''Smooth as a baby's butt, isn't it?''

''That's right, Lemmy, smooth as a baby's butt.''

''It's a bitch to keep up.''

''Fashion's got a price, Lemmy. Nobody ever said it was easy to be way cool.''

19

Question: If there really were a Tochin College and a Brenda Miller in its sociology department, what would Ms. Miller wear while gathering data from amateur strippers in New York City where the temperature had plummeted to five below? Answer: Anything and everything that would fit under her coat topped off by a hideous bile-colored knit hat with a pom-pom on top that somebody gave me as a joke. That hat was a challenge to my oft-stated belief that with a twist and a turn any hat could be made to flatter any face. Well, I twisted and turned and utterly failed. When Jackhammer saw it on my head, he backed away and growled.

"Ugly, isn't it?"

Jackhammer wagged his stub in agreement.

"I've got to wear something to keep my ears from cracking off my head," I said. "Besides, it looks like something Brenda Miller would wear back home in Tochin, Iowa. If I'm gonna pull this off, I've got to be believable."

Irene had given me the names of three strippers. I started with the one who worked close to the Village, Peg Smith. She worked at Two Jays Litho down on Varick Street, a fifteen-minute walk. I made my way down Seventh Avenue against the wind, glad to have the hat firmly on my head.

Two Jays was located in a twelve-story building that

sprawled over an entire block. Ten years ago most of the businesses in this building and in the surrounding area had been printers. Recently, though, many printers had gone out of business. I wasn't surprised to see a hand-lettered sign in the drab lobby: AUCTION TODAY—FIFTH FLOOR.

A tired-looking guard slumped on a stool by the elevator. I approached and said, "Two Jays Litho?"

"Follow the auction signs," he said.

All of a sudden I had a bad feeling about this interview.

The door to Two Jays was wide open. Just inside a burly man in a green sharkskin suit sat at a desk. He jabbed his forefinger at a piece of paper taped to the desk. "Sign in here."

"Can you tell me if Peg Smith is in today?" I asked.

He ignored my polite inquiry. "Look, lady, you going to the auction or not? 'Cause if you're not, you're gonna have to leave."

I signed in as Brenda Miller from Tochin College. The man handed me a number and a piece of paper with an illegible smear of words. "Read these rules," he said. "Auction begins at eleven sharp."

"What happened to Two Jays?" I asked.

"How the hell would I know?"

I'd been to enough bankruptcy auctions in the garment district to get the picture. For whatever reason, Two Jays Litho had lost the battle.

I felt like I was intruding at a stranger's funeral. I peeked into a tiny office full of beat-up Selectrics. Another room had telephones and gray metal in/out trays grouped together in lots. A promotional calendar from a Chinese restaurant was tacked to a wall, turned to November. Two Jays hadn't made it through the holidays.

A few people wandered through the office cubicles, poked at the typewriters, and occasionally scribbled down a lot number, but most of the action was in the larger rooms toward the back. One entire room was filled with light tables, another had skids of paper. There were cameras the size of rooms and a smelly darkroom where pooled chemicals had evaporated from sinks, leaving behind crystallized gunk. At the very back, in the largest room of all, were the presses—small presses, medium-size presses, and one press the size of a semi truck.

I asked around for Peg Smith. Finally a man who was demonstrating one of the presses pointed to a door off the press room. "She's probably in there," he said.

According to a sign on the door, that was the typesetting department. Inside, a tiny woman, presumably Peg, sat on the floor sorting through a pile of metal type. She was surrounded by typesetting equipment at least three generations behind the times. When she saw me in the doorway she looked up. Tears rolled down her freckled cheeks. "Can you believe it?" she said. "They're gonna sell it for scrap if no one makes an offer. All this history, lost forever."

I copped out. I couldn't possibly ask this distraught woman about amateur stripping. "I'm sorry," I said, and left.

On the way down to the lobby I remembered Chuck's reverence for expired technology. I called him from the street and told him there was a roomful of metal type about to be melted down if there were no bidders.

"Are you sure it's metal type? Like lots of little letters."

"I know what metal type is," I said.

"Has the auction started yet?"

"Not until eleven."

"Nobody's scrapping type while Chuck Riley still has money in the bank," he said. "What's the address?"

I told him. "If you get a chance, introduce yourself to Peg Smith. She's just your type."

"Very funny," said Chuck.

Maybe I'd do better with Ruth Dorsey, the next stripper on my list. According to Irene, she was office manager of a small engineering consulting firm on Third Avenue. I caught a bus up Sixth Avenue to midtown and walked across. I was set to give the receptionist the Brenda Miller research assistant spiel, but as soon as I introduced myself she told me to go right back to see Mrs. Dorsey.

It looked like a bomb had gone off in Ruth Dorsey's office. There were piles of paper everywhere, dead flowers drooped out of dusty vases, cartons overflowed with booklets. Her bulletin board was three layers thick with colorful job-tracking charts. In the center of it all sat a frazzled woman with a sweater knotted around her neck. "Miss Miller?" she asked.

"A pleasure to meet you," I said. When we shook hands, I saw that her fingernails were chewed down to the quick.

She gestured at a chair. "Have a seat, Miss Miller. Sorry about the mess. As you can see, we are in desperate need of help."

I moved a coffee cup and an old newspaper off the chair, sat down, and dug through my purse for my Tochin College credentials. Before I found them Ruth Dorsey asked, "Which agency sent you?"

"Agency?" Finally I retrieved my Brenda Miller business card and letter of introduction and handed them across her desk. "We're conducting a research study."

She squinted at the card. "You mean you're not from the employment agency?"

"I'm sorry if there's been a misunderstanding," I said, "but no, I'm not from the employment agency."

Ruth Dorsey beamed at me. "So much the better. I'd just as soon not pay the agency fee. How soon can you start?"

I tried to explain who I was pretending to be and why I was there, but she misinterpreted my reluctance, interrupted, and offered me more money. At last she said, "Twenty-seven, and that's the absolute best I can do. Now let me describe our benefit package."

Twenty-seven. I didn't know if that was the hourly rate or annual salary. She rattled off the benefits. The firm offered both an HMO-type healthcare plan and a traditional plan, a generous vacation and holiday schedule, profit sharing, and tuition refund for job-related courses. "I think you'll like working for us," she said. Before I could get a word in edgewise, her phone rang and she picked up. She said a few words, clamped her hand over the receiver, and looked at me. "I'm sorry, Miss Miller, but I have to take this call. We'll see you first thing tomorrow morning."

So far, as Brenda Miller, I had a dismal track record of talking to amateur strippers. I'd brokered a pile of metal type and landed a job I didn't want, although if the hat business didn't pick up, it might be worth considering. Not once had I even mentioned the word "stripper."

From Ruth Dorsey's office I walked up a few blocks and then took a bus across town to the Upper West Side: Daria Covington, the last stripper on my list, worked at home. She lived in a plain but well-kept eight-story building. There was no doorman, so first I had to get past the buzzer system. No sweat. I buzzed her and she buzzed me in without bothering to ask who I was. Then I took a painfully slow, dimly lit elevator to the seventh floor.

I didn't want to blow another interview. As soon as she opened the door I blurted out, "I'm Brenda Miller, with the sociology department of Tochin College. I'd like to talk to you about your performance in amateur strip clubs." I held my breath and waited for her to slam the door in my face.

"Fantastic," she said, stepping back to let me in. "You must be freezing. I'll make us some hot chocolate."

Daria Covington's long brown hair was the only neutral in the apartment. Everything else was saturated with color. She wore a stretch catsuit in a wild red and pink print, pink lipstick, and bright blue eye shadow. She led me through a bright yellow foyer to a bright orange couch.

"I'm flattered you want to talk to me," she said. "Of course, I've heard of Tochin College, but I'm embarrassed to say, for the life of me, I can't remember where it is."

I handed her a Brenda Miller business card. "The college is in Iowa, but I'll be at this New York number for the duration of the study."

She put the card down on a red cube that served as an end table. "I'm pleased someone is finally recognizing the amateur stripper. Now, Miss Miller, you make yourself comfortable and I'll get that hot chocolate.''

I needed sunglasses to look around her apartment. A grass-green rug clashed with vermilion walls, a taxicab-yellow plastic chair, and hot pink semi-gloss ceiling. There were scads of brightly colored pillows and knickknacks. Elaborate gold-framed mirrors on every wall multiplied the vivid color. The effect was nauseating.

Daria stuck her head out of the kitchen. ''Marshmallows?''

''If it's no trouble.''

She brought out steaming cups of hot chocolate and a bag of mini marshmallows. I dropped a few in my cup and watched them melt.

''I must say,'' said Daria, ''I'm flattered you want to interview me. But I am curious. How did you find me?''

''Your name came up in association with Buddy Needleson's amateur strip club.''

She shook her head. ''Such a shame, his murder. I simply could not believe it when I heard the news. Who would want to kill a nice man like that?'' She slipped her foot out of her shoe, rotated her foot about her ankle. Her feet were full of bumps and bunions.

I took a sip of hot chocolate. ''I can't imagine either. From what I've heard, he ran a good clean club.''

''The best. It's too depressing to talk about. Do go on, I'm anxious to hear more about your study.''

I cleared my throat, took a deep breath, and launched into bullshit mode. ''It's all part of a larger motivation study. The professor in charge is seeking a correlation between the desire to remove one's clothing and—''

Before I ran out of misleading language, Daria interrupted. ''I get it,'' she said. ''You want to know what in the world would possess me to stand bare-ass naked in front of a bunch of drooling slobs.''

''I guess you could put it that way,'' I said.

Daria put her foot back in her shoe. ''I can't speak for the other strippers, but I do it because ever since I was a little girl, I wanted to be a dancer. I took tap, ballet, modern, jazz, and, if I say so myself, I'm pretty damned good, but hardly professional. Do you know that in this entire city, there's not one single venue for amateur dancers? I mean, you've got your amateur comedy clubs, joints where amateur singers can let loose, there's even amateur mud wrestling, but dancers, nada. Amateur strip clubs give me the opportunity to dance in public. For me, it's not about undressing, it's about The Dance."

"What do your friends and family think?"

"They think it's great, even my boyfriend. Of course, not all the girls are so lucky. There was a recent incident. In fact, it was at Buddy Needleson's. This stripper, she was one of the regulars, got some dippy new boyfriend. He threw a hissy fit, jumped up on stage and tried to pull her off. It was funny, though. During the tussle she pulled his toupee right off his head. You should have seen the expression on her face."

Bingo. "She'd be wonderful for the study," I said. "You know, kind of as a contrast to your situation. You don't happen to know that stripper's name, do you?"

"Sure, like I said she was one of the regulars. Her name is Lisa Markham. I think she lives somewhere in Chelsea."

"Thank you so much," I said. You've been a great help." I got up to leave.

"Do you have to go so soon? I could show you my commemorative videotape."

I'd seen enough strip tapes for one lifetime. "We'll have to save that for my follow-up visit," I said.

"Follow-up visit?" said Daria.

"Oh yes," I said, "Tochin College's standards are stringent. That's how they got to be one of the leading research organizations in the world."

"I'll certainly look forward to seeing you again," said Daria.

20

I caught the number eleven bus in front of Daria Covington's apartment and rode to the end of the line, home, otherwise known as Abingdon Square, a confusing complex of streets. Abingdon Square is not a square by any of the known rules of geometry—it's got three sides. The streets around this misnamed hunk of land go haywire. At Abingdon Square, Hudson Street butts into itself and changes direction from downtown to uptown, Bethune Street starts its four-block dash from Hudson Street to the Hudson River, and Bleecker Street ends its crooked path through the Village with a fifteen-degree twist into the beginning of Eighth Avenue. Even mapmakers fudge when it comes to drawing Abingdon Square.

Adding to this confusion is the ever ongoing construction along Hudson Street. Both Hudson Streets—the uptown-headed version and the downtown-headed version—have been dug up, filled over, dug up again, and filled over again, making it a patchwork of old road, new road, old dug-up road, new dug-up road. Thick metal plates cover gaping holes.

It made for some pretty rough terrain. When old number eleven finally shuddered to a stop at the tip of Abingdon Square I felt like my pioneer ancestors who'd wagon-trained it out of Kentucky, ultimately stopping in Missouri when their vehicle rolled down a ravine and smashed into a walnut tree.

After that ride, in need of sustenance, I stopped at the deli. Dweena was there, in the middle of negotiations with the guy behind the counter.

The guy, a surly sort with heavy-lidded eyes and a sliver of mustache, held a turkey on rye in one hand. He made a two-fingered V sign with the other hand and shoved it in Dweena's face.

Dweena leaned over the counter and stomped her patent leather platform boot on the tile floor. "No way," she said emphatically. "For *one* lousy turkey sandwich, you get *one* free pass. Who the hell do you think you are? We're talking the hottest club in town. I can't just let anybody in. One turkey sandwich, one pass."

"Two," said the man. He dangled the sandwich over a plastic garbage can, threatening to let go.

Dweena banged her fist on the counter. "You wouldn't dare."

"Try me," said the man.

With a toss of her head, Dweena strutted toward the door. "If that's the way you want it, you know what you can do with that turkey sandwich."

"All right, all right," said the man. "It's a deal. One turkey sandwich, one pass, even steven."

"Hmpf," snorted Dweena. She traded him the ticket for the sandwich. "And, Bozo Breath, because you've been such a pain in my ass, throw in a side of cranberry sauce."

Between her job as a bouncer and some astute investments in high-tech start-ups, Dweena had plenty of money. Even so, she preferred the barter system. This was the first time I'd seen her in action.

"Cool," I said. "A ticket for a sandwich."

Dweena turned and saw me for the first time. "Brenda, how long have you been here? Let me get you something."

"That's okay," I said, "I just came in for a cup of coffee and a bran muffin."

"No, I insist. It's my treat." said Dweena. "How do you want your coffee?"

"Black," I said.

"Yo, Bozo Breath," she said to the counterman, "did you hear that? Add a black coffee and your freshest, most succulent bran muffin to my order, *s'il vous plaît.*"

The man glared at her. "This club had better be worth it."

"Would I steer you wrong?" asked Dweena.

I invited Dweena up to my apartment. While she devoured her turkey sandwich and cranberry sauce, I climbed up on my step stool, wrested the two-pound Manhattan white pages out of the top of my closet, and looked up Lisa Markham. There was one listed on West Fifteenth Street. It had to be her. How many Lisa Markhams could there be in Chelsea?

Dweena was anxious to hear about my progress in finding Brink LeHalle. "The sooner you nail that bastard, the better. What's the plan?"

"My next step is to try to meet Lisa Markham and see if she's still hanging out with LeHalle or knows where to find him. I guess I have to stake out her apartment. When she comes out I'll follow her and try to figure out some way to meet her."

"Sounds like a good plan. You be sure and let me know if there's anything I can do to help."

"Don't worry," I said. "I will."

Dweena gave the last bite of her sandwich to Jackhammer and stood up to leave. "I've got to run now to clue in this new DJ. You'll keep me informed, won't you?"

"Of course," I said.

After Dweena left I called Irene Finneluk. "Ever heard of Lisa Markham?" I asked. "Daria Covington says she was one of the regular strippers."

"Not by name, but I'd probably know her if I saw her."

Next I called Chuck and gave him an update.

"Thanks for the tip on the type," he said.

"Did you buy any?"

"Yep, the whole lot down to the last four-point ampersand. I also got a date with Peg Smith."

It was too cold for Jackhammer to go out, so I took him on a hike through the building for exercise. We walked up five flights, zigzagged back and forth between the north stairs and the south stairs, then down five flights. We weren't gone more than fifteen minutes, but when I got home there was a message from Naomi on my answering machine.

She started right in without so much as a hello. "Do you think insanity is hereditary?" she asked. "Because if it is, I can truly say after spending an entire day and night with my lunatic brother and crackpot parents locked up in a no-tell motel in Queens, that I'd better give some serious thought before starting my own family. Bonkers. All of us, except Aunt Babette, which makes sense because she isn't related by blood. No, my poor Aunt Babette had the misfortune of marrying into this family of wackadoodles. I tell you, Brenda, I'm serious about this. Fred wants the whole shebang American dream, two kids, station wagon, house in the burbs. Which is why I called, to find out how things went when you met him at La Reverie. Was he terribly, awfully disappointed I couldn't make it? I can just see him, all set to pop the question and no one to pop it to. I hope he didn't make a scene and cry or anything. Please call as soon as you get home. I want to talk to you before I call Fred. I'm a little surprised he didn't leave a message for me. If he's mad, I know how to make it up to him. Oh, oh, one more thing before I hang up. Did Fred show you my engagement ring? Were you dazzled?"

I was dazzled, all right, and exhausted from listening to her message. As soon as I got a little extra cash, I was going to have to invest in one of those answering machines that cuts off incoming messages after ten seconds.

Meanwhile, I didn't have the heart or the guts to tell Naomi that beloved, perfect Fred had stood her up. So I put off calling her back. She didn't need me to tell her that her boyfriend was a cad. She'd find out sooner or later.

My stomach growled. That bran muffin wasn't much of a lunch. So I ate some cheese and crackers to tide me over until dinner. That not only whetted my appetite, it reminded me that I had no dinner plans. After the debacle at La Reverie I sure as hell wasn't about to go out alone, not even to Angie's. Under no circumstances would I call Johnny. Elizabeth was still in Chicago. Renard hadn't asked me out yet. So, it looked like I was on my own at home, but my cupboard was, if not actually bare, for the moment unappealing.

I reevaluated. I figured that under certain special circumstances it was okay to call Johnny. After all, I needed to tell him that, while he had been off gallivanting around town with his guest starlet, I was single-handedly discovering who killed Buddy Needleson, a selfless act which ultimately would prove the innocence of his agent, and therefore boost Johnny's career. Johnny didn't even know about the stripper videotapes or Brink LeHalle. I decided to call, but not mention my hunger or lack of food in the apartment. Nor would I dare mention that I'd seen him at La Reverie. I'd let him bring up the subject of dinner. He always did.

I picked up the phone, took a deep breath, and placed the call.

Johnny didn't answer. I slammed down the receiver without leaving a message. Where the hell was he? With whom? Or, more accurately, whomette?

For dinner I found a long-forgotten box of wild mushroom ravioli stuck in the back of my freezer. I boiled it, slathered it with butter, and grated a chunk of Reggiano over it. For wine, I twisted the top off a bottle of Chateau la Rotgut I'd been saving for just such an occasion. After dinner I listened to Muddy Waters sing the blues, then switched to talk radio. I fell asleep listening to the sound of New Yorkers complaining bitterly about another proposed hike in the transit fare.

21

There I was, bright and early the next morning with that dreadful pom-pom hat pulled down over my ears, standing in front of a dreary building waiting for Lisa Markham to come out. It was my first stakeout and, I hoped, my last, because once again, real life proved a whole lot different than a *Tod Trueman* episode. Whenever Tod did a stakeout, Johnny got to sit in a late-model sportscar next to a glamorous guest starlet, sipping champagne and engaging in sophisticated repartee. I, on the other hand, wondered if the savage wind would pick me up and throw me against the side of Lisa's building.

I hugged myself and stamped my feet on the sidewalk in a futile effort to keep warm. Across the street a cozy coffee shop beckoned me, the yellow glow from its window washed out over the street. I fought the temptation until a gust of wind ripped a six-foot branch off a tree. It hurtled toward me, missed me by half an inch, and finally slammed into a metal garbage can with a clang. Dodging flying debris, I fled across the street and into the coffee shop.

The place smelled great and was as inviting on the inside as it looked from the outside. Half a dozen customers sprawled out on mismatched chairs and couches, thumbing through newspapers and magazines. I threw my coat over an armchair by a window that had a good view of Lisa

Markham's building, then headed to the counter to order coffee.

Of the millions of blends and styles of coffee available, I asked for their house blend, plain and black, then settled into my chair and resumed the stakeout. In this rotten weather everybody who came out of Lisa Markham's building looked the same, zipped up in puffy nylon coats with hoods up, exposing the smallest amount of face possible. It was hard enough to tell the men from the women, the tall from the short, the fat from the skinny, let alone if any of them was Lisa Markham.

I was on my third cup of coffee, about ready to give up, when a woman burst through the door of the building who looked a little like the woman on the video. The longer I watched, the more I was sure it was her. She bent over at the waist, put her hands on her thighs, and breathed, long and deep. She was dressed in sweats and earmuffs. Her jet-black hair was pulled back into a fat springy ponytail. She bounced down the steps, ran in place for a moment, then took off fast, headed north. Just what I needed; Lisa Markham was a runner.

I threw on my coat and took off after her. Not much of a runner, I somehow managed to slip along on the snow and ice well enough to keep her in sight. She trotted a few blocks north, turned and went several blocks east, and finally ducked into a health club. I'd heard of the place. Who hadn't? Their full-page ads, posters, and TV commercials showed high-contrast close-ups of sweaty tattooed biceps and assorted pierced body parts.

I waited outside until I caught my breath. Then, with a half-baked plan, I pushed through the revolving doors and entered into the world of fitness.

A woman behind a long counter smiled sweetly at me. "Can I help you?" She wore a hooded sweatshirt with the gym's logo.

"I've seen your ads," I said, "and I was thinking about maybe joining, but I'm not sure."

Another smile, sweeter than the first. "We have several

new member plans. I'll have one of our salespersons show you around."

"Great."

She spoke into her telephone. Moments later a square-jawed muscle-bound man with intense dark eyes and short blond hair shook my hand. He wore a sleeveless T-shirt emblazoned with the same logo.

"I'm Glen," he said. "I think you'll be delighted with what we have to offer."

Glen walked me through the facility, never once missing the chance to catch his reflection in one of the floor-to-ceiling mirrors. We passed by scores of treadmills and bicycles and skiing tracks and rowing machines. He yelled over the throbbing techno disco pop, "These here are good for your cardiovascular system." Half the machines were being used by sweat-drenched people. I didn't see Lisa.

In an exercise studio about twenty people jumped around, flinging their arms, while a zealous instructor shouted instructions. "High impact," explained Glen, "for burning calories. Our instructors are the best in the city. They have their own followings. Just like hairdressers." Again, no Lisa.

Next Glen led me into one of the gym's four professionally equipped weight rooms. That's where I spotted Lisa, the only female in a room full of grunting men. She was pulling a handle on some sort of contraption that was hooked up to a pile of weights.

"How long does it take to get arms like hers?" I asked.

"Lots of hard, consistent work," said Glen. "That lady never misses a day."

"Wow, that's dedication," I said. And good news, I thought. Lisa would be easy to find again.

Glen hoisted a barbell and admired his biceps in yet another mirror. He then led me into a tiny office and shut the door, muffling the music. The walls of the office were bright red, the furniture all black.

"Have a seat," he said, motioning me toward a sleek canvas sofa. He took some forms out of a desk drawer, fastened them to a red plastic clipboard, and sat down next to me, maneuvering so that he brushed against my knee ever so slightly. "Sorry," he said, then launched right into his sales pitch. "Now, Brenda—is it all right to call you Brenda?"

"Of course."

Glen smiled, showing too many perfect white teeth. "Well then, Brenda, depending on your personal goals, we offer several different plans." He ran his eyes over my body, enough to make me uncomfortable, but not quite enough to be flat-out offensive. "*You* obviously don't have any kind of weight problem," he said.

"Thank you," I said. "I believe in staying healthy and fit. I'd really like to have arms like that woman we just saw."

"You're in the right place."

He ran through a long-winded confusing spiel so fast I had trouble focusing. For classes only it was one price, another price included boxing lessons from a pro, but if I wanted to use the Olympic-size swimming pool I'd have to go to their other location, which was a higher price. Then Glen hit me with the additional issues of personal trainers, towel service, and locker space. "I'll bet your head is absolutely spinning with all the possibilities," he said.

"You could say that," I said.

Glen smiled. "I've saved the best for last. This is the best gym in the city to meet people of the opposite sex, primo people."

"How much is this going to cost me?" I asked.

"Much less than you imagine, I'll bet."

Glen was dead wrong about that. He half whispered a price, and it was about four times what I imagined and eight times what I was willing to pay.

"Hmm," I said, "it seems like a pretty good deal, but I don't know. I mean, it's just, uh—"

"Tell you what I'll do," said Glen. "You're the kind of person we like to see around here—makes the place look good, if you know what I mean. So to entice you to come on board, I'll give you a free pass. It's good anytime for one visit. When you use it, stop by to say hello. I'd love to get to know you better."

I took the pass and split.

I felt a sense of accomplishment. Things, it seemed, were finally moving in the direction of clearing Lemmy. I'd use my free pass and go back to the gym early the next day. If Lisa Markham showed up, I'd figure out a way to talk to her and get her to tell me about her boyfriend. If she didn't show up? Well, I'd worry about that later.

I spent the rest of the day at Midnight Millinery assessing just how far behind I was on spring. I had one enormous coiled straw braid hat like the one Irene Finneluk used in her strip act. Aside from that, zilch. The situation was bad. The rent was due. My custom clients weren't exactly beating down the door in this weather.

Jackhammer sniffed around the corners of the shop, then curled up on his pile of fabric beneath the antique vanity and snoozed. I doodled in my sketchbook. There was always the possibility that a random scribble would turn into The Idea for spring. But this time wasn't one of those times. I filled up ten pages and gave up.

Outside, the wind howled up West Fourth Street like it was in one mighty big hurry to plow into Eighth Avenue. I looked out the window at the combination snow, slush, and ice and tried to think spring. Pink. Green. Yellow.

The phone rang. "Midnight Millinery," I said, picking up automatically, before I had a chance to decide if I should. In this case, I certainly shouldn't have. It was Naomi.

"Dammit anyway, Brenda. Where the hell have you been? Why didn't you call me back?"

"Sorry, Naomi, but you know how it is. I've been real busy. I'm behind on spring."

"Don't give me any of that crap. I know you too well, Brenda Midnight. You're always behind on spring, or fall, or summer, or winter, or early spring, or pre-fall, whatever.

I know exactly why you don't want to talk to me. You've been moping around again about Johnny. You can't deal with the fact that there are some couples in this world, like me and my Fred, who are blissfully happy."

The truth would crush Naomi, but I didn't see any way to avoid telling her. I took a deep breath and said, "Uh, about Fred—"

She interrupted, "So what happened when you told my Freddy I was stuck in Queens? I can just see the expression on his face. I bet it was like one of those poignant moments where everyone in the place got lumps in their throats."

"Not exactly, Naomi. I don't think anybody knew."

"Okay, so my Fred played it low-key. The man's got nerves of steel. I hope he bought you a drink for your trouble."

"Well—"

"Did he show you the ring? Come on, Brenda, you can tell me. Am I gonna need a splint to hold my finger up? I still haven't heard from him, so I thought maybe he was angry. I guess I'll go ahead and call him now and apologize. Before I do, I've gotta ask you for a special favor. Now, I know how much you hate to do weddings, Brenda, but you've really got to design my veil. I mean, how could I possibly walk down that aisle with a stranger's veil on my head?"

The thing that finally shut her up was a click on the phone.

"Oops," she said, "somebody's beeping in. Hang on a sec."

I hung on, thinking how much I despised call waiting. It's nothing but a modern excuse for rude behavior. However this time, I was saved by the beep.

Naomi came back on the line. "Sorry, Brenda. I've got to take this. It's business. I'll get right back to you."

When she finally called back, much later, I was sitting at Angie's, alone, eating a grilled cheese, wondering where Johnny was.

22

Hoping Lisa Markham was a creature of habit and worked out at the same time every day, I got to her gym at eight the next morning. I flashed my free pass to the woman at the sign-in counter. She handed me a long sheet of paper and a ball-point pen. "Sign here," she said, pointing to a line at the bottom.

I scanned the tiny print. Basically it said that if anything happened to me while I was on the gym's property, it wasn't the gym's fault.

"Do I have to sign this?"

The woman smiled. "It's nothing, just a formality."

I signed.

The free pass didn't quite live up to its name. I had to shell out five bucks for a temporary locker and another two to rent a towel. The woman shoved the money into a drawer. "Enjoy your workout," she said.

My temporary locker was off in a dark corner of the dressing room. It was small, about one cubic foot. I peeled off my coat, boots, and outer layer of clothes and stuffed them inside. I didn't have a padlock, so I had to leave my temporary locker temporarily unlocked. A sternly worded sign informed me that the gym was not responsible for any of my belongings.

Dressed in black leggings and an old T-shirt, with three-dollar sneakers on my feet, I was ready to work out. I didn't want to leave my purse in the unlocked locker, so I dragged it along with me.

I checked all the rooms to be sure Lisa wasn't there yet, then stationed myself in the cardiovascular room near the front door so I wouldn't miss her when she came in. I did fifteen minutes on a stationary bicycle, got bored to death, switched over to a scary-looking climbing device, got bored again, switched to a treadmill, cranked it up to four miles an hour at a fifteen-degree incline, broke out in a sweat, caught a glimpse of myself in the mirror, and almost died of embarrassment. My hair was out of control, frizzed out worse than Chuck's, worse even than my grandfather's, from whom I'd inherited the stuff. But that was one great thing about being a milliner. I could usually figure out a stylish way to hide my hair problems. Fortunately, I had a swatch of cotton pique in my purse from my last trip to the garment center. I got off the treadmill, tied my hair back with the fabric, tucked in the ends, and got back down to business on the treadmill. Now I could sweat without further embarrassment.

As I'd predicted, Lisa Markham came in at the same time as the day before. She said a couple of words to the woman at the counter, then passed right by me. The readout on the treadmill claimed I had burned two hundred twenty calories. I stayed on until it hit three hundred, then I headed to the weight room, where I hoped to find Lisa.

On my way I ran into Glen preening in front of a mirror.

"Glad to see you back so soon," he said. "Have you decided which one of our packages to take advantage of?"

"Not yet."

"When you do, you let me know." He lowered his voice and moved in close. "I'm not really supposed to do this, you know, but if you sign up today, I think I can arrange for a little discount or throw in an extra couple of months."

"Thanks," I said. "I'll keep that in mind."

Just like yesterday, Lisa Markham was in the weight room. I looked around at the machines. Mounted on each was an illustration that outlined in red the specific muscles, or collection of muscles, the machine supposedly strengthened. Beneath the illustrations were step-by-step, not-so-easy-to-follow instructions.

I settled on a machine that looked like a cross between a tractor and a barbell. According to the picture, it was for the chest and shoulder muscles. I didn't care what it exercised. For me the important part was that it was next to Lisa Markham.

I studied the instructions for a minute or so, then turned to Lisa and said, "Excuse me. This is my first time here, and I can't figure out how to use this contraption. Could you help?"

Lisa stopped exercising. She looked at me, then at the machine. "Yeah, I guess so, sure."

She untangled herself from her machine to demonstrate. "It's easy," she said. "Sit down here and adjust the height so your elbows line up with the pivot point over there. See? Then put the pin in the weight stack." She looked at me again. "Judging from your size, you should probably start out with about twenty pounds."

"Thanks," I said.

"Anytime," she said, and went back to her machine.

Overloaded with instructions, I tried to correlate what she said with the illustrations on the machine. The pivot point was beyond comprehension. I hoped it was already in the right place. The weight stack adjustment was easy once I figured out that I had to push a plunger on the end of the pin to pull it out. All set to go, I lined up my twenty pounds and began pumping iron. I slammed that stack of weights up and down, up and down as fast as I could, making so much noise that everyone in the room gave me a dirty look.

"Slow down," said Lisa. "You're supposed to hold your contraction all the way down. Otherwise all you're doing is putting pressure on your joints."

"Oh," I said, slowing down. "It's so much harder this way."

Lisa laughed. ''That's the point. You know what they say: No pain, no gain.''

I tortured my muscles for ten minutes, then ventured, ''Hell of a lot of trouble just to keep looking good for my boyfriend.''

Lisa rested her stack of weights. ''He's worth it, isn't he?''

''I'm not sure yet. It's a new relationship. Already he's too possessive.''

''Mine too,'' said Lisa, ''but I don't mind. Not really. Even with his hot temper, he's worth it. You see, my boyfriend's an investment counselor. If the romance part doesn't work out, it doesn't matter. I've only known him for six months and already I've made a pile of money by listening to his advice.''

Sometimes my luck amazed me.

I called Chuck the instant I got home.

''It's not luck, Brenda,'' he said. ''It's skill. People trust you. They'll tell you anything. In fact, I've been thinking what a good con artist you'd be, that is, if you ever want to make a career change. In fact, I've been planning this scam, nothing bad really, it's like a quasi-legal caper. The computer model runs without a hitch. With your help I could pull it off for real. Just think, Brenda, you'd never have to make another hat. It would be legal. Sort of.''

''Making hats is sort of even more legal,'' I said. ''Besides, I love my work.''

''I hate to see you waste your potential.''

''Tell you what I'll do. If I decide to turn to a life of quasi-legal crime, you'll be the first to know. Meanwhile, we've got a legitimate bad guy criminal to worry about, Brink LeHalle, only now he goes by the name Trent Paterson. That's the name on the card his girlfriend Lisa gave me. I'm pretty sure he's our guy.''

''Trent Paterson. Now, that's an original name. He must have been looking at a map of New Jersey to come up with that. What's his middle name, anyway, Ho-Ho-Kus?''

Chuck laughed at his own joke. "What's your next move?"

"Pose as an investor and call him. Play it by ear. See what I can find out."

"Be careful, Brenda. Remember, if he's who we think he is, and if he did what we think he did, you're dealing with a killer."

Right. Pose as an investor. Call a killer. Play it by ear. It sounded so simple when I said it, but it took two hours to get up the nerve to call Trent Paterson.

He picked up on the first ring. "Paterson here." His voice was all business.

"Mr. Paterson, my name is Brenda Midnight. You don't know me, but Lisa Markham gave me your card. I'm interested in investing a little—"

He cut me off. "I'm afraid there's been a misunderstanding. Lisa's a wonderful girl, but sometimes says things she shouldn't. I don't handle individual investors. They're not worth my time. Lisa's a special case."

"The misunderstanding is all my fault," I said. "You see, when I said 'I,' I didn't mean 'I' as in me, I meant 'I' as in 'I represent a pool of rather well-heeled investors itching for some action.' "

He liked that version better and agreed to meet me for lunch the next day.

As soon as he clicked off, I called Dweena and asked her to come to the restaurant when I met Paterson. "I need to know positively if he's LeHalle."

"I'll be there," said Dweena. "No matter what kind of disguise the bastard's got on, or what New Jersey towns he's named himself after, I'll be able to ID him for you. Do me a favor and give me a wake-up call. Noon is like kind of early for me."

Sweaty and disgusting from my workout, I headed straight for the shower and was surprised by what I saw in the bathroom mirror. The swatch of cotton pique was still tied around my head. It looked great. The more I looked at it, the more it began to look like spring.

I eased the fabric out of my hair without disturbing the knot, skipped the shower, grabbed Jackhammer, and got myself over to Midnight Millinery.

I sat in front of the vanity mirror for an hour, messing around with the fabric. I put it back on my head, took it off, put it on again. All the time I was thinking, it can't be a hat, it's a scarf. It's more like a headband than a hat, but if I stiffen it up, define the bow knot . . . There were all sorts of possibilities.

My pulse quickened. I pulled out my design head block, some fabric, and a piece of buckram and hacked it all together, in the process losing track of time and everything else. When I was done, I had a prototype spring hat on the block held together by seven pushpins and a couple of dozen big basting stitches. It wasn't the whole line, not even a finished hat, but finally, at long last, a start. Spring. I could almost hear the chirp of little birds.

Depending on the fabric, it could look perky, casual, sexy, elegant, or dressy. It was easy to wear, flattering. It was a shape that would work way beyond spring, and it didn't take a week to make either.

I finalized the prototype and tried it on. I checked it out from all angles, including the top. I shook my head to make sure it stayed in place. I smiled. In my own humble estimation, the hat, or whatever it was, was somewhere between not too bad and truly brilliant.

I wanted to celebrate. I considered calling Johnny. I had a million things to tell him. He didn't know about the videotape or Brink LeHalle, but mostly I wanted to tell him about my spring line. When I called all I got was his machine. I didn't leave a message. What good would it do? He hadn't returned my last call. I didn't understand. No matter how many guest starlets were in his life and no matter what he felt about me, I'd have thought he'd be more concerned about Lemmy.

I was on my way out the door when the phone rang. I

had a hunch it was Johnny and dove for the receiver. So much for hunches.

Naomi tore right into me. "Brenda Midnight, you lied to me. How could you? I thought you were my friend."

She must have found out about Fred. I didn't even try to defend myself. "I'm sorry."

Naomi snorted. "Yeah, right. You can imagine what happened when I finally got in touch with Fred. Why didn't you tell me he stood me up? I made a complete fool of myself. *I* apologized to *him* for getting stuck in Queens. So the bastard listens to my stupid apology, then he goes, 'I don't know what you're talking about, Naomi. I had to work late that night. I never even went to La Reverie.' Imagine how I felt, Brenda. Do you have any idea, any idea at all? So, after I get over the shock, I ask Fred why didn't he call and he says the whole reason he was meeting me in the first place was to end the relationship. Get that? End the relationship, not pop the question, end the relationship. He went and got himself engaged to his old girlfriend, who's this bitch and a half and a fat pig to boot. When he couldn't make it to meet me, he decided it would be easier in the long run if he just plain old stood me up. Easier on who, I want to know. Certainly not easier on me."

I didn't know what to say.

"Brenda? Are you still there? Can you hear me?"

"Yes, Naomi, I heard you." I was really sorry. I'd made the wrong decision, copped out, hoped the problem would go away on its own. I should have known better. Problems never go away on their own.

She went on and on. "How could he leave me for that whore? I'm never going to speak to another man again. Never ever ever. I'm going to go sulk now and when I'm done sulking I'm going to pierce my nose. That'll show Fred."

Not that anyone seemed the pierced nose type, but Naomi *really* didn't. "Don't do anything rash," I said.

She slammed down the phone.

I went home, made a cheese, onion, and tomato sandwich, called Johnny again, got his machine again, and hung up again without leaving a message. I was upset, but unlike Naomi, I had not even the slightest urge to pierce my nose.

23

I tossed and turned all night. Every time I closed my eyes I had visions of Johnny dressed as a bunny rabbit with guest starlets on his arm, visions of Naomi with a pierced nose, visions of Lemmy behind bars, visions of Brewster Winfield's snake Myrtle, and, the most disturbing vision of all, that I was meeting a murderer for lunch. Bad enough to have to break bread with a killer, but he'd insisted on a restaurant located in midtown. From the get-go I would be out of my element.

I called Dweena at noon. She was already up.

"I'm so excited about busting LeHalle," she said. "I couldn't sleep a wink, so I got up and procured us a car. I'll pick you up in an hour."

Hoping Dweena's "procured" meant borrowed from an old friend who owed her a big favor, I agreed.

To convince Trent Paterson that I represented a bunch of filthy rich, morally destitute people who were willing to be taken for a ride, I needed to dress to look either wealthy or eccentric. Wealthy was out of the question, so I opted for the eccentric look—a severe long black sheath, gray gloves, and a gray wool hat with a brim that swept down over my left eye.

For the first time in days, the sun was actually peeking through the clouds, so I went outside to wait for Dweena. That turned out to be a mistake. Detective Turner screeched up in his unmarked car. There was nowhere to hide.

He rolled down his window. With a smirk, he said, "My, my, don't we look fetching?" From the tone of his voice, I knew there was some kind of trouble and that whatever it was, I was right smack in the middle of it.

"Why, Detective Turner, how nice to see you again. Out soaking up some rays?"

"Hardly. I'm looking for that boyfriend of yours, Johnny Verlane."

"Afraid I can't help you with that, Detective. You see, it's ex-boyfriend, with a lot of emphasis on the ex. Johnny and I don't keep tabs on each other."

"Bullshit," said Turner. He opened his car door and stuck his leg out so that he was half in, half out. "When you see him tell him I'd like to talk to him about the whereabouts of his agent Lemon B. Crenshaw, who happens to be a fugitive from the law."

Damn. It sounded like the detective had finally put two and two together. "Lemmy?" I said. "A fugitive? You've gotta be kidding." I feigned a look of surprise.

"Aha," said Turner. "You admit that you know Mr. Crenshaw."

"Of course I know Lemmy. He's been Johnny's agent for years. But a fugitive? Lemmy? I can't believe it. What'd he allegedly do, park in a loading zone, litter, jaywalk?"

My attempt at levity had no effect on the detective's scowl. "What really pisses me off," he said, slapping the car door for emphasis, "is that you and Mr. Verlane actually expected me and Detective McKinley to believe that the two of you just happened to show up at Buddy Needleson's funeral, the very stiff who'd been offed by Mr. Crenshaw, who just happened to be Johnny's agent. Despite your subterfuge, it didn't take us long to uncover the truth. You and Johnny Verlane know more than you're telling. In fact, I wouldn't be at all surprised if you know the whereabouts of Lemon B. Crenshaw."

Turner's surprising use of the word "subterfuge" had me going for a moment. Then I remembered how Johnny, as Tod Trueman, used it a lot, often in the next to last scene when he confronted the guilty party. "That's absurd," I said. "I went to Buddy Needleson's funeral because I'm a friend of the family. Johnny came along as my escort."

"Whatever you say, Ms. Midnight, but remember I don't believe a word of it. Do yourself a favor and get word to your ex-boyfriend that I'd like to talk to him. Soon. I don't care how many favors Detective McKinley and I owe the two of you, murder is damned serious business."

"I understand that, Detective, but I really haven't seen Johnny. If I do, I'll be sure to let him know you want to see him."

"See that you do," said Turner.

Dweena picked that moment to zip around the corner in a very expensive Japanese car that looked like a highly polished egg. She didn't recognize Turner's Chrysler for what it was—an unmarked cop car—or Turner for what he was—a detective. She pulled up behind his car and stuck her head out the window. "Yo, Brenda. Hop in."

"Looks like my ride's here," I said.

"Nice car," said Turner. "Who's the babe at the wheel?"

I gave him a look of contempt as if to say, You disgusting sexist pig, jumped in, and told Dweena to step on it.

She made a quick left onto Eighth Avenue and nudged the shiny egg car over into the right lane. "Who was that?"

"That was Bad News, Real Bad News, otherwise known as Spencer Turner, *Detective* Spencer Turner. After all this time, he and Detective McKinley figured out that Lemmy is Johnny's agent. From that tiny bit of information he has deduced the most awful things, all of them true."

"You didn't tell him where Johnny was, did you?" she asked.

"I don't know where Johnny is," I said.

"Oh." Dweena flatlined her mouth and kept her eyes straight ahead on the traffic.

From the way she dropped the subject and avoided my

eyes, I was positive she knew something about Johnny. Since I wasn't ready to hear all the whos, whats, and wheres, I didn't press the subject. We drove along in uncomfortable silence until Twenty-third Street, where a cab cut us off. In a beautifully choreographed three-part movement, Dweena slammed on the brakes, gave the cabby the finger, and shouted, "Jerkhole." Her action went unnoticed by the cab driver, but it broke the ice between Dweena and me.

"If Trent Paterson really is LeHalle," I said, "he's got a lot of guts to meet me in a public restaurant. I'd think he'd want to keep a low profile. You recognized him. Don't you think someone else might?"

"Part of it is unabashed arrogance," said Dweena, "although there's really no way anyone would recognize him, not with that hairpiece. It gives him an entirely different look. Besides, most of the people he screwed never saw him. His operation was strictly backroom. He did his ripping off by phone. As for his co-workers, except for me, they're all, uh, how shall I say? They're up the river, doing time."

"So LeHalle got other people in trouble besides you?"

"No. Those currently incarcerated got busted in the second wave of scandals. Had nothing to do with LeHalle."

When we got near the restaurant Dweena turned to me and said, "Let me know if you see a good place to double park."

"Won't the car get towed?" I asked.

She rolled her eyes toward the heavens. "Of course it's gonna get towed. That's the idea. Towing, however, takes forever. Before the car gets towed, we've got a chance to get even."

"Get even?"

"Brenda, you're so naive. We can stick it to someone by pinning them in. So, who you got a grudge against?"

"No one."

"God, Brenda, Johnny was right about you. How about the cable company, or the phone company?" Before I could answer, Dweena banged her hands on the steering wheel. "Look, up ahead. Hot damn. This is too good, too, too good to believe. What did I do to deserve this? Tell me, Brenda, do you believe in instant karma?"

"I'm not sure," I said. I didn't see anything special up ahead.

"Well," said Dweena, "I do. That dark green sedan up there is living proof that what goes around, comes around. See the one I mean, brazenly parked in a tow-away zone? Check out the plate. Diplo-freaking-mat. I love it. We're gonna pin in a diplomat."

Dweena risked our lives, darted across three lanes of angry horn-blaring traffic and double-parked next to the diplomat's car. "There," she said, turning off the car. "I'd like to see that bastard get out of this space."

We split up. I went into the restaurant first, Dweena stayed behind pretending to window-shop.

According to my *Zagat,* Garadom's food wasn't what it used to be, its formerly to-die-for pesto now merely passable, the once famous steaks now ho-hum. Despite the food, it remained one of the city's premier business luncheon spots.

I gave my name to the hostess. She ran her finger down a list of names in a large leatherbound book. "Ah yes, Mr. Paterson is expecting you." She signaled for an assistant to show me to the table.

Paterson was definitely the man on the videotape, smarmy, bewigged, and unseasonably overtanned. All that remained to be seen was if he really was Brink LeHalle.

I managed to shake his hand without flinching. "Pleased to meet you, Mr. Paterson."

"Call me Trent," he said.

"Trent," I said.

He held out the chair for me. Out of the corner of my eye I saw Dweena come in and sit at the bar. She was dressed conservatively for Dweena, but since we were in midtown, she turned a few heads.

A waiter came to take my drink order. They had several wines by the glass. I chose a midpriced California red.

Paterson flicked his finger at his empty glass. "Another martini."

Then the waiter hustled off, leaving us alone. We checked each other out, neither saying a word, until his eyes lit on my hat. He grinned, showing a row of tiny, perfectly even teeth. "That's a stunning hat."

"Thank you." It was hard for me to make polite conversation and not blurt out accusations, but I made it through an inane exchange about the weather and another about how the proposed transit hike would affect the investment business. I was rescued from further chitchat when the waiter came back with our drinks and stayed to take our orders. I ordered the pasta primavera, Paterson got a sixteen-ounce porterhouse steak. "Charred and crusty on the outside," he said, "bloody red in the middle."

While the waiter was taking our order, Dweena casually walked by the table, signaling me to join her in the ladies' room.

"If you'll excuse me," I said to Paterson, "I need to powder my nose."

"Of course," he said, taking a sip of his drink.

The ladies' room was down a long flight of stairs, next to a cigarette machine, a pay telephone, and a potted palm. I laughed when I saw Dweena because she really *was* powdering her nose, dramatically, with a big fluffy pink puff. Powder flew everywhere. I sat down next to her and rooted through my purse for a lipstick. "Are we alone?" I said softly.

"Not quite," said Dweena. She jutted her chin in the direction of the second room.

I heard a toilet flush. A fat woman came out and washed her hands, then left.

"Now we can talk," said Dweena. "He's a couple of years older, a few pounds heavier, a hell of a lot tanner, and he's covered his sizable bald spot, but you're having lunch with a dead man. Trent Paterson is, beyond the shadow of a doubt, the former Brink LeHalle."

"Buddy Needleson's killer," I said.

"I sure wouldn't put it past him," said Dweena.

"I've got to trap him, trip him up, turn him over to the cops," I said.

"How?" asked Dweena.

"I'm not sure yet."

"Here's a suggestion. Use your feminine wiles, Brenda. You'll have him eating out of the palm of your hand."

"I couldn't. I mean, what about Lisa?"

"His girlfriend? Forget it. You'd be doing her a favor."

Finally I found my lipstick.

She watched me put it on. "Red is a good color for you."

"Thanks." I stood up to go, straightened my dress. "I'll call you later and let you know how it went."

"Good luck, Brenda."

Halfway out the door, I turned back. Since I'd primped in the mirror next to Dweena, I felt we'd bonded enough for some real girl talk. "Uh, Dweena, one more thing."

"Shoot," she said.

"You know where Johnny is, don't you? You've seen him."

Dweena looked down at the floor.

"Come on, Dweena. I know he's your friend and all, but sooner or later I'll find out."

Dweena sighed. "You've got to understand that I haven't seen him, but he's a celebrity and word does get around. The buzz is that he's been making the rounds of the strip clubs. No one quite knows what to make of it."

Neither did I. Johnny hanging out in strip clubs made about as much sense as—oh, I don't know what. It didn't make any sense at all.

"Thanks, Dweena. You're a pal," I said.

When I got back to the table, our food had already arrived. Garadom's food may not have been what it used to be, but the portions were enormous. Paterson's steak hung over the edge of his plate and there was enough pasta on mine to feed me for two days. The sight of so much food killed my appetite, so I moved the mound of overcooked noodles from one side to the other. Occasionally I picked out a chunk of broccoli and ate it. Paterson, meanwhile, ripped into his steak until all that remained was a pool of blood in the bottom of his plate. He sopped that up with a piece of bread.

Throughout the meal we made small talk. I didn't want to be the one to bring up business. Finally, halfway through coffee and dessert, he did. "You say you represent several investors?"

I had my story ready. "Yes, I do. They're not satisfied with their current adviser. They feel with the amount of money they have, they should be doing much better. From what Lisa told me about you, I got the impression you were, uh, more capable than most brokers."

"As I said before, sometimes Lisa says more than she should." He leaned forward, rested his elbows on the table, and interlaced his fingers. He looked at me as if he were trying to make up his mind whether or not he could trust me. "How much money are we talking about?"

"Plenty." I hoped he wouldn't ask me to be more specific.

"I'm sure you know that to make any kind of decent return, you have be willing to take risks," he said.

I nodded. "Of course."

"These investments I have in mind, these instruments, if you will, aren't traded on the Big Board."

Since I didn't know what the Big Board was, that didn't bother me at all.

Paterson went on, "These instruments, derivatives really, are based on a little-known quirk of the market. The SEC—"

"The SEC? We don't want to do anything illegal."

"Trust me, Brenda. I would never ask you or your friends to break the law."

"That's a relief," I said.

"What these instruments are," said Paterson with a wink, "is gray area. So far the SEC hasn't caught on. Once they do, who knows? That's why we have to act fast. Naturally, I'll need to meet with everyone involved. How quickly can you set up a meeting?"

I wasn't prepared for this. "You want to meet the investors?"

His eyes narrowed. "Because of the irregular nature of these instruments, I need to know exactly whom I'm dealing with." Then he broke into a smile. "Besides, I'd like to give the investors a chance to meet me, to give them a sense of security. So, can you do it by the end of the week?"

"I guess so. Sure."

"Fine. You let me know when and where."

Once I took a second to think about it, I couldn't believe my good fortune. Paterson had just handed me an opportunity on a silver platter. A fake investor meeting would be a perfect way to trap him. Of course, there were a million things to do to prepare. I was busy scheming in my head when Paterson interrupted my thoughts.

"Now, Brenda, since we're going to be partners, I'd like to get to know you better, a lot better."

I smiled nicely, remembering how Dweena told me to use my feminine wiles.

"How about tomorrow night?" he said.

I hadn't meant to smile that nicely. "I thought you and Lisa—"

"What Lisa doesn't know won't hurt her."

"I'm afraid I've got—"

He leveled his eyes at me. "You better make up your mind, Brenda. Are you in this deal or not?"

I took a deep breath and said, "I'm in."

He signaled to the waiter for the check, paid it quickly with plastic, and stood up to leave. "Meet me tomorrow night at eight at La Reverie. After, we'll go back to my place and I'll give you a preview."

24

Preview? I tried to convince myself Paterson didn't really mean anything by that. Maybe he just wanted to explain his derivative whatevers in the privacy of his own home. Fat chance.

I let Paterson squeeze my hand in a good-bye gesture, then tore out of Garadom's. Worried as I was, I couldn't help but notice a big commotion on the street.

Dweena would have been thrilled to see the results of her double-parked car. A man in a fur-trimmed topcoat sputtered and bellowed at a cop in a language I didn't understand. However, his frantic gesticulations transcended the language barrier. He made it clear that he was a big-wheel diplomat and that some double-parking son of a bitch had pinned in his car, causing him to miss a crucial meeting and thereby destroying hope for peace in the free world. Or maybe the unfree world. It was hard to pick up every nuance from his gestures.

I watched the drama until the tow truck came. Then I took the Lexington Avenue line down to Astor Place and from there walked to Chuck's. I caught Chuck and Lemmy in the middle of screaming at each other about which radio station to listen to. Chuck wanted country western. Lemmy wanted top forty.

"It's my apartment and my radio and I do not allow top

forty to pollute my air,'' said Chuck. His face was as red as his hair.

''I hate that twangy shit,'' said Lemmy. ''Don't forget, I'm a guest.''

''An uninvited guest,'' said Chuck.

I turned the radio off before they came to blows. ''Knock it off, both of you guys. We've got developments to discuss.''

''It better be good,'' said Lemmy. ''This place is driving me nuts.'' He slumped into the red beanbag chair.

Chuck rolled his computer chair over and straddled it backward, resting his chin on the back support. ''I'm all ears,'' he said.

''Here's the deal,'' I said. ''At lunch today Dweena made a positive ID of Paterson. He's definitely Brink LeHalle and he fell for my investor story. What's really great is that he wants to meet with the investors. It's a perfect setup to expose him. I figure a bunch of us can pose as investors—Dweena, Winfield, Elizabeth if she's back, maybe some others. I'll get Turner and McKinley to come, and they'll bust him for whatever sleazy scam he's got going now. To really cook his goose, Dweena can ID him.''

''It could work,'' said Chuck.

''I like it,'' said Lemmy.

''I thought you would.''

''Where are you going to have the meeting?'' asked Chuck. ''You're going to need a swank venue to pull this off.''

''I've got something in mind,'' I said.

''So, everything's set,'' said Lemmy.

''Not quite,'' I said. ''Paterson wants me to meet him at La Reverie tomorrow night.''

''Back so soon?'' teased Chuck. ''You're getting to be a regular there.''

''It's not funny. He wants me to go home with him after dinner for a 'preview.' He insinuated that if I didn't go, he wouldn't go through with the investor meeting.''

''Preview?'' said Chuck.

"That's what he said. Maybe . . ."

Chuck looked at Lemmy and they both shook their heads.

"No way," said Chuck. "It's too dangerous."

"It'll be okay," I said. "I've got it all figured out—well, partially figured out. I'll meet him for dinner. La Reverie is a public place. Nothing can happen there. I'll just think up some excuse not to leave with him."

"What kind of excuse?" asked Chuck.

"I'll come up with something that won't make him mad."

Chuck frowned. "What if you don't? Or what if you do and he doesn't go for it? What if he's armed? He could stick a gun in your back and march you right out of La Reverie. What then? I won't let you go."

"Excuse me?" I said. "You won't *let* me go."

Lemmy dismissed us both with a wave of his hand, then eased himself out of the beanbag chair, ambled over to the refrigerator, and grabbed a beer. He took a long swallow, wiped his mouth with the back of his hand, and smiled. "Calm down, kiddies. I've got an idea. Brenda goes along with the dinner. Meanwhile, we call Paterson's girlfriend, the chick in the video."

"Lisa," I said. "Lisa Markham."

Lemmy nodded. "Yeah. So we call this Lisa Markham chick and say that her boyfriend's two-timing her and give her all the particulars of where and when. If she's half a woman, she'll storm La Reverie and make a scene. That way, Brenda won't have to leave with the creep and the girlfriend will get the blame. I've got to hand it to me, the plan is brilliant. I'm really cooking."

"The plan is half-baked," said Chuck. "What if Lisa Markham doesn't give a hoot that her boyfriend's running around? What if she isn't home when we call? What if she doesn't believe it? What then?"

"Plan B," said Lemmy.

"What's Plan B?" I asked.

"Plan B is where we get Johnny to pretend to be your

boyfriend. It's a role he's familiar with. He waits in the wings. If, by the time you order dessert, Lisa hasn't shown, he storms in, causes a scene, and whisks you away. Then in a couple of days you can call Paterson and apologize, and say how sorry you are the date ended before it even began. Lay it on thick with a lot of suggestive sweet-talking crap. Then tell him your boyfriend's gonna be out of town on such and such a date and why not reschedule for then. Just make sure that such and such a date is after the fake investor meeting."

"Not bad," said Chuck, "not bad at all."

Lemmy beamed. "Why, thank you, Chuckeroo."

"There is a problem," I said. I paused a moment, trying to come up with a better way to say what I didn't want to say. "It's like this: I don't exactly know where Johnny is."

"No big deal," said Lemmy. "Call him later. We don't have to talk to him this instant. I'm sure he'll do it."

"I mean I *really* don't know where Johnny is, not for the last couple of days."

"What do you mean you don't know where Johnny is? He's in the middle of the most important shoot of his career."

"All I know is that he doesn't answer his phone, doesn't return my calls. Dweena says he's been cruising the strip clubs late at night. I don't know if he's showing up at the shoot or not. The last time I saw him . . ." I trailed off. I didn't want to think about the last time I'd seen Johnny.

"You're telling me he's out carousing, not getting his rest. Do you understand how much is at stake here? We've got Sal Stumpford directing. Do you know who Sal Stumpford is?"

"Johnny said he was from the West Coast," I said.

"For your information, Sal Stumpford is the biggest cop show director of the last two decades. A true innovator. We never would have got him except Stumpford's daughter, who married my dentist's son, happens to be a big *Tod Trueman* fan. She convinced Sal to come out of retirement to do a few *Tod Truemans*. Based on Stumpford's name alone, we resurrected the show. If Johnny doesn't show up to shoot, or if he shows up baggy-eyed and hungover, he's gonna piss off Stumpford. If Stumpford's pissed off, Stumpford will quit, and if Stumpford quits, we'll lose our backing, and that means no more *Tod Trueman, Urban Detective*—and that means Johnny will be back washing dishes."

"Johnny never washed dishes," I said.

"You know what I mean," said Lemmy.

"You left out the part about your percentage," said Chuck sarcastically.

Lemmy gave him a dirty look. "If Johnny's disappeared, we've got to call the cops. Get those detective friends of his working on this."

I shook my head no. "I didn't say Johnny disappeared. I just said I didn't know where he was. As for Detective Turner and Detective McKinley, they're already looking for Johnny, but for all the wrong reasons. They finally figured out that Johnny is your client. They think Johnny knows where you're hiding out."

Lemmy buried his head in his hands.

I continued, "So you see, it's actually better if Johnny doesn't show up at the shoot, because if he does and Detective Turner gets wind of it, the cops will interrupt the filming to bring Johnny in for questioning, and if Johnny talks—"

"You're screwed," said Lemmy.

"Huh?" I said.

"You heard me," said Lemmy. "You're screwed. Because if Johnny blabs about where I am, then I'm gonna have to talk and tell who was in my car that night, which was you and him, your geeky feather friends, that tranny Dweena, and one dead guy in the trunk."

That was the first time Lemmy had directly threatened to rat on Johnny and me. I didn't blame him one bit.

"It would seem," said Chuck, "that it's better all around if Johnny stays lost for a while."

"This could be the end of *Tod Trueman,*" said Lemmy.

I kept my mouth shut, but deep down I didn't think that would be such a bad thing.

After that, nobody said anything for a while. Lemmy, with a gloomy look on his face, thumbed through an old issue of *Backstage*. I felt sorry for him. He'd worked as hard as Johnny to make *Tod Trueman, Urban Detective* happen. Now the show might be in crisis, and here was Lemmy, a fugitive, holed up in a boarded-up East Village storefront, unable to help or even find out what was going on.

Chuck went into the other room and banged on the computer keyboard, his way of letting off steam. I leaned back in my chair and shut my eyes. I did not have pleasant thoughts.

Pretty soon, Chuck came back in and said, "I can solve one part of the Johnny problem. I'll play the role of your boyfriend tomorrow night. If Lisa Markham doesn't make a scene, I will."

That roused Lemmy from his funk. "You?" he shouted. "I bet you don't even have a suit. You won't get through the door at La Reverie."

Chuck dragged one of the ugliest suits I've ever seen out of the back of his closet. It half hung on the hanger like it couldn't make up its mind what it was supposed to do. He tried to slap the wrinkles out. "It needs a pressing," he said.

Lemmy hated the suit but relished cutting it down. "It's not only a brown suit," he said, "it's a brown suit made out of a petroleum product, for chrissakes. If ol' Chuckadoodle passes too close to a candle, that thing'll melt into a pool of dinosaur blood."

"The suit's fine," I said. It was good enough to get Chuck into La Reverie to rescue me. I hated to admit it, but having Chuck there as backup made me feel a whole lot better.

25

I walked all the way home from Chuck's, through gritty black slush, worrying about where to hold the investor meeting. Like I told Chuck and Lemmy, I had something in mind, but now I had to make it happen. That meant calling Irene Finneluk. As a real estate broker she had access to the kind of apartment that would be perfect for an investor meeting. All I needed to do was convince her that she should risk her career to help a complete stranger out of a jam. I didn't know what kind of laws and how many she'd be breaking if she let me use one of her listings for the meeting. At the very least it was unethical. At the very worst it was aiding and abetting a fugitive, something I'd been doing so long I barely gave it a second thought. Irene, on the other hand, might not be so blasé. I decided to run it by Brewster Winfield. Let him actually do something to earn his money. I had to call him anyway to ask him to pose as one of the investors.

I passed by Johnny's building. From inside the vacant storefront I heard the thwack of a nailgun and the high-pitched wail of a saw. It had been rented fast. The windows were still covered with paper so I couldn't tell what it was going to be.

I looked up at Johnny's window. His lights weren't on, but it was just beginning to get dark so that didn't mean much. Maybe he wasn't home. Or maybe he was pursuing an activity that didn't require a lot of light, like going over a script with a guest starlet.

That thought stayed with me the rest of the way home and put me in a lousy mood. I perked up when I saw Elizabeth in the lobby. Her hands were full with the hatboxes I'd given her and she was struggling to kick a big cardboard carton into the elevator.

"Welcome home," I said.

"There you are," she said, "a friend in need. Help me with this, will you?"

"Boy, is it ever good to have you back," I said. The box was caught on the elevator door runner. I got it over the bump, then shoved from behind. "It weighs a ton."

"Not quite a ton," said Elizabeth. "I've got Dude Bob's Vietnam books in there. He had to leave the convention in a hurry. As soon as the airport reopened, he split. He didn't have time to pack this stuff up."

"How come he was in such a hurry? I thought you two were having a great time."

"We were. What happened is he got in a fistfight with this young fellow who was wearing a Kill for Peace T-shirt. I'm afraid my Dude knocked out one or two of the fellow's teeth. Dude Bob cleared out of town before anybody decided to press charges."

"Your boyfriend is still a bigot, I see."

"He is not. The Dude's a changed man. He even paid a ridiculous price for an antiwar book."

"You're kidding."

"Well, it had a picture of me in a flowered micro-miniskirt leading a rally, so that might have had something to do with it. This fight had nothing to do with politics. The Kill for Peace fellow was hitting on me. When I spurned him, he got downright offensive. Dude Bob took action. He claims he hadn't had so much fun in thirty years."

"I'll bet."

I helped her drag the box into her apartment. "Want to

come over later?" she asked. "I've got lots to tell you."

"I've got lots to tell you too." So far the only thing I'd told Elizabeth about the Lemmy mess was that I'd dumped a body at the morgue, and she hadn't believed that. I definitely had a lot to tell her.

"Good," she said. "Come over later. I don't feel like dinner but I'll make a batch of cookies. How's oatmeal jalapeño sound?" she asked.

"Awful."

Elizabeth laughed. "I knew you'd love it. Bring Jackhammer. I'll whip up a little snack for him too."

I must be nuts, I thought, as I dialed Irene Finneluk's phone number. I hated to ask anybody, even my best friends, for favors. Irene would have to be equally nuts to agree to do it. Since she didn't appear to be the least bit nuts, I figured this was a waste of time. But life is full of surprises.

"Brenda," said Irene, gushing, "I'm thrilled you called. I've been meaning to ask you to do me this gigantic favor, and, well, I was kind of embarrassed to ask, given the fact that I barely know you."

"You needn't be embarrassed, Irene. Go ahead. Ask me anything."

"If you're sure it's okay. You see, I finally got around to having my strip tape duped and I had an extra copy made. I'd be forever grateful if you'd give it to Johnny Verlane."

"No problem," I said.

"You're a doll, Brenda. This could be my chance of a lifetime. I'm sure you know that Johnny's been cruising the strip clubs. Rumor has it that he's scouting for new talent to use on *Tod Trueman, Urban Detective*. I've been going out every night, hoping to run into him, but so far no luck."

"You know, it's ironic," I said. "The reason *I* called *you* was to see if you could do me a favor, except it's not really a favor for me, it's actually for Johnny and it'll help catch Buddy Needleson's killer."

I explained the situation to Irene, glossing over a few of

the details. She was thrilled to help. "When you put it that way," she said, "how could I say no? Remember that Central Park West apartment?"

"Of course."

"The owner's gone now, in the clink, so to speak. The apartment is still on the market. I think it would be quite nice for the meeting you have planned."

"It's perfect," I said. "Is there enough furniture left to make it look lived in?"

"Actually, no," said Irene, "but that's not a problem. I can get furniture. An interior decorator friend owes me a big favor for a tip on a magnificent rent-stabilized two-bedroom with a view, tons of light, and a working fireplace. He'll loan me something appropriately opulent for the occasion."

"A room or two is all we'll need," I said.

"It's as good as done. One more thing, Brenda."

Here it comes, I thought, the reason I hated asking for favors. "What's that?"

"Since I've already got to be in the apartment to let everyone in, could I play one of the rich investors? It might help me get the *Tod Trueman* gig."

I accepted her kind offer.

Next I called Winfield. He agreed to act as one of the rich investors, but emphasized it would count as billable time. I hung up disgusted with lawyers in general and him in particular. I was so mad I forgot to ask him about our legal status with the vacant apartment. I figured it couldn't have been too bad or he wouldn't have agreed to do it.

I had my fake investors and the swank apartment. It looked like the investor meeting was a go, which meant I had one more call to make before going to Elizabeth's. This call I particularly dreaded.

Somehow I had to let Detectives Turner and McKinley know enough to entice them to come to the investor meeting, without letting them know enough to put two and two together. I knew Turner already smelled a rat. As he'd hinted in our last encounter, he may have owed me a lot from an incident a while back where he took all the credit after I bopped an international hit man on the head with a hat block, but his goodwill had its limits.

I dialed the precinct and got right through to Turner.

"So, who *was* that babe driving the spiffy car?" he asked.

I ignored his question. "I've got a line on a fugitive for you," I said.

"It's about time you and Johnny came clean," he said. "I presume the fugitive in question is Lemon B. Crenshaw? You tell Mr. Crenshaw that if he turns himself in, things might go easier."

"No," I said. "It's not Lemmy. Like I already told you, I haven't seen or talked to Johnny and I have no idea where Lemmy Crenshaw is." I tried to keep my voice steady throughout the entire sentence, both the truthful part and the lie, but I think it changed to a higher pitch on the lie. If Turner noticed, he didn't say anything. I wondered when he was going to get angry enough to haul me in for a serious grilling.

"Well then, Ms. Midnight, if not Mr. Crenshaw, then which fugitive are you talking about?"

"A man named Brink LeHalle murdered Buddy Needleson."

"Never heard of him."

"Think back a few years ago, a big Wall Street scandal."

"Oh yes. I do remember. He died, didn't he, in some kind of accident?"

"Convenient boating accident," I said. "A little too convenient. The boat smashed to smithereens. His body never turned up, and for good reason. Brink LeHalle is alive, only now he calls himself Trent Paterson. Buddy Needleson found out. LeHalle killed him to shut him up."

"So you've got the case all solved."

"That's right," I said, glad Turner could see it my way.

He didn't. A sarcastic edge crept into his voice. He said, "I suppose that after bashing in Mr. Needleson's head with a blunt instrument, Mr. LeHalle convinced Lemon B. Crenshaw, a complete stranger, to dump the corpse at the morgue. Excuse my French, Ms. Midnight, but you're full of shit. I've got a good mind to bring you in for questioning."

"Look, Detective Turner, I've got a way to trap Paterson. I can prove he's LeHalle. If you and Detective McKinley will show up at a little gathering I have planned, I promise you won't be sorry. You and Detective McKinley will get the glory for bringing LeHalle to justice, not just for the Wall Street stuff, but for murder too."

Turner sighed. "I'd much rather you tell me the whereabouts of Lemon B. Crenshaw, the whereabouts of Johnny Verlane, and what the two of you were really doing at Buddy Needleson's funeral."

It's widely known that I don't do weddings. I'm adamant about this. Some people don't do windows, I don't do weddings. Period. But in this case, I had nothing else to bargain with. "Detective Turner," I said, "remember what you asked me at Buddy Needleson's funeral? Do this for me and I'll make your sister's kid's wedding veil."

In the end we compromised, or rather, Turner called it a compromise. I called it something else entirely. The deal was that even though I had to make the veil, Turner and McKinley still wouldn't go to the meeting. However, if I came up with any hard evidence, they'd take a look at it.

Elizabeth put a tray of fresh-baked cookies on her boomerang-shaped coffee table. I took one and looked it over carefully, then took a tiny test bite. On the second bite I hit a jalapeño. "Whoa, that's hot." Immediately my scorched tongue was soothed by a sweet cool sensation. "What else is in here beside jalapeños?" I asked.

Elizabeth smiled smugly. "That's my little secret." She held out a cookie-shaped chunk of food to Jackhammer. He trotted over, sniffed it, and was all over her in an instant, wiggling and vibrating his tail stub. She made him sit, then gave him the treat. He carried it off into the corner. Whatever she'd concocted, it must have been rock hard. I could hear him grinding away from clear across the room. "It'll help clean his teeth," she said. "Now, tell me what the hell's been going on while I was in the boonies."

I started from the beginning. "Remember how I told you I'd dumped a body at the morgue?"

"I remember thinking it wasn't nice of you to tell such whoppers to an old lady."

"It wasn't a whopper."

I got her to believe that, then told her the rest of the story.

She sat quietly and listened. When I finished she said, "That's some mess you've got there, Brenda."

"Want to help out and play the role of a filthy-rich investor?" I asked.

"My deah," she said, affecting a highfalutin' manner of speech, "I thought you'd never ask. I'll be there with bells on."

Eating jalapeño cookies for dinner hadn't been the best idea. When I got home from Elizabeth's I stretched out on the floor flat on my back and waited for the pain to go away. I chided myself for indiscriminate eating. I was as bad as Jackhammer.

The phone rang. For once, I remembered to let the answering machine pick up.

"Brenda, it's Naomi. Please pick up, I need your help."

No way, I thought.

She went on, pleading. "Come on, Brenda, I know you're there. Pick up the damned phone. I *really* need to talk to you."

I hesitated. My hand hovered over the receiver like it was a hot potato.

"Brenda, please."

I gave in and answered. "Does this mean you're not mad at me anymore?" I asked.

"Of course I'm still mad at you," said Naomi, "but I've got a big problem. I think my nose is infected."

"I guess that means you went through with the piercing,'' I said. No matter how hard I tried, I couldn't visualize Naomi with a gold hoop through her nose.

''It may have been a mistake,'' she said. ''It doesn't feel very good and it looks weird.''

''Isn't the purpose of getting your nose pierced to look weird?'' I asked.

''No, I mean my nose looks *really* weird. It's all red and puffy. Do you think it's infected?''

''Sorry, Naomi, I'm hardly an expert on infected noses. Where'd you get it pierced?''

''This guy, Norbert's friend, did it. He said it's *probably* okay and to wait a few days and see what happens.''

''Probably? He said *probably*?''

''My reaction exactly,'' said Naomi. ''You better believe I gave him a piece of my mind.''

''What did he say?''

''Nothing. He hung up on me.''

''You'd better go to a doctor, to be on the safe side.''

''I guess so.''

''Aside from your nose, how's everything else?''

Naomi sighed. ''Status quo, I guess. Business is business, Fred is marrying that whore, Mommy and Daddy are back in Florida. Aunt Babette is still pissed at all of us. Norbert has the flu and he's grouchy as all getout. 'Naomi feed me, Naomi cover me up, Naomi, Naomi, Naomi.' I swear I could wring his skinny little neck. He doesn't give a goddamn about my nose.''

26

It's no wonder I woke up in a rotten mood. Not only did I have to go back to La Reverie, the scene of my recent humiliation, but I had to go there with a lecherous murderer. Dinner wasn't until eight, so I had the entire day to worry myself into a tizzy. I figured Lemmy's foolproof plan would work, if not Plan A with Lisa Markham, then Plan B with Chuck, but still I was a little queasy. It could have just been those jalapeño cookies.

To distract myself I took Jackhammer over to Midnight Millinery and worked on my spring line. The millinery part of my life was back on track. Spring was really taking form. I deconstructed my prototype and used it to draft a paper pattern. Then I made a hat from the pattern. It came out nicely, so I made a permanent cardboard pattern from the paper pattern.

Even as I concentrated on the hats, ugly thoughts from deep in the back of my brain percolated to the forefront of my consciousness. I worried about all the possible things that could go wrong to screw up both Plan A and Plan B.

I called Chuck for reassurance. Too proud to let on that I was uneasy, I dreamed up a technical question for him. "Chuck," I asked, "how much memory do I have in my computer?"

"You mean the computer I set up that you've never once turned on?"

He didn't have to be so sarcastic. "Yes, Chuck, that computer. I was just thinking how I might like to use it, you know, to keep track of suppliers or customers or something."

"Okay, Brenda. Whatever you say. Your computer's got twenty-four megs, far more memory than you'll ever need. Now, will you please stop worrying, I'll be at La Reverie tonight. If Lisa Markham doesn't take care of the situation, I will."

I should have known I couldn't fool Chuck. He knew me too well.

I worked until noon, then called Dweena to make sure she'd be at the fake investor meeting. "Wouldn't miss it for the world," she said.

I hated getting ready to go. What a stupid turn of events. I figured something had to be dreadfully wrong with my life if the only way I could go to La Reverie was either as a stand-in for Naomi or as bait for a con man murderer. If this had been a real date, getting dressed would have been a pleasure. However, it was anything but a real date and getting dressed was downright depressing.

I got out a small satin clutch purse, threw in lipstick, several quarters for phone calls, a ten-dollar bill for cab fare home, a fifty-dollar bill in case of an emergency, a credit card in case of a bigger emergency, a miniature canister of pepper spray disguised to look like perfume for an even bigger emergency, and a hatpin in case I needed to jab it into Paterson's eyeballs.

I put on a super slinky off-the-shoulder black velvet dress that was appropriately elegant and seductive, and a dramatic black satin cocktail hat with a big velvet flower on the side. Tiny rhinestones scattered over the flower would catch the candlelight. I searched the bottom of my sock drawer and dredged up a pair of elbow-length red kid gloves. Little by little I eased them on. Then I smoothed my dress and took a look in the mirror. I'd never looked better or felt lousier. What a tragic waste of a fabulous ensemble.

It took some going to force myself out the door. I thought of all the things that could go wrong. I fought the urge to call Chuck again. Finally, I put on my coat, stepped out into the hallway, and locked the door. The elevator took forever to come, an eternity for its doors to open and an eternity and a half to get me down to the lobby. Once there, I took a deep breath and marched straight out the front door, without even a nod to Ralph the doorman, and into more snow.

New-fallen snow had erased the black-tinged slop and smoothed over the hard edges of the city. An ambulance zoomed along in a scooped-out rut down the middle of Bleecker Street, its wail muffled. I passed by Johnny's building and looked up; still no light in his window. I had a new awful thought to add to my pile of other awful thoughts: What if Johnny showed up at La Reverie with another guest starlet?

I got to La Reverie early. I didn't want to wait in the bar again, so I hung out in a recessed doorway across the street until Paterson arrived. Right on time, he slid around the corner in an expensive champagne-colored sedan. In one swift maneuver, he beat out a less combative driver to a parking place only two doors from the restaurant. I watched as he locked up his car, checked his watch, and strutted inside. A couple of minutes later I followed.

Last time, I never got past La Reverie's bar. This time, I was ushered through it and down the long dramatic curved staircase to the main dining room. I was engulfed in peachness. Everything that could possibly be peach, was peach—enameled peach walls, vaulted peach ceilings, peach light sconces, tall slender peach candles, peach table linens, paper-thin peach china, fresh peach-colored gladiolus. The wait staff was outfitted in starched peach oxford shirts tucked into high-waisted black trousers. Of course, all the diners wore black. This was, after all, downtown Manhattan.

"You look luscious," said Paterson. He stood up and leered as I approached the table. "Lovely, a vision."

If he'd laid it on any thicker I would have puked on the peach rug. "Thank you," I said.

As soon as I was seated a team of waiters surrounded the table. One brought menus, one announced specials, one asked for drink orders, one splashed crystal-clear water into faceted goblets, and one wanted to discuss the wine list in great detail. "No thanks, nothing for me," I said.

"Are you sure?" asked Paterson.

"Yes." You're not going to get me drunk, you slime mold, I thought.

He ordered a martini.

To avoid conversation I studied the gigantic peach-colored menu, which had surprisingly few listings, all elaborately hand-lettered and virtually impossible to read in candlelight.

"They do up a fine steak here," said Paterson.

"Hmm," I said, nodding my head. I tended not to make a big deal of not eating meat. I closed the menu. "The linguini in creamy morel sauce sounds good."

"Then you shall have it."

The waiter came back and talked us into appetizers, a salad of baby greens for me, a liver pâté for him. Then, before I could protest, Paterson ordered an extravagantly priced French wine.

"You'll love it," he said.

"I'm sure I will," I said.

The waiter left. Paterson leaned forward, gave me a piercing stare, and said, "Let's dispense with the business right up front. Did you set up that meeting for me?"

"How does tomorrow around sevenish sound?" I asked.

He smirked. "I like my women efficient."

Paterson wrote the Central Park West address down in a small gilt-edged leather book, which he then tucked back in his jacket. "Fine neighborhood," he said. "Now that we've got business out of the way, we can enjoy the rest of our evening together. I see you're wearing another lovely hat,'' he said.

That made two ''lovelys'' in one evening. I never trusted that word or the people who used it. ''Thank you,'' I said, trying to sound as positively lovely as possible.

A waiter returned with Paterson's martini, another dropped off a basket of steaming hot bread, and yet another brought our entrées. Paterson busied himself with eating and drinking and bragging about his cars and boats, properties and conquests. All I had to do was nibble, nod, smile occasionally, and, of course, worry about why Lisa hadn't shown up yet.

It was way past time for Plan A to begin. Lisa should already have come crashing down the stairs. Somewhat anxious, I glanced around the room. No Lisa anywhere, but I saw two guys hand over huge diamond rings to their girlfriends. Naomi was right about the place. It was highly conducive to proposals. It drove me crazy to know that Johnny had been here with someone else.

Where was Lisa? For that matter, where was Chuck? I didn't have a good view of the bar. I hoped he was up there ready to initiate Plan B.

The waiter came by, decrumbed our table, and gave us the rundown of dessert specials.

We both ordered a white chocolate mousse. Paterson got an after-dinner brandy.

Dessert was supposed to have been Chuck's signal to do something. Dessert came, still no Chuck. I took tiny bites. Paterson slurped up his mousse and ordered another brandy. ''You sure you don't want an after-dinner drink?'' he asked. To stall, I said yes. However, I could only drag things out so long. By the time the waiter brought my second after-dinner drink, I faced the fact that I was on my own. Scrap Plans A and B. I had to come up with Plan C.

I interrupted Paterson's bragging and excused myself. On my way to the ladies' room, I walked through the bar. Definitely no Chuck. This wasn't like him at all. I used one of my emergency quarters to call him and got his machine. "Condition red," I said. "Help."

I sat down on a bench and put on more lipstick. How was I going to get myself out of this mess? Maybe if I got drunk as a skunk, danced on the table, made a fool of myself, threw up, and passed out, Paterson would get as repulsed by me as I was by him.

On the way back to the table, I passed through the bar again on the slim chance Chuck would be there. He wasn't. The piano player was griping to the bartender that nobody could hear his songs over the squealing car alarm outside. "Son of a bitching alarms should be outlawed," he huffed. "No alarm ever stopped a car thief anyway."

"Yeah, well," said the bartender. "If you really wanted quiet, you wouldn't be in New York."

That gave me an idea how to dump Paterson graciously. I rushed back to the ladies' room and called Dweena. Fortunately she was home.

"I'm in trouble. Think you can make Paterson's car disappear?"

"It would be my pleasure," she said.

I gave her the particulars.

"Give me twenty minutes and that bastard's vehicle will be history."

I returned to the table feeling lighthearted and confident. For the next half hour I pulled out all the stops. I ordered another drink. I let Paterson paw at me. I flirted. I hinted. I even teased my toe up and down his leg. Then, as we walked out of the restaurant, I let him hold me close. When we got to the street, he saw the empty space where he'd left his car and freaked out. "My car, somebody stole my goddamned car."

I called Dweena as soon as I got home. "You should have seen the look on Paterson's face when I said I'd be happy to go to the police station with him."

Dweena laughed. "That's the problem with being a dead

crook with an assumed identity. Somebody rips off your car and you can hardly go crying to the local gendarmes. How'd he weasel his way out?''

''He told me the police station was no place to take a lovely lady such as myself and put me in a cab. I thanked him for a lovely evening and promised that we'd get together some other time *after* the investor meeting.''

''Good going, Brenda.''

''Thank you, Dweena. You saved me from—''

''I know, I know, from a fate worse than death. You're welcome, but it was nothing.''

Much later that night Chuck called. He sounded frantic. ''Are you all right?''

''No thanks to you,'' I said. ''Where the hell was Lisa? Where the hell were you?''

''Thank god you're okay. I couldn't call Lisa. I couldn't get to the restaurant. Brenda, you won't believe what happened.''

''Try me.''

''I got busted.''

''Busted? Did the cops find Lemmy?''

''No, no, nothing like that. I was actually more like detained than busted. It started when I went out to pick up a pepperoni and mushroom pizza, with pepperoni on half and—''

''Get to the point,'' I said.

''When I got back, Fifth Street was in turmoil. You know the squatters across the street? How once or twice a year the city boots them out? Well, the city issued another ultimatum and sent the cops in to enforce it. The squatters fought back. They poured paint off the rooftops and threw M-80s and bottle rockets at the cops. Man, it was like a war. I got picked up in the confusion. I was afraid to give the cops my address because if they checked it out they might see Lemmy. I'd still be there except one of the cops recognized me from the time I installed a multi-gigabyte hard drive in his girlfriend's computer. He got me released, no questions asked."

"Lemmy must have been terrified."

"Lemmy didn't know a thing about it. He was upstairs at an Urban Dog Talk rehearsal the whole time."

27

The next morning I bolted out of bed with a great idea. I called Chuck to see if it was possible. I got his machine. "Wake up, Chuck. You owe me big."

He picked up. "You know, Brenda, on one hand you're right. I screwed up last night and I owe you big. On the other hand, I'm looking at this chrome dome blob of humanity snoring in my beanbag chair and I say to myself: 'Chuck, that over there, that's all Brenda's fault.' "

"That's why I called," I said. "I've got this idea. If it works, Lemmy will be home by tonight."

"Keep talking," said Chuck.

"I should have thought of it last night at dinner."

"Thought of what?"

"Fingerprints. Paterson's fingerprints were all over the place. I was so worried about getting away from him and so caught up in his general loathsomeness that it didn't occur to me until five minutes ago that fingerprints would prove who he is. I could have swiped a wineglass and proved Paterson was really LeHalle."

"That would depend," said Chuck, "on if his prints were on file."

"He must have had them taken to get a security clearance for his Wall Street job. Once he was a known criminal, wouldn't those records get turned over to the police?"

''Probably,'' said Chuck.

''I'll check with Dweena later, but for now, let's just assume his prints are on file. If I bring some nice smooth glasses for the fake investor meeting, can't we do something?''

''Sure,'' said Chuck. ''I can lift 'em, scan 'em, and modem 'em to your detective friends.''

''That'll get Turner and McKinley to sit up and take notice.''

A quick call to Dweena confirmed it. ''Every employee in the firm had been fingerprinted,'' she said. ''After the trouble, all that junk went to the authorities.''

I took Jackhammer for a walk and picked up everything we needed except champagne flutes. Those I borrowed from Elizabeth. Then I zipped uptown to meet Irene Finneluk at the Central Park West apartment. She and her friend had done a magnificent job furnishing the entry hall and main room.

They'd hung a six-foot-high gold-framed mirror in the entry. A crystal bowl and vase of fresh roses sat on a delicate table in front of the mirror. Off to the side was an umbrella stand complete with two bamboo-handled umbrellas. They'd done up the main room with plush chairs, Oriental rugs, oil paintings, and artful arrangements of collectible doodads. It looked like a picture from a home design magazine.

''It's perfect,'' I said. ''How can I thank you?''

Irene handed me a videotape. ''Here's the dupe of my strip tape. Give it to Johnny.''

''I'll make sure he gets it.'' I dropped off the champagne flutes, plates, a bottle of Dom Perignon and a box of selected hors d'oeuvres from a nearby specialty food shop.

''See you at the investor meeting,'' said Irene.

I needed to talk to Detective Turner again. I took Jackhammer with me to the precinct to break the ice. With his help, I charmed my way past the main desk, sneaked up to the second floor, and surprised Detective Turner in his cubicle. He was on the phone. When he saw me he made a face and motioned for me to sit. I rolled an office chair over and listened in on the last part of his conversation.

"Right, right, got that," he said. He scribbled something on a pad of paper. "Unh-huh, okay." He slammed down the receiver, turned to me, and sighed. "What is it now, Ms. Midnight? I thought I made it clear. Detective McKinley and I are not going to your little party this evening."

Jackhammer jumped up against Turner's leg and wagged his tail.

Turner reached down and scratched Jackhammer on the head. "He's not going to pee, is he?"

"He's very well trained."

"Well, trained to what—to pee or not to pee? That is the question." Turner slapped his desk and laughed at his own joke.

I rolled my eyes and managed a weak smile before going on. "As it turns out, we don't need you and Detective McKinley at the gathering tonight. In fact, it's probably better that you stay here where you have access to your fingerprint data. I've got this friend, Chuck, he's like this computer and electronics genius. He's figured out a way to get LeHalle's fingerprints and modem them to you."

"Your friend Chuck's gonna do what?"

"Modem, you know, like when one computer calls another computer."

Turner groaned. "I know what a modem is, Ms. Midnight. Go back to the part you mentioned about the fingerprints."

"Chuck's gonna lift the fingerprints and—"

Turner buried his face in his hands. "You people watch too much TV. It may come as a surprise to you, but life is not one long *Tod Trueman* episode. Regular civilians don't just go 'lift' fingerprints. It's not easy. It takes training. There's a hell of a lot more to it than tape and black powder."

"You don't know my friend Chuck," I said. "If Chuck

Riley says he can get a fingerprint, Chuck Riley can get a fingerprint. Once he gets it, he'll scan it into his computer and modem it to you. So he needs the number of your modem."

"All right, all right. I don't know what good it's gonna do you, but here." Turner wrote the number on a piece of paper and handed it to me. "Don't let this number get out. All we need is a buncha flaky citizens clogging up the computers sending us crap."

"I'll keep it to myself," I said. I folded the piece of paper and put it in my purse. "Thanks, Detective. Now, promise that you and Detective McKinley will check out the prints the minute you get them."

Turner pursed his lips and glared at me. "All right, Ms. Midnight, but after this, no more favors."

"Thank you, Detective Turner. You won't be sorry." I gave him the Central Park West address and the number for Irene Finneluk's cellular phone. "Call and let me know when you're on your way. I'll make sure LeHalle stays in the apartment."

While Turner and I had been talking, Jackhammer busied himself nosing around, searching for edibles. I called him over and gathered my things to leave.

Turner leaned back in his chair and folded his hands across his admirably flat stomach. "Hold on there a minute, Ms. Midnight. When are you gonna tell me the whereabouts of your ex-boyfriend, or better yet, the whereabouts of Lemon B. Crenshaw?"

"I already told you," I said, "I don't know where Johnny is. I don't know where Lemmy is. I wish I knew, but I don't."

"Yeah, yeah, yeah," said Turner, waving his hand in front of his face. "I hope you know that you're walking pretty damn close to the edge, Ms. Midnight. We've got penalties for obstruction, aiding and abetting, all kinds of stuff. You could be in a shitload of trouble."

"Thanks for the warning," I said on my way out.

So that was it. The investor meeting was on.

* * *

At six I went back to the Central Park West apartment. Irene Finneluk met me at the door. She was turned out elegantly in beige couture designer slacks and a matching silk sweater. She'd softened her usual look with subtle makeup and styled her chin-length blond hair in a gentle pageboy. She looked pretty and wealthy and understated and like she belonged there, not at all like a stripper or a real estate broker.

Chuck arrived soon after I did. He set up his equipment in a small room off the kitchen. I had a small panic attack when I saw him hooking up the modem. "What if the phone service has already been cut?" I asked.

"It's on," he said, "but even if it weren't, I could have hooked into something. I know my way around wires."

Dweena got there decked out in a matronly dark green two-piece outfit with a skirt that ended unflatteringly at midcalf, humongous tortoiseshell glasses above which she'd penciled skinny arched eyebrows. LeHalle/Paterson would never recognize her as his former boss Edward. Her wig was uncharacteristically conservative, mousy brown with a fringe of bangs. I thought maybe it was her real hair and made the mistake of asking. Offended, she assured me it was not.

Elizabeth and Winfield arrived at the same time. She looked every bit the wealthy widow in a blue and green print silk dress. Winfield, of course, always dressed in fine haberdashery. For the occasion he'd pulled his dreadlocks back off his face and stuck a red carnation in his lapel.

I introduced everyone to Irene. We milled around, admired the view, and chatted. At precisely seven o'clock the doorman rang and announced that Mr. Trent Paterson was on his way up. A wave of tension swept over the room. The filthy rich investors had a case of opening-night jitters.

"The show's about to begin," I said.

Chuck went to man his computer; the others took their places.

I answered the door. Paterson flashed a smarmy smile

and kissed me on the cheek. "Sorry about last night," he said.

"Think nothing of it," I said. "Did you get your car back?"

"No."

I introduced him to Irene first, since it was supposedly her apartment. "Lovely apartment," he said, taking her hand.

"Why, thank you, Mr. Paterson. We're so glad you agreed to meet with our little group," said Irene.

I got the rest of the introductions over quickly and showed Paterson to the chair I had picked out for him. Elizabeth and I sat on a couch directly opposite, Irene on a chair to his left, Winfield next to her, and Dweena next to Winfield.

When everyone was situated, I handed Winfield the champagne, excused myself, and went to the kitchen. I waited until I heard the cork pop and then came out with a tray of hors d'oeuvres just as Winfield was pouring champagne into Paterson's glass. When he finished pouring, he turned to everyone and said, "May I suggest a toast to new and profitable friendships."

Using silver tongs, I distributed hors d'oeuvres, two for each investor placed on tiny plates. When I got to Paterson I tripped. I ended up in his lap, a stuffed mushroom flew into his champagne flute.

"Oh, I'm so clumsy," I said, giggling. "Here, let me take your glass. I'll get you a clean one."

"There's nothing like throwing yourself at a man, now, is there?" teased Dweena.

I carried the glass to the kitchen, careful to touch only the very bottom.

Chuck was waiting for me. He made an okay sign with his thumb and forefinger, took the glass, and disappeared into his computer room. If all went as planned, he'd get the prints taken, scanned, and modemed in less than half an hour. I grabbed another champagne flute and returned to the meeting in time to hear Paterson begin his spiel.

"I take it," he said, "you're all here today because you want to see your money work for you."

The fake investors nodded their heads with great enthusiasm.

"From what I hear, you're all disappointed with conventional investment programs?"

More nodding.

"If interest rates don't pick up soon," said Dweena, "I'll have to sell my summer place. Or get a job."

Elizabeth laughed. "A job? Who would hire you? You've never worked a day in your life."

Irene looked around at the other investors. "For that matter, neither have any of us."

I thought maybe they were laying it on a bit thick, but Paterson ate it up. His nostrils quivered with excitement like Jackhammer's did whenever he spotted food on the street.

"I'm not sure how much Brenda told you," said Paterson, "but you must understand I can't guarantee results."

Elizabeth interrupted. "Brenda told us you doubled her friend's money in a few months."

"Well," said Paterson, smiling smugly, "to be honest with you, Brenda is not exactly right there."

Winfield let out a disgusted sigh. "Here comes the BS. I knew it was too good to be true."

"Wait," said Paterson, "and hear me out. The reason I said Brenda was not exactly right is because as of yesterday around two o'clock in the afternoon, that particular investment had tripled. You hear me? Not doubled, but tripled."

The fake filthy rich investors gasped in unison.

"That's more like it," said Dweena. "Those are the kind of numbers I like to hear."

"You can say that again," said Irene. "Please, Mr. Paterson, show me the dotted line."

"Please call me Trent. After all, we're all going to be partners."

"Not so fast," said Winfield. "I wouldn't be signing anything so quick. I need to know more about what I'm getting into, before I let go of even a measly half a million."

The mention of Winfield's measly half a million set Paterson's nostrils aquivering again.

"And I," said Elizabeth in her haughtiest voice, "would like to know a wee bit more about Mr. Paterson before entrusting him with my dear beloved dead husband's fortune."

If Paterson was offended, he didn't show it. He looked Winfield straight in the eye, then Elizabeth. "I don't blame either of you. To tell you the truth, I wouldn't expect anything less of shrewd investors like yourselves. That's why I brought these along." He reached into his briefcase, took out several presentation folders, and handed them out. Before he could explain them, Irene's cellular phone rang.

"Hello," she said. She listened for a moment, then held out the receiver to me. "It's a Mr. Turner for you. He says he and Mr. McKinley can make it to the meeting after all."

"Oh, goody," I said, taking the phone.

For a nerve-wracking fifteen minutes we went on with the show. We looked over Paterson's presentation, nodded seriously, and mumbled among ourselves. The graphs and bar charts and pie charts showed how our money would grow in leaps and bounds. Of course, it was complete hogwash. Quasi-legal instruments, gray area—what a crock. Paterson intended to take our money and run.

Before anybody signed on the dotted line, Detectives Turner and McKinley rode in and saved the day. They dressed better than most cops. For that matter, they dressed better than most guys. To me, they looked exactly like filthy rich potential investors. But when Trent Paterson, aka Brink LeHalle, saw them standing in the entryway, his expression changed from cocky to fearful in a nanosecond. Crooks have an uncanny ability to ID cops no matter what they've got on.

Turner and McKinley wasted no time. They marched over to Paterson. McKinley snapped the handcuffs on.

"Brink LeHalle," he said, "you're under arrest. You have the right—"

Seething, Paterson said, "My name is Trent Paterson."

"Your mouth might be saying Trent Paterson, but your fingerprints are saying Brink LeHalle," said McKinley.

"You'll be sorry," said Paterson. "I have friends in high places."

Dweena couldn't restrain herself any longer. She took off her glasses, got eyeball to eyeball with the LeHalle, and said, "I'll just bet you do, Brinky Brink."

Paterson did a double take. "Edward?"

As Turner and McKinley led him away, Paterson inveighed, "You're making a big mistake."

"The only mistake," I said, "is the one you made when you murdered Buddy Needleson."

"Murder?" he said with a look of utter befuddlement.

"That's right, murder."

"Don't worry, Ms. Midnight," said Turner. "We'll get it out of him."

28

The fake investors gathered around the window and watched Turner and McKinley lead Brink LeHalle, aka Trent Paterson, across Central Park West. LeHalle's mouth was flapping a mile a minute; his handcuffs gleamed in the glow of a street lamp. The whole drama played against the backdrop of the snow-covered park. The detectives stuffed the bad guy into their car and pulled away.

"Hope he gets the hot chair," said Dweena.

"Not likely," said Winfield.

"I've got Lemmy on the phone," said Chuck. "He's happy as a pig in mud. He wants to meet us all for a celebration. His treat."

"Not so fast," said Winfield. He took the phone from Chuck and spoke into it. "Now, look, Lemmy, from a legal point of view, you've got to lay low until the dust clears. All we gave the authorities was the fact that this Paterson character is really Brink LeHalle. Ergo, LeHalle didn't die in a boating accident. Unfortunately, that doesn't prove LeHalle *is* a murderer. Therefore, it doesn't prove you are *not* a murderer. It's not safe for you to come out of hiding yet."

Much as I hated to admit it, Winfield was right. I was glad I couldn't hear Lemmy's end of the conversation.

Winfield continued, "I'm sorry, but as your legal counsel

I must advise you to stay put.'' He hung up the phone.

''What's this mean?'' asked Chuck.

''It means you've still got a roommate,'' I said.

Elizabeth spoke up. ''Lemmy may be stuck at Chuck's, but I think the rest of us should go celebrate.''

Chuck agreed. ''I'd just as soon stay away from Lemmy for a while.''

Dweena didn't have to be at work for hours. Irene Finneluk said she was game for anything. Brewster Winfield went along because it extended his billable time. I was the only one who didn't want to go. It didn't seem right without Lemmy. Elizabeth told me, ''Lemmy would understand.''

''Bullshit,'' I said, but I went along anyway.

We tramped through to the snow to a place Irene knew of near Lincoln Center. Winfield sprung for the first round of drinks. While I moped, the fake filthy rich investors got drunk and patted themselves on their backs.

''The test of a good actor,'' said Winfield, raising his glass high, ''is that you can't tell that they're acting.''

''How did you like my bit about my summer home?'' asked Dweena.

''Not bad,'' said Elizabeth, ''but my favorite was the way Brew played devil's advocate.''

The lawyer beamed. ''Thanks, Liz.''

Brew? Liz?

Dweena had changed into a red wig done up in banana curls and doffed the bottom portion of her matronly outfit. She asked Chuck how her club could get a web page up on the Internet. He launched into a long-winded technical explanation. Elizabeth joined in and the three of them came up with this idea to start their own Internet service. Winfield and Irene got into a discussion, which they seemed to find fascinating, about an obscure real estate law. It always amazed me that people could feel passionately about such things.

To use Lemmy's words, I was bored as a gourd.

The celebrants polished off another round of drinks.

Winfield walked Irene home. The rest of us shared a cab downtown.

We got stuck in an inexplicable late-night gridlock by the Lincoln Tunnel, so by the time I got home it was after eleven. Jackhammer begged to go out. I told him it was too late, the weather was rotten, and the streets would be deserted and dangerous. My protests had no effect on him. He jumped up and down in front of the door and made a trilling noise deep down in his throat that sounded like Urban Dog Talk's synthesizer. "All right," I said. I bundled up, grabbed my hatpin for protection, and snapped on his leash.

On my way out, Ralph, the doorman with the seemingly perpetual shift, told me I was nuts. "It's freezing cold out there. Only weirdos and creeps'll be out now."

"I know," I said, "but he has to go."

"Don't say I didn't warn you." He turned his attention back to the tiny television he wasn't supposed to have at work.

Once we got outdoors it didn't seem so bad. There was no wind, so the cold didn't cut through us. The Chinese restaurant across the street was still open and filled with people. Emboldened by that and the fact that I'd seen a couple of other dogwalkers, I let Jackhammer pull me west to the edge of the city. While he frolicked on a pile of industrial garbage bags, I stared across the frozen Hudson River at New Jersey. I wondered what Johnny was doing. I wondered how long it would take Turner and McKinley to get the truth out of Brink LeHalle. I stood there far too long, wondering about a lot of things. The next thing I knew, Jackhammer was pawing at my leg. I looked down and the little guy was shivering. He vibrated from head to tail stub. I picked him up, tucked him under my coat, and started back.

By then, the streets really were deserted. The electric buzz that constantly pulsed through New York wasn't there. It could have been another time, another place. But it wasn't, so I took my hatpin out of my pocket, just in case, and walked as fast as possible over the ice, snow, and slop.

When the door of my building was in sight, I relaxed and watched my sigh of relief turn to white smoke in the air. Before it had fully dissipated, I got grabbed from behind.

I've been in New York long enough to know what was happening. It was scarier than the time I'd had a gun pointed at me. It was scarier than the time someone had pointed a cigarette lighter at me that I thought was a gun. It was scarier than the time a loser in a filthy nylon ski parka threatened me with a crudely sharpened screwdriver. It was scarier because I couldn't see my assailant, couldn't look him in the eye, couldn't see what kind of maniac I was dealing with.

Elaborate scenarios flashed before me in gory bloody detail. I held on tight to Jackhammer, who, deep inside my coat, seemed oblivious to the danger. My attacker's grip relaxed for a second. Okay, Brenda, I thought, here's your chance. I grabbed the hatpin with my free hand, summoned up all my strength and courage, spun around, and confronted my attacker.

"Johnny!"

My fear evaporated and into the vacuum surged a confusing mess of emotions. There were a million things I wanted to say to Johnny. I wanted to thank him for not being a mugger. I wanted to ask who he was with at La Reverie. I wanted to ask why he hadn't returned my calls and where he had been. I wanted to tell him I was never going to speak to him again. What finally came out of my mouth was: "I could use a drink. How about you?"

Ralph nodded to Johnny as we passed through the lobby. "I told you she was out there," he said. "Much too late to be walking all alone with that pipsqueak dog, if you ask me."

The myth of New York is that everyone is anonymous, lost in the mean streets, the shuffle and hustle-bustle. In reality New York has got seven million busybodies, all with my best interests in mind.

When Johnny and I got upstairs, I opened a bottle of Chateauneuf du Pape. We sat down on the couch, close but not touching. "I guess you're wondering why I haven't return your calls," he said.

"I figured you were busy, what with filming and all, not to mention your busy social life." I spat out those last three words like they made a bad taste in my mouth.

"We haven't been filming. Stumpford's flu turned into pneumonia. He went back to the coast."

"You could have at least told Lemmy. He's worried sick. He told me Stumpford was extremely important for the show."

"What Lemmy doesn't understand is that the *Tod Trueman* show is just as important for Stumpford as Stumpford is for the show. Everybody thinks Stumpford retired. Truth is he made colossal blunders. They sent him out to pasture. So, Lemmy doesn't have to worry. Stumpford will be back. Soon Lemmy won't have to worry about those bogus murder charges either. I've been doing a little investigating on my own, undercover. I'm sorry, Brenda. I should have told you."

"Undercover?" He didn't look too undercover at La Reverie.

"Yeah, like in that *Tod* episode where Tod pretends to be a junkie. Remember?"

"I remember. It's not one of the better *Tod*s."

"Maybe not. I thought it was pretty good. Anyway, it's where I got the idea. I've been visiting all the amateur strip clubs, talking up people. I pretended to be a new impresario in town from Chicago. Nobody had the foggiest idea who I was."

I didn't have the heart to tell him that everybody who was anybody on the New York night scene knew that Johnny Verlane, TV's own Tod Trueman, had been hanging out in the clubs. Nor did I have the heart to tell him that while he was gallivanting around making a fool of himself, I had solved the murder. "So, tell me, Johnny, what did you find out?"

He leaned back and looked me in the eyes. "Let me tell you, Brenda, Johnny Verlane has seen the seedy underbelly of things. It ain't pretty. I've met people who'd rub you out just for looking at them cross-eyed. And those people saw Buddy Needleson as competition. You know how Jackhammer marks his territory?"

"Sure, he lifts his leg."

"Buddy Needleson's fatal problem was that he didn't sniff around enough before opening up his club. Some bigger guys had already lifted their legs on that turf. When the goons confronted him, he played tough guy, a stupid move for a feather salesman. The mob had no choice but to whack him."

Johnny had been playacting too long. "That's absurd, Johnny. Buddy Needleson wasn't 'rubbed out,' he wasn't 'whacked,' he was bopped over the head with a baseball bat. The mob doesn't bop people. The mob would have used a gun and then cut off his tongue or something."

"Brenda, Brenda, Brenda. Don't you know anything? The mob isn't what it used to be, not by a long shot."

Johnny tried to convince me that the mob was now made up of a bunch of young drug-addled crazies who no longer played by any rules. "They're quite capable of a messy hit."

"Johnny, you're on the wrong track."

I told him what I'd learned in the last few days and how I'd captured the killer. As usual Johnny was stubborn and pigheaded. He stuck with his theory. "You've got no proof, Brenda. It's a big step to go from investment scams to murder."

It was pointless to argue. "I'm going to bed."

Johnny said it was too late to walk home. He spent the night on my floor, turned on his side like a jackknifed eighteen-wheeler, with Jackhammer curled up in the crook of his knee.

I lay in bed, silently fuming. He could have at least told

me I'd done a good job with LeHalle. It wasn't every day I turned over a crook to the cops. He was too wrapped up in his own stupid theory and so-called undercover activities to grasp the enormity of what I'd done, single-handedly, while he was running around at strip clubs and taking guest starlets to La Reverie. I asked him about that too, but he didn't answer. I couldn't tell if he was asleep or ignoring me. I was afraid to find out.

29

I woke up to the smell of freshly made coffee. Johnny stood by my window, sipping from a steaming mug, looking at me with a vaguely sad expression.

I pulled the covers over my head. "Go away." Jackhammer jumped up on the bed and pushed at the covers with his nose.

"I've got a pan of oatmeal on the stove," Johnny said. "I'll bet anything you haven't been eating properly."

"I've been eating just fine, thank you." It was the perfect opportunity to bring up the subject of La Reverie—either his dinner there with the guest starlet or my dinner with a murdering con man—but I let the moment slip by.

Johnny tossed my white terrycloth robe on the bed. "Here, put this on. Your oatmeal will be ready in a couple of minutes."

Johnny had set the table with bright red place mats and napkins I'd tucked away and forgotten. He'd folded the napkins into perfect triangles. Sometimes Johnny displayed a domestic side that was truly frightening. He ducked back into the kitchen for a minute and came out carrying bowls of oatmeal.

"I couldn't find your raisins," he said.

"That's because I don't have any. I hate raisins."

"I thought you liked raisins in your oatmeal."

"Well, I don't." I bit my tongue to keep from accusing him of confusing me with somebody else, some guest starlet who liked raisins in her oatmeal.

"In that case," said Johnny, "I've fixed the oatmeal exactly the way you like it—plain."

"Thank you." With or without raisins I wasn't all that crazy about oatmeal. The only reason I kept it around was in case I had the urge to make oatmeal cookies.

We chewed in silence. To avoid Johnny's eyes, I looked out the window and studied a rusted-out fire escape that ran down the building next door. Before the silence became significant, Johnny put down his spoon and said, "Did you think any more about what I told you last night?"

"About how you think the mob killed Buddy Needleson?"

"Yeah."

"Didn't give it a moment's thought." I wasn't going to either. "You know," I said, "Turner and McKinley have been looking for you."

"I'm not surprised," said Johnny. "They made the connection between me and Lemmy, right?"

"Right."

"I'll drop by to see them today to explain."

"Fine, and when you do, they'll tell you that Brink LeHalle has confessed to the murder of Buddy Needleson."

"You don't have to get so huffy about it," he said.

"I'm not huffy; I'm right."

He didn't say anything more. Neither did I. We finished our oatmeal and did the dishes. Johnny washed; I dried. Then he headed for the door. "Let me know when you want to tell me what's bugging you," he said on his way out.

What bugged me was that I didn't know what he'd been doing or who he'd been doing it with. What bugged me even more was that it was none of my business. After all, we were just friends.

* * *

As far as the Lemmy problem went, there was nothing left to do except sit tight and wait until LeHalle confessed. At last I could work on my spring line without feeling guilty that I should be doing something else. The line was pretty much designed. The next step in the process was sales. I couldn't retail enough hats out of Midnight Millinery to survive, so I sometimes wholesaled part of the line to a few select stores. This late in the season it was going to be tough.

"You've got to be kidding," said the first buyer I called, a woman who'd bought lots of hats from me in the past. "Spring? Now?"

"I just thought—" She'd already disconnected.

The second buyer I called said, "This is some kind of a joke, right?" before she slammed down the receiver.

It was pretty much the same story everywhere. Even my close personal friend Margo, who owned a classy Soho boutique, let me down. "If I sold summer hats I'd take your spring line and say it was summer, but all my customers flee this steamy smelly hellhole in the summer, so I'm already thinking forward to fall. Call me in July."

I should have known better. I did know better. Designers are allowed to be late and make dramatic entrances. They can be late for dinner, the hairdresser, the doctor, the trainer at the gym. Designers can show up when everyone else is leaving the party. But what designers can't do—and no designer would ever dream of doing—is be late for a season. Here I was trying to peddle spring at the tail end of winter. The second buyer was right, I must have been joking. All I could do was fill Midnight Millinery's windows with spring hats and hope I'd get enough walk-in sales to keep my head above water. It meant I would have to keep the store open regular hours.

When the phone rang I hoped it was one of the buyers calling back with a change of heart. "Midnight Millinery, Brenda Midnight speaking," I said in my most professional voice.

"So," said Naomi, "I go to this doctor, this fancysmancy Park Avenue skin doctor, the same one Aunt Babette uses to get her wrinkles puffed up. I mean the guy is very very la-di-da, if you know what I mean. In the waiting room he's got every foreign *Vogue* imaginable, fresh flowers, and real leather chairs. So the doc, he gives me this junk to rub on my nose, smells like I don't know what. He tells me the swelling should go down in a week or so and that I'm lucky I wasn't permanently disfigured. Can you believe it? Aunt Babette says I should sue Norbert's friend, the butcher. Which reminds me, as soon as the estate gets settled, Babette's moving to Connecticut. She's selling a whole bunch of her stuff. Want to go look at it with me?"

"What kind of stuff?"

"You know, furniture, household items. The poor woman needs to make a fresh start. It's rough losing a spouse like that. So, you want to go, or not?"

I remembered the solid oak table from the time I'd snooped around Buddy and Babette Needleson's apartment. I could use a table like that; my worktable had seen better days. "Maybe, if I get caught up on my work."

"Okay," said Naomi. "I'll call you before I go."

"Thanks."

I thought that was the end of the conversation, but as I lowered the receiver, Naomi's voice continued. "So, do you think I should sue?"

"The nose guy? Nah. But maybe you should let him think you might. Shake him up so he won't poke holes in anyone else's nose."

"Good one, Brenda. I like that. I could have Norbert tell him he'd heard me talking to a lawyer."

Naomi would have gone on all day and night if I'd let her, but I put my foot down, told her I absolutely had to get back to work, and hung up. I spent the rest of the day hanging my spring hats in the window. Time passed quickly. Before I knew it, my stomach was growling and the phone was ringing. It was Johnny. "Meet me at Angie's."

* * *

Johnny was at our favorite booth in the back, blowing at the foam of his dark beer. The waiter had already brought a glass of red wine for me. Johnny smiled broadly when he saw me. "Do you want the good news first or the bad?"

"Hit me with the bad stuff. I can take it."

"You're sure?"

"Positive."

"Okay. I went to see Turner and McKinley today."

I nodded.

"I hate to be the one to tell you this," said Johnny, seriously wrinkling his forehead, "but I was right. Brink LeHalle did not kill Buddy Needleson."

The waiter brought an order of fries, my grilled cheese, and a burger for Johnny. I ordered another red wine. It was going to be that kind of night.

Johnny continued, "LeHalle has an ironclad alibi for the entire two-day period surrounding Needleson's time of death."

"Yeah, and what was that?" I pounded out a giant blob of ketchup on the side of my plate.

"Emergency appendectomy. Brink LeHalle was in St. Vincent's. Of course, he was calling himself Trent Paterson."

"So, big deal," I said. "He could have faked it, sneaked out of the hospital, bopped Buddy Needleson, and then sneaked back in again. That'd be premeditated. Maybe he really will get the chair."

Johnny shook his head. "You don't fake appendicitis. Apparently this one was pretty messy. Poison had been leaking into his gut for several days, almost killed him. Turner and McKinley are satisfied your guy didn't kill Buddy Needleson. However, they're extremely happy to have nabbed him on the investment scams. They'll probably get another commendation for wrapping this one up. They send their best to you."

"Damn it to hell," I said, in lieu of some choicer words that were running through my mind. "What about Lemmy?

We're back to square one. He's your agent; I don't know what you look so damned happy about."

Johnny touched my cheek with his hand. "Now, now. Don't get so upset."

I hated it when he babied me. I knocked his hand away and glared at him.

He ignored me and went on. "I still say the mob did it. Give me a couple more nights in the clubs." He brought his thumb and forefinger together so they almost touched. "I tell you, Brenda, I'm this close to cracking the case."

When was he going to stop acting like Tod Trueman and start acting like Johnny Verlane? I washed down the last few bites of my grilled cheese with the rest of my wine and made a move to put my coat on.

"Don't be like that, Brenda. Face it, your theory is wrong. For a nondetective, you've done a fantastic job. Turner and McKinley said so themselves. Anyway, you can't leave before I tell you the good news."

I'd forgotten all about the good news. I shoved my coat back into the corner of the booth, put my hands on the table, and smiled. It was not a sincere or a happy smile.

"The good news is that I—we—are off the hook with Turner and McKinley for that funeral thing. I convinced them that we didn't know that Lemmy was a fugitive, that you attended out of respect for the Needlesons, and that I was your escort."

"I told Turner the exact same thing and he didn't believe me." If I sounded petulant, it was because I was. It burned me up that no matter what I said to some people, I had no credibility.

"I gave them a good reason to believe me. I told them that Lemmy wouldn't want his number one client to find out he was a fugitive."

I got home late and took Jackhammer for a short walk in front of the building. He was miffed when I dragged him back inside, and refused to get out of the elevator until I promised him a green bean. When we got inside I made good on my promise. He swallowed it whole and begged for more. I let him have three; more than that and he'd have gotten a bellyache.

I played my phone messages before going to bed. Jammed between another long-winded call from Naomi about her nose and one from Lemmy telling me he was bored as a gourd was a message from Daria Covington, the stripper I'd interviewed when I was pretending to be Brenda Miller, Tochin College researcher.

"Sorry to bother you," she said, "but I didn't know who else to call and you did leave your card. See, I sent in my tape with the signed release in that blue postpaid box just like the letter instructed. Now I can't find the letter. I want to know when it's going to be on."

I had no idea what she was talking about.

I fooled around for a while, caught up on some paperwork, then went to bed early. I drifted off thinking about Babette Needleson's oak table. It really would be nice in Midnight Millinery. I tried to visualize it to get an idea of how big it was. I remembered what was on it: a computer, a laser printer, and, off to the side, a stack of blue boxes.

Blue postpaid boxes.

I sat bolt upright in bed. Then I played Daria Covington's message again.

Seven A.M. was kind of early to call. I dialed the number anyway.

"Hrrro," said a voice.

"Daria?" I said.

"Yes. Who is this?"

"Brenda Miller, returning your call."

"Of course. Brenda Miller, the researcher from Tochin College. Thanks for getting back to me. I was afraid you'd already gone back to Iowa."

"I'm still in New York. I apologize for calling so early."

"Don't worry about it. My alarm is set to go off any minute. I called because I haven't heard anything from that production company yet. I thought you might know something about it.''

''Production company?''

''The company that wanted my commemorative strip video for the cable show. I don't remember when it's going to be on and I lost the letter. I don't want to miss it, especially after paying all that money. I found your card and since you're studying the strip clubs, I thought you might know how to contact the production company.''

''You mentioned you sent the tape in a blue box?''

''Yes, a real light blue. Powder blue, I'd call it.''

''I'm sure I have the name of the production company somewhere in my files,'' I lied. ''I'll look around and get back to you as soon as I find it.''

''If it's not too much trouble.''

''Oh, it's no trouble at all. And Daria, thank you so much.''

I made a cup of coffee, then called Irene Finneluk.

''Irene, remember when you gave me a copy of your strip video for Johnny?''

''Did he look at it yet?''

I ignored her question. ''You mentioned you had another dupe. What did you do with it?''

''I sent it along with a money order to the production company that was doing that cable show. I guess the whole thing is off now. I should probably try to get my money back.''

''How much money?''

''Three hundred, I think.''

''How'd you send the package?

''I just shoved it in the box and dropped it in a mailbox. It was postpaid.''

''Do you remember what the box looked like?''

''Yes. It was a pastel blue, like a fuzzy sweater I had in high school.''

''What was the name of the production company?''

"I don't know but I think I saved the letter. If it's important, I'll get it."

"It's important."

"Okay, hang on a minute."

In the background I heard footsteps, drawers opening and closing, then footsteps again. "I've got it," said Irene. "Lucky Liberty Productions."

"And the address?"

"There's no address printed on the stationery, but I remember the address on the box."

"You remember?"

"Of course I remember. Addresses are my business. It was down at Battery Park City. I handled an apartment in that building in the B line. I think the production company was in the C line, because I remember thinking it must have been next door to the B, which would mean it would have a nice view of the Statue of Liberty, hence the name."

"Irene, you don't happen to remember the floor, do you?"

"No, but it was pretty high."

"Thanks, Irene."

As Chuck would say: Hot dog. I'm on a roll.

30

Details distinguish a fine piece of millinery from a piece of junk. Show me a hat I've never seen and the first thing I do is turn it over to examine its guts. I look along the edges, under the lining, see what holds it together. Stitches or glue? Hand or machine? Surface decoration—feathers, baubles, and silk flowers—may distract, but it can't hide a bad hat.

The larger truth is that details matter in everything in life, not just millinery. Like the details that mattered in Buddy Needleson's murder, the details I ignored. His murder would have been solved sooner if I'd only turned the problem over and looked under the lining. I'd been misled by surface decoration. I was convinced Buddy Needleson was blackmailing somebody, if not strippers then Brink LeHalle, aka Trent Paterson. The truth was under the lining, much closer to home. Babette Needleson had killed her husband. Like most spousicides, she'd done it for a stupid reason, unpremeditated, out of anger.

Despite what the Ns thought, despite what Howard and Zorema thought, Babette Needleson had known about the strip club all along. She was far too clever to let anybody know that she knew. That way she could squeeze money out of the club for herself. She must have gone nuts when she discovered that softhearted Buddy gave the strippers commemorative videos that he could have charged for. She fixed his wagon. She found a way to get the strippers to pay by coming up with the Lucky Liberty Productions scheme. One thing I'd learned hanging out with Johnny is that everyone wants to get discovered. Babette, through Lucky Liberty, promised the strippers they'd be on cable TV. All they had to do was send in their commemorative tape, along with a hefty money order, and Lucky Liberty would take care of the rest.

The way I figured it, Buddy Needleson must have discovered Babette was exploiting the strippers. They argued, she clobbered him with the baseball bat.

Simple. Now all I had to do was prove it.

I called Naomi. "When are you and Norbert going to look at the stuff your aunt's selling?"

"Later today. Why, did you decide you want to go?"

"Yeah. I could really use a good worktable for Midnight Millinery."

I met the Ns in front of Babette's building.

"That's a funny-looking hat," said Naomi, eyeing the cloche on my head.

"Doesn't look like a Brenda Midnight," said Norbert.

"It's kind of an experiment," I said. Actually I'd thrown it together that morning, after talking to Naomi. If I was going to Babette Needleson's, I needed a hat that would change the look of my face in case her doorman had a good memory.

I needn't have worried. A different doorman was on duty. He told the Ns that Mrs. Needleson was expecting us.

In the elevator Naomi checked her red, swollen nose in the security mirror. "How's it look?"

I thought a white lie would be best. "Not bad."

"It's still a little tender," she said.

"My baby sister is imagining things," said Norbert.

"No, I'm not. Don't think your friend's off the hook just because the swelling is starting to go down."

Babette came to the door dressed in a stretchy gold lamé

jumpsuit. Her bleached blond hair showed an inch of gray and black at the root.

I hung back while the Ns and Babette air kissed each other.

"Remember my friend Brenda?" asked Naomi. "She was at the funeral."

"Of course I remember," said Babette. "You were with that handsome Tod Trueman."

She directed us to put our coats on a chair. "I'm selling almost everything, so if you see something you want, ask. Norbert, will you give me a hand in the kitchen? The shelves are so damned high and I'm scared to death of ladders."

Norbert shrugged and followed his aunt into the kitchen.

I walked around the living room, looking at the sleek glass, chrome, and leather furniture. There were large cardboard cartons all over, most already sealed. I hoped I wasn't too late. My plan was to find those blue postpaid boxes and peek inside. If my theory was right, I'd find a stripper's videotape inside each one. I just hoped Babette hadn't already packed them up.

I sat on the long leather couch. "I don't suppose this makes into a bed, does it?"

"I don't know," said Naomi. "You'd have to ask Babette."

"Later. I don't want to bother her now. I'm really more interested in a good strong worktable for Midnight Millinery."

"She's got something in the office that might work." Naomi cocked her head toward the hallway. "Come here, I'll show you."

The table was there just as I remembered, but it was bare. The computer, printer, and blue boxes were nowhere in sight. There were no cartons anywhere in the room, unless they were in the closet.

Naomi kicked a table leg. "What do you think?"

"Solid," I said. It was a great table, but I had other things on my mind. "Naomi, do you think you could find me a yardstick or something? I'm not sure there's room for this at Midnight Millinery.''

''Sure,'' said Naomi. ''I'll be right back.''

When she was gone I tiptoed over to the closet and opened the door. As I'd hoped, it was filled with cardboard cartons, and inside those were small blue boxes.

''Those aren't for sale,'' said Babette sharply, startling me. She'd popped out of nowhere. She marched into the office and snatched the box out of my hand.

''Is this software?'' I asked. ''My friend Chuck gave me a computer, and—''

''I'm not selling software.'' She threw the box back into the carton and tucked the flaps in. The look she gave me was not exactly friendly.

''Sorry, I just thought—''

''These are personal items. Not for sale.''

''Oh. How about the table? I could sure use a table like this in my shop.''

''It's solid oak,'' she said. ''You can have it for twenty-five hundred cash.''

''That's more than I wanted to spend. Solid oak, you say?'' I bent down and lined up my eyeball with the top of the table. ''Looks like a good flat surface. No warpage. I'll have to think about it.''

Babette glared at me.

Ignoring the bad vibes, I wandered back into the living room. Babette followed right on my heels.

''Does this couch pull out into a bed?'' I asked.

''Of course not,'' said Babette icily. ''That would be rather tacky, don't you think?''

Ever since I'd been in New York my beds had folded out of a couch. That is, except for the time I'd slept in a sleeping bag under the blocking table at Midnight Millinery.

The Ns poked around awhile longer. Babette never once took her eyes off me. No way was she going to let me back into the office. I pretended not to notice her stares and helped Naomi decide which lamps to buy. She finally picked three. Norbert, meanwhile, snagged a huge leather recliner.

I helped the Ns drag the recliner and lamps into the foyer. Then, as we were putting on our coats, in a fit of desperation, I had an idea—not the best in the world, maybe, but better than nothing. The idea depended on Babette being a proper hostess, which fortunately she was. As a proper hostess, she maneuvered her way through the narrow foyer to unlatch the door for her guests. I waited until she'd squeezed by the Ns, the recliner, and the three lamps. When all that stuff was between us, I said, "Just let me take one more look at that table."

I darted into the office, leaving Babette behind to negotiate her way through the obstacle course of three lamps, one recliner, one niece, and one nephew.

By the time Babette puffed into the office, I already had two of the blue boxes tucked away in my purse. She found me innocently running my palm along the top of the table. "It *is* a nice table," I said, "but I'm afraid I have to pass on it."

Babette's eyes darted around the room. "Two thousand," she said.

"That's still way out of my league."

She motioned for me to follow her out of the office. She must have known I was up to something. I was relieved when she didn't confront me.

"You getting the table?" asked Naomi.

"Not unless I win the lottery," I said.

With a lot of pushing and pulling the Ns and I got the recliner and the lamps into the elevator. On the ride down I worried that Babette had alerted the doorman and he'd stop me, but he didn't even glance up when the Ns and I hauled their booty through the lobby, out to the curb, and into a waiting cab. While Naomi and I put the lamps in the trunk, the cabby helped Norbert wedge the recliner into the backseat, leaving just enough room for Naomi if she sat sideways. Norbert got in the front seat.

I didn't care that there was no room for me. I took the

next vacant cab straight to Chuck's. He and Lemmy were surprised to see me. I always call first.

"I hope you're here to tell me the cops finally beat a confession out of LeHalle," said Lemmy.

"Afraid not," I said. "Here." I tossed one of the blue boxes to Chuck.

"What is it?" asked Chuck.

"If it's what I think it is, it's Lemmy's way out of here. It's proof that Babette Needleson killed her husband."

"What the hell are you talking about?" asked Chuck. "We just proved that Brink LeHalle, aka Trent Paterson, killed Buddy Needleson."

"Well, things have changed."

Chuck opened the box. Inside, just as I'd hoped, was a videotape. He played it.

"Oh boy, a naked babe," said Lemmy, moving closer to the screen.

We watched the tape to the end. When it was over, Chuck hit the rewind button. Lemmy plopped himself into the beanbag chair and said, "Thanks for the thrill, Brenda, but I don't see how this proves Babette Needleson killed her husband."

"It doesn't," I admitted, "but it does prove that she was lying when she claimed not to know about the strip club. I'll explain it all, but first let's try and get Brewster Winfield over here."

"He won't want to come," said Chuck. "He's all worked up because Myrtle has an audition tomorrow."

"Remind him that he hasn't been paid yet. He'll come."

While Chuck made the call I talked to Lemmy. "I saw Johnny," I said.

Lemmy bombarded me with questions. "Where the hell has he been? What's going on with the *Tod Trueman* shoot? Please tell me he didn't screw up with Sal Stumpford."

"Everything's okay. Johnny didn't screw up anything. Stumpford got sick and had to go back to the coast. Johnny used his time off to cruise the amateur strip clubs, playing undercover detective. At least that's what he thinks. According to Dweena and Irene, he hasn't fooled anybody. Everybody knew it was him. They thought he was scouting for talent. Johnny thinks he's about to prove that the mob killed Buddy Needleson.''

''That's ridiculous,'' said Lemmy. ''The mob doesn't bop people over the head.''

''Try telling Johnny that.''

We didn't have to wait too long for Winfield. He rushed in with his dreadlocks swirling. When he took off his cashmere coat, Myrtle was underneath, draped around his neck like a long scaly scarf. I backed away.

''She's looking good, isn't she?'' said Winfield.

''Pretty as a picture,'' I said. I showed him the blue boxes, played the tape, then explained why it was important. Summing up, I said, ''Babette Needleson did it.''

''What about LeHalle?'' he asked.

''Ironclad alibi,'' I said. ''Emergency appendectomy.''

Lemmy leaned back in the beanbag chair, making a whooshing sound. ''You know, Brew, this Babette thing makes sense to me.''

''I don't know,'' said Chuck. ''It's going to be hard to prove.''

''Maybe not so hard,'' I said.

''Do you have an idea?'' asked Winfield.

''Yes,'' I said, ''but you're not gonna like it.'' I waited a couple of beats for that to sink in, then took a deep breath and said what they wouldn't like. ''Lemmy's got to turn himself in.'' I was right. They didn't like it.

Lemmy popped out of the beanbag chair. ''You been sniffing mercury or something? I thought they took that stuff outta hats.''

''Calm down,'' I said. ''It's not half as bad as it sounds. If we go directly to Turner and McKinley, they'll listen. They owe me one for Brink LeHalle.''

I pleaded and argued until Lemmy agreed to go. ''On one condition, Brenda. If you're so positive this will work, put your own butt on the line. Tell the cops the whole truth.

Tell them who dumped Buddy Needleson's body at the morgue."

I agreed, which meant I was pretty sure of my theory.

Winfield was still doubtful. "I don't know," he said to Lemmy. "As your attorney, I must warn you of the extreme risk."

"Look at it this way," I said. "It'll make a smashing end to the *Fugitive Agent* property. I can see it now: 'In order to achieve truth and justice for all, Fugitive Agent risked everything, including his own freedom.' "

Winfield got a dreamy look in his eyes. "I'm liking it," he said. "Definitely liking it."

31

Winfield didn't want to take Myrtle to the precinct. "Cops have a thing about snakes," he explained. On the way there he double-parked in front of his loft, ran upstairs, and dropped her off. Chuck, Lemmy, and I stayed in the BMW, on the lookout for traffic cops and tow trucks.

Lemmy slouched in his seat but the tension showed in his face. "I'll be glad when this is over," he said.

"You and me both," said Chuck. "No offense, but I like living alone."

"I hate living alone," said Lemmy, "but if anything like this ever happens again, I'm gonna be damn sure I get taken in by a breathtakingly beautiful, big-breasted, love-starved blond, not some weirdo wise-ass computer geek."

"If I have anything to do with it," I said, "nothing like this will ever happen again."

I spotted a tow truck two blocks up Broadway. Before its driver saw us, Winfield was back. He jumped in the car and took off. When we got there, we couldn't find a parking space anywhere near the precinct. Winfield circled the block for ten minutes before giving up and pulling into a parking lot.

"Put it on your bill," I said to Winfield.

"Wouldn't dream of doing otherwise," he said.

It was a two-block walk to the precinct. The closer we

got, the slower Lemmy walked. "Maybe this isn't such a good idea," he said.

"What'sa matter, Chrome Dome, getting cold feet?" asked Chuck.

Defiantly, Lemmy said, "No, I'm not."

I kept my mouth shut. This had to be Lemmy's decision.

"You want my advice?" asked Winfield.

"What else are you getting paid for?" said Lemmy.

Winfield cleared his throat. "All right, then. As far as the risk factor goes, there is most certainly an element of risk, but I say great art always has an element of risk. Like Brenda said, it would make a heroic ending to our *Fugitive Agent* property."

"*My* property," said Lemmy.

"Everything's negotiable," said Winfield.

By that time we were in front of the precinct. Lemmy turned toward the door, sighed deeply, and said, "What the hell. Let's do it."

Talk about shocked cops. Turner and McKinley both dropped their jaws in amazement when the four of us clomped into their grim office cubicle. Lemmy went first, followed by Winfield, then Chuck, then me.

McKinley said, "Well, well, well, if it isn't Mr. Lemon B. Crenshaw, escaped felon. So good to finally see you again."

Winfield stepped in between Lemmy and the cops. "My client did not escape. You released him."

"In error," said McKinley.

"That's all water under the bridge," said Winfield. "My client wants to deal."

McKinley raised his eyebrows and looked at Turner. Turner gave his partner a tiny nod.

We had decided I should do the talking. So, while Lemmy paced back and forth like a windup toy, Winfield watched Lemmy pace, and Chuck watched Winfield watching Lemmy, I told the story.

I started with Naomi's frantic call to me for help and

ended with seeing the light blue boxes at Babette's. I went real fast over some of the more legally questionable parts. For instance, I said I didn't know the bundle in the trunk was a dead body until it was too late and I totally left out the part about all the places I broke into in pursuit of the truth.

From the look in Turner's eyes, I wasn't fooling anybody for a second. "Ms. Midnight," he said, "that's the most cockamamie story I've heard since your last cockamamie story, but—"

"That cockamamie story turned out to be correct," I reminded him.

McKinley took over. "What my partner is trying to say is that we feel we owe you something for the exemplary work you did in the capture of Brink LeHalle."

Not to mention the fact that I'd promised to make Turner's sister's kid's veil, I thought.

"So that's why," continued Turner, "despite everything, we're gonna go down there and interview the lady in question. We're gonna play good cop/bad cop and see where it gets us."

"On one condition," added McKinley ominously. "You people, Mr. Crenshaw in particular, stay put until we get back."

Chuck whispered something to Winfield. Winfield nodded his head and started acting like a lawyer. "We want a pizza," he said.

"Pepperoni," said Chuck.

"Sausage," said Lemmy.

While McKinley ordered the pizza, Turner pulled me aside. "How long does it take to make a veil? My sister's kid decided on a May wedding."

"That's plenty of time," I said.

The cops left; the pizza came. Lemmy seemed fine. He and Brew Winfield sat at McKinley's desk and spoke in low tones. At first I thought they were talking about the possibility of an appeal if something went wrong, but when I heard phrases like "film rights" and "percentages" I knew they were hacking out the details of their *Fugitive Agent* agreement.

Chuck started fooling around with Turner's computer. After a couple of minutes he said, "I'm in." After that it was impossible to get his attention. He sat glued to the monitor, fingers flying over the keyboard.

Left all alone, the enormity of what I'd done hit me smack in the head. What if I was wrong about Babette Needleson? Or what if I was right and the cops didn't go for it? What if, because of me, Lemmy went to jail? What if, because of me, I went to jail?

Before I worried myself to death, Turner and McKinley came back. It was hard to tell which cop had the bigger smile.

"Good cop/bad cop worked?" I asked.

"Mr. Crenshaw is free to go," said McKinley.

"Your cockamamie story was right on the mark," said Turner.

"Hot dog," said Chuck. He slapped Lemmy on the back and whooped. Lemmy hugged me and whooped. Winfield hugged Lemmy and whooped. Chuck hugged me and whooped. I hugged Winfield.

When all the hugging and whooping was done, I asked, "What happened?"

"The short version," said Turner, "and that's all you're gonna get because we've got a shitload of paperwork to do . . . the short version is that we found the grieving widow in the garbage room of her building. She was standing on a ladder dropping certain household items into a Dumpster."

Poor Babette, I thought, remembering how she'd said she was scared to death of ladders.

McKinley picked up the story. "Among those household items were the baby blue boxes you described and a baseball bat, the probable weapon, which contained probable bloodstains and probable particles of brain matter that forensics will confirm." McKinley went on to say that Babette broke down under their good cop/bad cop ploy and confessed.

On the way out I asked, "Who played the good cop?"

"That, Ms. Midnight, is a professional secret," said Turner.

The first thing I did when I got home was call Johnny. The second thing I did was hang up on his answering machine. Then I took Jackhammer out. Then I took a long hot bath. Then I called Dweena and told her the good news. Then I called Elizabeth and told her the good news.

Then, pretending again to be Brenda Miller the Tochin College researcher, I called Daria Covington and told her the bad news. "Turns out the production company was a scam."

"My video won't be on cable?"

"I'm afraid not."

"Well, thank goodness for that."

"I thought you'd be disappointed."

"The thing is, I watched my copy again and, you know, my routine needs some work. I'm back to the drawing board, choreographically speaking."

I climbed into bed embarrassingly early, but I figured no one would ever know. I was in the middle of an animated hat dream when the phone woke me. All the little hats stopped singing and dancing. In a poof they were gone.

"What is it?" I said into the receiver.

"Trouble," said Dweena.

I threw a coat on over my pajamas and ran the two blocks to St. Vincent's Hospital. Dweena met me in the emergency room.

"Where is he?" I asked.

She pointed down a corridor toward a set of double doors. "Back there. Every hour on the hour they let us in for ten minutes."

I checked my watch. It was twenty after three, which

meant a forty-minute wait. I didn't think I could stand it. "How bad is he?" I started to cry.

The waiting room was full of people in various stages of distress. A television mounted on the wall was tuned in on an infomercial for an all-in-one kitchen device.

Dweena sat me down in a plastic chair. "It's all right, Brenda. Johnny's going to be fine. He's got a nasty cut above his left eyebrow, maybe a couple of cracked ribs, and bruises all over, but it doesn't look like he's got any serious internal injuries."

"What happened?"

"I don't know. I was working the door of the club and these people came up and said there's some guy in pretty bad shape sprawled out in the gutter over on the corner of Washington and Horatio. I got somebody to watch the door for me and went right over to check it out. When I got there, I saw it was Johnny, so I ran back to the club, called nine-one-one. The ambulance scooped him up and here we are."

"Johnny didn't say what happened?"

"Mostly Johnny groaned."

Time creeped along. I looked around at the other people. It was hard to tell the injured and sick from the friends of the injured and sick. At this hour, in this environment, everyone looked sick. Even Dweena was a mess. Whiskers poked through her fastidious makeup and her wig, a saucy blond ponytail with flirty eyebrow-length bangs was slightly off center. I was glad there were no mirrors around. I probably looked pretty scary myself.

At four o'clock Dweena and I were the first through the double doors. Dweena led me into a room down a long hallway to the left. Johnny was stretched out on a steel examination table. He held a bloody gauze pad on his forehead.

When he saw me I think he said, "Brenda, what are you doing here?" but it was hard to make out. It obviously hurt him to move his mouth. From the looks of things it hurt to move anything.

"I called her," said Dweena.

"I came right away," I said.

He tried to smile.

"What happened?" I asked.

With great effort, he said, "Got too close to the truth. Mob tried to rub me out."

I patted his hand. I couldn't believe he was still hanging on to his stupid mob theory. Later I'd have to tell him that Babette Needleson had confessed to killing her husband, but I'd let him have his fantasy for a while.

A doctor scurried into the room and clipped Johnny's X-rays up on a viewer.

"Mr. Verlane," he said, "you're a lucky man. Nothing's broken. I'm just going to sew up your forehead so you don't get a scar."

"No," said Johnny. That came out loud and clear.

"Huh?" said the doctor.

"No stitches," said Johnny.

"You'll have a scar."

"I don't care. I want a scar."

"You'll have to sign a release."

"Fine."

The doctor left the room.

"Are you crazy?" I said.

Before Johnny answered, it was ten after four and a guard kicked Dweena and me out.

"He's out of his mind," I said to Dweena as we looked for empty chairs in the waiting room. "We can't let him do this. His career."

"It's his career he's thinking of," said Dweena. "A scar will give him an edge. Especially once word gets out that it's a mob-induced scar that he got while solving a real-life crime."

"Look, Dweena, you and I both know this was no mob-induced scar. Johnny didn't solve any crime. Johnny got mugged."

"Nobody else has to know that," said Dweena with a wink.

32

Johnny's scar was a big hit. He and Lemmy cooked up a story about how Johnny had gone head to head with the forces of evil. Johnny thoroughly enjoyed his recovery. On his doctor's orders he spent a few days in bed. Then for two weeks he sat on his couch reading true crime books, the gorier the better. At night I brought him food, mostly takeout and lots of Elizabeth's cookies. By the time Sal Stumpford got back to town, Johnny and his scar were ready to resume filming. The new *Tod Truemans* stayed on schedule.

I opened up Midnight Millinery on time every day and stayed until at least six. My spring line attracted some walk-in sales, but it hurt not having any other stores carrying my hats. I'd never recover my losses.

One morning I was sitting in the shop worrying about the landlord's latest threat when Lemmy called. I hadn't had much contact with him since the big party he'd thrown. Even there, I'd barely talked to him. He'd been too busy chatting up Irene Finneluk and I'd been too busy talking to Renard and trying to see if Johnny noticed.

It was good to hear from Lemmy.

"Congratulations," he said.

"For what?" I asked.

"Didn't you see the article in the *Times* about your hats? That's quite a coup. I didn't know you had a publicist."

"I don't."

"In that case," said Lemmy, "somebody did you a mighty big favor."

I hightailed it over to the newsstand and picked up the paper. There, on the front page of the third section, was a six-inch, two-column article about me and Midnight Millinery. The headline read, HATS OFF TO MIDNIGHT MILLINERY. It was just the basic hats-are-coming-back-into-style article that had been appearing two times a year for as long as I could remember, but this one credited the resurgence of the industry to "innovative designers like Brenda Midnight." I went back to the newsstand and bought up the remaining fourteen copies.

When I got back, the phone was ringing. It was Detective Turner. I figured he was calling to nag me about his sister's kid's veil, but he surprised me. "See the paper yet today?" he asked.

"I'm walking on clouds," I said. "I just found out about it."

"I thought it would be a nice surprise," he said.

"You?"

"Ms. Midnight, you never know who has a sister who knows someone at the *Times*."

"Your sister got them to do the article?"

"No, but she pointed out to someone that you make a fine hat, and that someone pointed it out to someone else, and so on down the line, or maybe in this case up the line."

"I don't know how to thank you," I said.

"I know how," he said. "Stick to millinery. Stay away from police work."

"Done." From the way he talked, you'd think I sought out trouble.

All day the phone rang off the hook. Even Brewster Winfield called. He turned out not to be such a bad guy after all. He was ecstatic when Lemmy got Myrtle a cameo in an aftershave commercial and absolutely beside himself when that led to a much larger role in a seductive perfume ad. Once he and Lemmy got going on *Fugitive Agent,* he magnanimously agreed to forget all the money owed to him for a bigger chunk of the action.

All that afternoon customers trickled in. By evening I'd sold ten hats. The next day I sold fifteen, and that was just the beginning. By night I made hats, by day I sold them. Jackhammer loved all the activity in the shop. He showed off for the customers, strutting around like he owned the place.

And so it went, day after profitable day.

It was my best season ever. I could even afford a new worktable. On a lark I called Naomi and asked what had happened to her Aunt Babette's oak table.

''It's still for sale,'' she said. ''Even if Babette gets off, she's going to move out of town. It's hard enough to get a date in this city without having murdered your husband, and Babette, she's the kind of person who needs to be married. Thank heavens I'm not like that.''

I agreed with her, carefully staying away from the Fred issue.

Naomi went on, ''Meanwhile, Norbert and I are in charge of her apartment, so if you still want the table—''

''How much, Naomi?''

''Um—''

''You owe me, Naomi.''

''Yeah, but—''

''Naomi.''

''All right, already. Take it. The table's yours, but I still say it's all your fault. You're the one who insisted we dump Uncle Buddy's body at the morgue. If we'd done it my way and dumped him in the alley, we wouldn't have needed a car, and none of that bad stuff with Johnny's agent would have happened. That is, none of it would have happened except Aunt Babette killing Uncle Buddy. Norbert says we've got bad blood, killer blood in our veins.''

I reminded her, ''You're only related to Babette by marriage.''

''Yeah, I know, but you know Norbert. He's always romanticizing.''

Myself, I had a tough time romanticizing murder.

* * *

On one especially hectic day, Elizabeth dropped by and invited me and Jackhammer over for dinner.

"I'm pretty pooped," I said.

"Oh come on. It'll be fun. Dweena and Chuck are coming. Dweena is buying a computer. Ever since someone pulled a gun on her at the club, she doesn't want to be a bouncer anymore."

"I don't blame her."

Elizabeth went on, "The three of us have resurrected our idea of starting an online service. With Chuck's computer expertise and Dweena's knowledge of clubs, it'll be *the* place to be. I, of course, will contribute good sense and strange cookies."

"Online?"

Elizabeth smiled. "Virtual cookies. So, shall I set a place for you?"

"Okay," I said.

"You can invite Johnny if you want. He's always welcome."

Once Johnny had gone back to work, he'd become less and less available. We almost never went to Angie's anymore. He always had some excuse or other, dinner with network executives, an interview with a magazine editor, guest starlet, something.

"Thanks, Elizabeth, but he's probably already got plans," I said.

"Okay then. Dinner's at eight. See you and little Jackhammer then."

Around seven o'clock I cleared the last customers out of the store and went home. I called Johnny on the off chance he was home. He answered, but I'd gotten so used to slamming down the phone on his machine that I hung up. When I realized I'd hung up on a real live person I was too embarrassed to call back.

When Jackhammer and I got to Elizabeth's, Chuck and Dweena were already there.

"Where's Johnny been lately?" asked Chuck. "Those

new *Tods* are great. That scar gives him an edge.''

''I don't know,'' I said as if I didn't care. Everybody knew better.

Dweena diplomatically changed the subject. ''So, Brenda, Elizabeth tells me Midnight Millinery is thriving.''

''You know what they say,'' I said, ''hats are back in style.''

''They're fetching,'' said Dweena.

''Chic,'' said Elizabeth.

''Sexy,'' I said.

''No,'' said Chuck, ''not sexy.''

''Excuse me,'' I said. I'd always thought Chuck admired my work. ''You're telling me my hats aren't sexy.''

''Look, Brenda, your hats are sculptural, architectural, gravity-defying, cool. They're good art, great style. Sexy, maybe a little.''

I glared at him.

''Okay, maybe a lot. But if you want super sexy, carry a hatbox.''

''A hatbox?''

''That's right.'' Chuck looked at Dweena and Elizabeth and got no reaction. He shrugged. ''It's a guy thing, I guess.''

I couldn't believe my ears. ''You, Chuck Riley, you're telling me a hatbox is sexier than the seductive curve of a brim over one eye? A hatbox is sexier than the allure of a veil?''

''I'm telling you there's nothing sexier than a hatbox.''

''It probably *is* a guy thing,'' said Elizabeth. ''Remember I told you about that fellow in Chicago, the one Dude Bob decked?''

I nodded.

''Well,'' continued Elizabeth, ''I was carrying one of your Midnight Millinery hatboxes full of buttons and bumper stickers when he tried to pick me up.''

''Oh, for goodness' sakes,'' I said. ''It doesn't mean a thing.''

''I know another time,'' said Dweena. ''Remember when

you and I were waiting for the Sixth Avenue bus?"

"Yeah, we were going to the Ns to get your feather boa."

"Right. I attracted a lot of attention. I was carrying a Midnight Millinery hatbox."

"You always attract a lot of attention. If I remember correctly, you had on a chartreuse wig and matching mini-skirt that day."

"This is New York," said Dweena. "People are used to that. It could have been the hatbox. It's like seamed nylons. Doesn't make any sense, but drives guys wild."

Chuck had a self-satisfied grin on his face.

I still didn't get it.

During dinner Chuck, Elizabeth, and Dweena talked about start-up costs for their online service. Jackhammer patrolled the floor underneath the table, on the lookout for crumbs. I thought about hatboxes and concluded Chuck had been spending too much time staring at his computer monitor. He was obviously out of his mind.

But what if he wasn't? What if just this once he wasn't talking through his hat?

I excused myself before dessert, claiming extreme fatigue.

I put on my long clingy black dress, sophisticated coat, and, despite what Chuck said, my sexiest hat, the one with the sweeping brim and mysterious swash of veiling. When I was ready to go I scoped out the hall through my peephole. I'd never live it down if Chuck, Elizabeth, or Dweena saw me. The coast was clear. I grabbed a Midnight Millinery hatbox and slipped out the door.

Ralph the doorman was on duty again. "Who's the lucky guy?" he said. I ignored him, figuring he was talking back to his TV, but when I turned onto Bleecker Street, a guy walking his dog winked at me, and then a bit farther on a wolf whistle pierced the cold night air. I began to think maybe Chuck was on to something.

The new storefront in Johnny's building was finished. A

sign promised live poetry seven nights a week. There was a light in Johnny's window. I paused for a moment to check out my reflection in the glass door. I adjusted the hat, arranged the hatbox just so, then rang his buzzer.

BARBARA JAYE WILSON writes the Brenda Midnight mystery series. She occasionally stops writing, rolls out the buckram and hat blocks, and turns her Greenwich Village apartment into a millinery studio.

JILL CHURCHILL

"JANE JEFFREY IS IRRESISTIBLE!"

Alfred Hitchcock's Mystery Magazine

Delightful Mysteries Featuring Suburban Mom Jane Jeffry

GRIME AND PUNISHMENT
76400-8/$5.99 US/$7.99 CAN

A FAREWELL TO YARNS
76399-0/$5.99 US/$7.99 CAN

A QUICHE BEFORE DYING
76932-8/$5.50 US/$7.50 CAN

THE CLASS MENAGERIE
77380-5/$5.99 US/$7.99 CAN

A KNIFE TO REMEMBER
77381-3/$5.99 US/$7.99 CAN

FROM HERE TO PATERNITY
77715-0/$5.99 US/$7.99 CAN

SILENCE OF THE HAMS
77716-9/$5.99 US/$7.99 CAN

And in Hardcover

WAR AND PEAS

Buy these books at your local bookstore or use this coupon for ordering:

Mail to: Avon Books, Dept BP, Box 767, Rte 2, Dresden, TN 38225 G

Please send me the book(s) I have checked above.

❑ My check or money order—no cash or CODs please—for $__________ is enclosed (please add $1.50 per order to cover postage and handling—Canadian residents add 7% GST). U.S. residents make checks payable to Avon Books; Canada residents make checks payable to Hearst Book Group of Canada.

❑ Charge my VISA/MC Acct#______________________________ Exp Date________

Minimum credit card order is two books or $7.50 (please add postage and handling charge of $1.50 per order—Canadian residents add 7% GST). For faster service, call 1-800-762-0779. Prices and numbers are subject to change without notice. Please allow six to eight weeks for delivery.

Name____

Address______________________________________

City__________________ State/Zip__________________

Telephone No.________________

CHU 0797

ANN GRANGER

The Meredith and Markby Mysteries

"The author has a good feel for understated humor, a nice ear for dialogue, and a quietly introspective heroine."

London Times Saturday Review

COLD IN THE EARTH 72213-5/$5.50 US

A FINE PLACE FOR DEATH 72573-8/$5.50 US

MURDER AMONG US 72476-6/$5.50 US

SAY IT WITH POISON 71823-5/$5.50 US

A SEASON FOR MURDER 71997-5/$5.50US

WHERE OLD BONES LIE 72477-4/$4.99 US

FLOWERS FOR HIS FUNERAL 72887-7/$5.50 US

CANDLE FOR A CORPSE 73012-X/$5.50 US

Buy these books at your local bookstore or use this coupon for ordering:

Mail to: Avon Books, Dept BP, Box 767, Rte 2, Dresden, TN 38225 G

Please send me the book(s) I have checked above.

❑ My check or money order—no cash or CODs please—for $__________is enclosed (please add $1.50 per order to cover postage and handling—Canadian residents add 7% GST). U.S. residents make checks payable to Avon Books; Canada residents make checks payable to Hearst Book Group of Canada.

❑ Charge my VISA/MC Acct#____________________Exp Date_______

Minimum credit card order is two books or $7.50 (please add postage and handling charge of $1.50 per order—Canadian residents add 7% GST). For faster service, call 1-800-762-0779. Prices and numbers are subject to change without notice. Please allow six to eight weeks for delivery.

Name____________________

Address____________________

City__________State/Zip__________

Telephone No.__________

ANG 0497

IRIS HOUSE B & B MYSTERIES

by

JEAN HAGER

Featuring Proprietress and part-time sleuth, Tess Darcy

THE LAST NOEL

78637-0/$5.50 US/$7.50 Can

When an out-of-town drama professor who was hired to direct the anuual church Christmas pageant turns up dead, it's up to Tess to figure out who would be willing to commit a deadly sin on sacred grounds.

DEATH ON THE DRUNKARD'S PATH

77211-6/$5.50 US/$7.50 Can

DEAD AND BURIED

77210-8/$5.50 US/$7.50 Can

A BLOOMING MURDER

77209-4/$5.50 US/$7.50 Can

Buy these books at your local bookstore or use this coupon for ordering:

Mail to: Avon Books, Dept BP, Box 767, Rte 2, Dresden, TN 38225 G

Please send me the book(s) I have checked above.

☐ My check or money order—no cash or CODs please—for $__________ is enclosed (please add $1.50 per order to cover postage and handling—Canadian residents add 7% GST). U.S. residents make checks payable to Avon Books; Canada residents make checks payable to Hearst Book Group of Canada.

☐ Charge my VISA/MC Acct#____________________ Exp Date_______

Minimum credit card order is two books or $7.50 (please add postage and handling charge of $1.50 per order—Canadian residents add 7% GST). For faster service, call 1-800-762-0779. Prices and numbers are subject to change without notice. Please allow six to eight weeks for delivery.

Name______________________________

Address____________________________

City________________ State/Zip________________

Telephone No.________________ JH 0897

by
TAMAR MYERS

LARCENY AND OLD LACE

78239-1/$5.50 US/$7.50 Can

As owner of the Den of Antiquity, Abigail Timberlake is accustomed to navigating the cutthroat world of rival dealers at flea markets and auctions. But she never thought she'd be putting her expertise in mayhem and detection to other use—until her aunt was found murdered . . .

GILT BY ASSOCIATION

78237-5/$5.50 US/$7.50 Can

A superb gilt-edged, 18th-century French armoire Abigail purchased for a song at estate auction has just arrived along with something she didn't pay for: a dead body.

THE MING AND I

79255-9/$5.50 US/$7.50 Can

Digging up old family dirt can uncover long buried secrets . . . and a new reason for murder.

Buy these books at your local bookstore or use this coupon for ordering:

Mail to: Avon Books, Dept BP, Box 767, Rte 2, Dresden, TN 38225 G

Please send me the book(s) I have checked above.

❑ My check or money order—no cash or CODs please—for $__________is enclosed (please add $1.50 per order to cover postage and handling—Canadian residents add 7% GST). U.S. residents make checks payable to Avon Books; Canada residents make checks payable to Hearst Book Group of Canada.

❑ Charge my VISA/MC Acct#____________________Exp Date________

Minimum credit card order is two books or $7.50 (please add postage and handling charge of $1.50 per order—Canadian residents add 7% GST). For faster service, call 1-800-762-0779. Prices and numbers are subject to change without notice. Please allow six to eight weeks for delivery.

Name____

Address______________________________________

City____________________State/Zip____________________

Telephone No.____________________

TM 0797